OF DELICATE PIECES

A. Lynden Rolland

Month9Books

This book is a work of fiction. Names, characters, places, and incidents are either products of the author's imagination or are used fictitiously. Any resemblance to actual persons, living or dead, business establishments, events, or locales is entirely coincidental. The author makes no claims to, but instead acknowledges the trademarked status and trademark owners of the word marks mentioned in this work of fiction.

Published by Month9Books, LLC.
Cover design by Najla Qamber Designs
Cover copyright © 2015 Month9Books

Month9Books

To anyone putting pieces back together

The world does not provide visibility.
The world does not create tangibility.
The imagination does.
That is the true reality.

Abigail Frank, "The Manual of Sight"

OF DELICATE PIECES

A. Lynden Rolland

Chapter One

In her dream, Alex was back in the desert, the one with the footprints, except this time the sky was green. The sand clung to her feet, weighing her down, and she worried how long she would have to endure it. Chase appeared and intertwined his fingers with hers, and a pleasant zap of electricity struck her palm. Alex heard a satisfactory *click* as their hands snapped into place. The light from the setting sun framed his silhouette, forcing Alex to blink several times, blind to his features. Warmth overcame her.

"Chase." His name tasted like sunlight, and the sky brightened. "Is this my dream or yours?"

"If I had to bet on it, I'd guess yours because we're back in this litter box again."

"You've had dreams like this before, too."

Chase glanced over his shoulder. "I have no footprints. Like I'm not really supposed to be here. And I've never had a dream that leads home to Parrish. Ready? Any minute now." They could hear the sound of the waves before the bay materialized next to them. "We're back."

The sand hardened with water, allowing them to walk without restraint. Never did the icy fingertips of the waves find a way to reach them. This world couldn't touch them anymore.

Chase looked out at the horizon. "What is it that you're looking for? There has to be some reason your mind is so adamant about taking you back here. Not that I mind long walks on the beach, but it's a little cliché."

He let go of her hand and instead wrapped his arm around the small of her back. In every place their bodies touched, Alex's nerves *zinged*, struck by the electricity between them. The sky winced in a snapshot of lightning.

She took a deep breath, expecting the familiar aroma of salt water and seaweed. Instead, sugar sprinkled the breeze like sweetened raindrops of comfort and home. It could be because this was where they were born, where they met and grew up together. Or it could be because Chase himself was her home no matter where the world placed them.

He gestured to some kids playing volleyball near a bonfire: four brothers and a sickly undersized girl on the sidelines. "There we are again. Your mind is like a movie on cable. You keep rerunning the same stuff. I think I'm going to start calling you Showtime."

"That's a horrible nickname."

"I could think of worse."

Alex slowed to observe the thirteen-year-old version of herself, deep in conversation by the fire. The younger version of Chase kneeled in front of her, reaching out to graze his fingertips along her temple, to tuck her unruly hair behind her ear. The surrounding children watched them, transfixed, envying them, but the dream version of Alex took no notice. It was the moment in life when Chase told her that she was perfect to him, broken and all.

Her biggest mistake back then was assuming he would always be around to gather what was left of her in his arms, to carry her. When death had reared its ugly head and snatched Chase by the collar, he'd dropped her. She couldn't pick up the pieces alone.

She hoped the meaning of her dream had nothing to do with the end of the night. She'd spent plenty of time trying to forget about that. If she knew then what she knew now, she wouldn't have questioned her sanity or the idea of spirits—now that she was one. She and Chase were stuck between alive and dead, in a mental world Alex loved more and more every day.

"I could be looking for you," Alex suggested.

"Impossible. I'm already yours."

When Alex first began to have this dream, she and Chase participated, like actors on a very lifelike stage. They knew it wasn't real, but they went along with it anyway. Now they were spectators, strolling past the scene and continuing down the beach, hand in hand. If she allowed herself to keep sleeping, she and Chase would walk along the coast until they reached the infamous Esker woods. Wind ripped from the waves and struck them. Even the world shivered thinking of those woods. She wouldn't allow the dream to go so far as to lead them there, not after what had happened. Their bodies were dead, and as spirits, their lives depended on the energy in their minds, something almost as fragile as the body. If that part of them died, too, where would they end up? And more importantly to Alex, would they find each other again?

Yes, her subconscious replied. *Chase will always find me.*

They had lived the entirety of their short lives together, and they found each other in death. It was hard to imagine something the two of them could not withstand between the iron vice of their grasp on one another, but this world never ceased to surprise Alex, to toy with her. She turned back for one last look at the bonfire, at the children they used to be.

Alex dug her feet into the sand, stopping.

"What's the matter?"

"Nothing." Alex allowed Chase to pull her forward once again. She leaned into his chest where she fit and where she couldn't look back. The light from the moon pooled around them like a spotlight.

She could have sworn she'd seen her old friend, Liv Frank, staring in wonder right at them, eyes wide, mouth ajar. Like she'd seen a ghost.

That was impossible, right? This was a dream. Then again, at one point, Alex might have believed that two dead kids walking down the beach hand in hand would also be impossible.

The mind is so deceptive.

***

Alex waited for the hesitancy to pass in the lull between sleeping and waking. In the wretched space between Chase's death and her own, she had lived solely for this moment each day, a split second when her mind hadn't had time to remind her of what made it splinter. At the time, her doctor insisted that this was a good thing; it proved her mind had the ability to heal, that her cracks wouldn't break her. She was reluctant to believe his psychobabble.

She did believe, however, in the power of the moment. It bestowed the mind a brief hiatus from the confines of reason. The world was not always such a beautiful place, and so Alex clung to blissful ignorance when she could. This morning, that little hiatus of time overflowed with whispers. A waterlogged echo warped the words, preventing Alex from understanding the overlapping voices. Her head felt heavy and overloaded.

The whispers soon dulled, and Alex gave in and sat up in bed. Chase wasn't there, but she had a feeling he had been. His fingerprints were all over the air. She couldn't be sure what time it was. Even if the towering trees surrounding Eidolon didn't create an artificial night on the sunniest of days, the white-gray fog clung to the air like the exhaust from a dying car. It lingered, a constant canopy, an appropriate setting for ghosts. But the sun was like a stubborn child, and often it would find a way to push its first bits of sunlight into her world.

This morning's rays found her nightstand and a photograph of Alex's mom next to Chase's mom, both of them glowing and pregnant. Propped next to the frame was a small square of paper. The handwritten drawing of an hourglass appeared in Alex's pocket after she'd been attacked last spring. She tried to throw it away, rip it up, burn it, and toss it from her balcony, but it always reappeared in her pocket. Her friend, Skye, told her it could have been there all along and she didn't know to look for it. If that was the case, perhaps her mind could be kind enough to explain the meaning. If only. In this world, "clarity" was like looking through a kaleidoscope.

Alex stared at the drawing like she did every morning. Chase's question echoed in her mind, *What are you looking for?*

Answers.

What answers could a stupid hourglass give her? She wanted to know what happened to her mother. The target on her back in the form of a dead prophet wasn't an acceptable answer. She wanted to know why she looked identical to that dead prophet, Sephi Anovark. An hourglass didn't help.

Last spring the ragged sketch depicted only a dusting of sand at the bottom of the glass, but now the grains were distributed evenly between the top and the bottom. Whatever it meant, it appeared she was running out of time to figure it out.

She slid from her bed, and a stream of sand shimmied to the floor like a dash of rain, and the soles of her feet felt soft as though she'd been shuffling along the beach. She still wasn't accustomed to living in a world the mind could manipulate. It felt all too easy to straddle the thin line between fantasy and reality.

She shook her head and gazed down to find that she was already dressed, a perk derived from the same mental manipulation. Duly noted. She'd take the good with the bad.

She left her bed in disarray, knowing it would be tidy when she returned. If she could imagine an ideal space for herself, this room satisfied her vision. She hadn't seen another spirit's room, even Chase's, but she assumed it would appear the way the occupant envisioned it. Her room with its thick, white throw rugs, sunken chairs, and fluffy blankets, felt shabbily quaint. It was always warm and smelled of extinguished candle flames. She found peace in the distressed white wood flooring, the chipped white brick, and fractured paneling bathed in light from a rickety chandelier overhead. It was so different from the dirty, mossy black exterior of Brigitta Hall, her home.

Morning yawned through the French doors leading to her balcony, smelling of earth and fog. She could see the crowds already hindering the main street of Eidolon's older shops. Lazuli Street's congestion deepened with each passing day that summer. Because Alex had a clear view of the street a mile away, she could zero in on faces and conversations if she wanted. But she didn't want.

The unsettling bout of tourism coughed its curiosity up toward her balcony, and so she shut the doors, sacrificing fresh air for the protection of the glass. Even from such a distance, she could be seen and heard, and she promised Romey, the Brigitta director, that she wouldn't step outside unless she wanted her room assignment changed. Due to accelerated senses and amplified vision, those spirits a mile away could see her as easily as she could see them.

She searched her mind for any signs of Chase. She assumed the whispers she heard in her head moments ago slid between the swinging gateway of her mind and his. The noises surrounding Chase often leaked into Alex's mind and vice versa. The more and more time she spent dead, the better Alex became at managing it, at shutting the floodgate when she so desired. Though it seemed impossible to latch it.

Chase might have gotten up early. He might be downstairs in the vestibule or outside in the courtyard. Considering the number of voices she'd heard, he was surrounded by people.

Her hair tied itself into a ponytail, a sign of impending productivity. She felt like someone was waiting for her. And as soon as she thought about it, her door swung open.

Despite the vibe, a vacant corridor awaited her. She moved down the crooked hallway of the seventh floor before turning the corner to find Skye Gossamer poised on the railing of the balcony overlooking the vestibule.

Skye waved and adjusted a blue and yellow flower tucked behind her ear. "Took you long enough."

"I woke up two minutes ago."

Skye raised her auburn brows as if to say, *Exactly.*

Each floor had a common area overlooking the grand entrance hall below. Skye perched on the decorative railing like a bird on a wire. With her blanket of hair, Skye reminded Alex of a redheaded Rapunzel.

"It makes me nervous with you sitting like that."

"I won't fall. Not that it would injure me if I did."

Alex peered down at the seven stories below. "You might not be strong enough to keep a fall like that from hurting."

"I know my way around my brain."

"It's distracting."

Skye gave her a pitying look that indicated how ridiculous she thought this was, but she dismounted nonetheless. Alex noticed a handful of newbury boys on an adjacent terrace staring at her unusual friend in fascination. Skye had that effect on people, especially boys.

Alex took a seat on one of the bistro chairs and rested her elbows on the matching table. "What are you doing up so early? Waiting for me?"

"I'm trying to be a good neighbor. If we had newspapers, I would have brought it in for you."

The idea of a newspaper was absurd in a world so brilliant in its technology. News would always be a constant, but the source of its distribution evolved steadily. In Eidolon, news traveled as spirits traveled: using frequency waves.

Alex looked out at the shimmering headlines suspended over the vestibule in a checkerboard of electronic media. The morning news scrolled across the room like projections of stray thoughts. In the hoopla following the attack last spring, newburies rushed to read every ration of news they could devour. Whoever would have thought that keeping up with the times would become the latest trend?

She doubted that most of the newburies had ever blackened

their fingertips with newspaper ink during life. Alex certainly hadn't, but she blamed this gossip fad on the simplicity of reading with accelerated mind power and the lack of effort. Although she scoffed at the articles, in actuality, she craved more. The afterworld was so sparsely populated that the news tasted as juicy on her lips as high school gossip, especially when so much of it involved her. She pretended that she hated the attention, but she couldn't deny that a piece of her enjoyed it. She tucked that secret into her pocket with the hourglass sketch.

The installation of the news projections in both Brigitta Hall and in the adjacent learning center sparked a lengthy debate among the staff. Half of the faculty argued that the center had always been closed to the outside world, shielding the newly buried until they were ready. For the sake of tradition, they believed the campus should remain primitive. On the other hand, some reasoned that this was a way to ease the newburies into the reality of the spiritual world outside Brigitta, and the familiar environment of a school was a great way to introduce the news.

The contemporary crowd claimed victory, and now dozens of newburies stood transfixed underneath the projections each morning. Fingers outstretched, they searched the feed by skimming the article titles in the frequency waves and pulling them from midair. With the constant crowd, the energy, and eagerness, the vestibule now reminded Alex of the New York Stock Exchange. If she desired, she could select an article from the reel, tug it away from its energy feed, and read it at her leisure, but something caused her mind to pound and pulse that morning.

She blamed the pollution of Skye's apprehension.

"Spill it." Alex sighed. "You might as well tell me what's on your mind." She poked the moving field of energy and it rippled in front of her.

"Do you want to go downstairs?" Skye asked, adjusting the flower behind her ear.

Alex glanced again at the vestibule, scattered with spirits wearing everything from sweatpants to eveningwear depending on their moods. If she went down there, they would watch her, and she'd rather be the one observing. Last year, she grew used to the teachers gawking at her, even interrogating her, but now after the attack, the entire world knew her secret. Her teachers encouraged her to steer clear of the negative articles, so she pretended not to care that her name appeared in the headlines like a celebrity on a binge.

But of course she cared. Of course she wanted to know what others said about her. Who wouldn't?

Alex tried to ignore the itch in her fingertips as she browsed the bylines. "How bad is it this morning?"

Skye shrugged. "It could be worse."

The itch intensified. "Sephi Anovark?"

"Of course."

What could they possibly have left to write about her? Alex wondered, thinking about Sephi's love letters coincidentally twenty feet away from them. The temperamental box containing those letters hibernated in Alex's room, stubbornly refusing to share any more of its stories.

"Am I mentioned?"

"Do you even have to ask?"

Alex grimaced at the projections but wondered how genuine it seemed because it took all her effort to turn away. She didn't know why she tried so hard. She would end up scratching the itch until she bled.

She could recite yesterday's article easily with her Wikipedia brain.

What is the Big Deal?
Sigorny L.
The Voice of the Newburies

Last spring, a photo went viral and our campus flooded with questions about prophets, crime, and violence. When it comes to the potential return of the infamous Josephine Anovark, many of you have been posing this question:

What's the big deal?

I've found myself wondering the same thing. If we have another prophet on our hands in the form of Alex Ash, so what? Isn't it a good thing to know where our future might lead?

What's all the hype about? Well, let me tell you a little bit about Sephi Anovark. Her gift. She was the Joan of Arc of the 1800s, using her visions to aid the Union Army during the American Civil War. When she was living, she was a myth, already a ghost in a sense, but her tall tale was no fairy tale. Her ending was far from happy.

She was a celebrity, a "Marilyn." They call her captivating, a vixen who rolled with the likes of General Ulysses S. Grant and Walt Whitman in life, and in death, the politically dynamic DeLyre brothers; the fallen genius, Syrus Raive; and our very own hero, Ardor Westfall. People were infatuated with her then, as they remain now.

What would the human masses do if a dead ringer (pun intended) for Marilyn Monroe waltzed into a coffee shop in Los Angeles? I'm willing to bet the reactions would be the same if Sephi Anovark strolled into Broderick Square. Pandemonium occurred the first time Alex Ash innocently tiptoed along the endless knot at the stoop of the tower. With the release of one portrait photo, Alex Ash became larger than (after) life.

This is not necessarily a good thing. I, for one, would not choose to switch places with her if given the opportunity. For as many people who loved Sephi, an equal number despised her. During her short stint as an Ardor aide, she helped to imprison forty-seven spirits, half of who never sat before a jury. The world simply accepted Sephi's accusations as the truth; the accused were indicted on her word alone. Scary. As a result, Sephi could not leave the city without an army of Patrollers flanking her side, led by Commander-turned-Professor Henry Van Hanlin.

Note: No Van Hanlin updates to report. He is actively listed as missing.

So what's to fear? Well, let's say Alex Ash claims you're planning to blow up a frequency wave. Will you automatically be arrested? By nature, we feel the need to protect ourselves, and does a Sephi sequel stand in the way of our freedoms or our comforts?

After all, Sephi part one sparked a change in our world to ignite a full-on restructuring in our way of living. Do we want another Restructuring? Is that what will happen? Will Alex be used to generate political fear? Societal fear? And if that's the case, should she be dealt with now? These questions seem to be at the center of our issue. Are we happy with the way the afterlife is run now? Or worse, are we not?

People fear the unknown.

And that's the big deal.

Alex couldn't fault Sigorny for bringing to light some important facts, but the girl enjoyed shining light in the darkest of places.

"Is today's article worse than yesterday's?"

Skye shook her head. "I don't think so."

"Is the article about watching my back?"

"You're getting closer. She didn't come right out and directly say that, but it's sort of implied."

"I'm done guessing."

"Drumroll, please. The article is about—" Skye paused for dramatic effect "—tourism."

"Oh. That doesn't sound so bad."

"Before I read it, I thought the same thing," Skye said. "You can probably guess why so many spirits are visiting the town."

"To see me."

"The gist of the article is that the city should prepare itself for even more tourism. Shop owners are ecstatic, townies are annoyed, and the visitors, yeah, they are here to catch a glimpse of you, and they aren't afraid to say it. Fame comes at a price."

"Are visitors allowed on the school campus?"

"Of course not, but are you planning to limit yourself to the Brigitta campus?"

Alex hadn't thought of this. As soon as she stepped foot through the alleyway leading to Lazuli Street and the city beyond, it was public domain. "Can anyone get into the city?"

"Any spirit? Yes."

"How do they find it?"

"Like the bodied would, genius. They follow a map. Supposedly, the sky shines brighter over our little city, and that helps, too."

"A map through frequency waves and following light. That's hardly traveling like the bodied."

Skye tapped her fingers along the edge of the railing, giving Alex a forced smile.

"What do you think? They won't try to keep me confined to Brigitta, will they?"

"Do you want to read the article?"

"Not really."

"Okay, then. I guess I'll tell you. This year marks the centennial of the current civility laws."

"In plain English please."

"Seriously? We have brilliant minds."

"I just woke up. Give me the plain and simple facts."

"Fine. One hundred years ago, the spirited and the gifted came to a truce about how they would interact."

"I thought there was no interaction."

"Exactly. That was the truce. Sephi Anovark was really close to changing it, but she died at the wrong time. Her ambitions died with her, so the agreement became that we would live peacefully but separately."

Alex heard her name whispered multiple times among the conversations seven stories below in the vestibule. They flew upward and fused together in a wavy question mark of light.

"It's some big thing called the Centennial, and it's going to bring in even more tourism."

"The gifted are going to come in to see the city?"

Skye put a hand over her heart. "They'd never let the gifted in here."

Alex assumed that once the summer was over, her fifteen minutes of fame would end. She didn't know whether to feel anticipation or dread, to know on which side the grass would be greener. The funny thing about being dead though was that these tourists had all the time in the world to tread on that grass. Especially tourists who wanted to sneak a peek at a newbury who was identical to one of Eidolon's most tragic figures.

Little did they know, she wasn't related to Sephi Anovark, and, most importantly, she had no psychic abilities. She wasn't special. "That's all that the article said?"

Skye nodded her head and then shook it. "There were a few quotes from witnesses who had already seen you. Freaking out. Are you aware that there's a map of where you usually go in the city?"

She didn't know whether to be flattered or afraid. "What a way to start the new season."

Skye hopped into movement. "Not until tomorrow! Let's get going. We have a lot to do today."

"We have nothing to do today."

"Don't you have group therapy?"

Alex followed Skye to the winding ramp leading down to the vestibule. "Like I said. Nothing."

She despised therapy. Wallowing in her feelings and whining about death was a waste of time.

At the foot of the ramp, Skye turned. "Here. I almost forgot." She plucked the flower from her ear, presenting it to Alex before descending down the stairs.

"What's this?"

"Morning Glory. It should bring you some peace."

Alex examined the blue flower in her palm.

"What?"

"Nothing."

Skye was contradicting herself. If Alex truly had nothing to worry about, why would she need something to invoke peace?

Chapter Two

Alex's definition for group therapy: a platform for complainers to do what they do best. She wished she could shove them from that platform one by one. She had plenty of compassion, a trait which often got her into trouble, but as someone who grew up with limitations, she'd never been able to stomach people who felt so sorry for themselves that they needed others to pity them, too.

Whining sounded different to dead ears. It shrieked and squealed, scratching its nails across whatever part of her mind still gave her the ability to hear. She slouched in her seat, grimacing, as the blond girl seated next to her sobbed into her fist. Alex wondered for the umpteenth time if Ellington Reynes had sentenced her to group therapy in order to test whether or not she was still clinically insane. If she wasn't already crazy, this would do the trick.

The only deterrent was a pair of cold blue eyes that snared her attention. Chase flinched every time the girl sobbed but didn't divert his gaze. Alex gladly fell into those icy pools, and he must have liked her thoughts because the corner of his wide mouth curled. The lights began to flicker and buzz like an impending power outage. The other newburies in the circle looked upward nervously, but Ellington sighed. He was familiar with the source of the surge. The energy between Alex and Chase caused electricity to go haywire. A few weeks ago, they caused a blackout all the way down Lazuli Street simply because Chase kissed her in the middle of the road.

Ellington's hair stood on end. He snapped his fingers at the lights, and they calmed. "Not to worry, my friends. Our emotions are difficult to control. After an event as traumatic as death, the intensity of our feelings makes the world around us react."

What a crock. He knew sorrow couldn't produce such energy—it devoured it—while the more powerful emotions, like anger or passion, fueled it.

"Moving on," Ellington said, smoothing down his hair and straightening his bowtie. "Let's continue where we left off last week."

Alex lowered her head, brushing the floor with her stare, hoping to be overlooked.

"Behavior patterns. Physical reactions. Anything to share?"

Swish, swish, swish. Alex swept the floor with her mind. She watched as the dust shifted under the strength of her concentration. She crisscrossed the pattern to make a tic-tac-toe board. Ellington really needed to clean his floors.

"Chase? How have your physical reactions been?"

Alex's eyes snapped up, and the dust rose with them. *What reactions?* Her thoughts were louder than she intended because Chase looked at her and shrugged.

"You aren't alone, you know," Ellington pressed. "Hardly anyone here died of natural causes. It is normal following a traumatic event to experience flashbacks. We are haunted by our pasts more than anything else. Chase, what usually happens to you?"

Alex's mind tingled as she felt Chase's thoughts twirl nervously, like the race of a heartbeat. The memory of her pulse began to race.

"May I share?" Gabe spoke up.

Chase visibly relaxed.

"I, um, *we* died in a car accident." Gabe cleared his throat, and Alex felt a lump develop in hers. They never spoke much about their deaths. This was why she hated this "therapy." She did not consider reliving pain to be a form of treatment.

"I didn't die right away." Gabe waved his hand at the dust still rising into the air. "And sometimes if I'm bumped from the side or if I hear something shatter or crunch, it's like I'm back there again. It's intense, like being stuck in a nightmare."

Ellington nodded. "Memories define us and destroy us. Trauma victims in life experience the same sorts of flashbacks but to a much lesser degree. Your minds are powerful now, and it intensifies your memories."

Heads bobbed around the circle in agreement.

"What do you see when it happens, Gabe?"

He ran a hand through his blond curls. "I'm not sure, but when we crashed, I think the bottom half of my body was stuck under some part of the car. I could see everything. One of my brothers had been ejected. He was lying in the middle of the road, but I couldn't tell who it was because he ... whoever it was, they weren't completely there. I think something else must have hit him after the initial crash."

Stills of their funeral flashed through Alex's mind like a series of snapshots. Each of the Lasalles had a closed casket. She felt herself collapsing. She remembered the blinding hatred she felt toward death and yet how much she wanted to crawl into those caskets with them. She heard herself screaming, her voice echoing through the church as though several people were screaming along with her. Everyone had covered their ears. Her mind flashed to an image of the field outside of the Eskers. Again, she was screaming. Again, they covered their ears. This time, she made the world freeze with the power of her despair. Like a banshee.

She studied the scars a banshee had lashed onto Gabe's face. The half-moon along his cheek stretched as he spoke. "I remember letting go of my life. Part of me wonders if I could have fought harder, if I would have lived. I didn't even try. And I feel guilty for that."

"How long does the flashback last?" Ellington asked.

"A few seconds? A few minutes? When I snap out, I'm drained afterward."

"Headache?"

Gabe nodded.

"It takes time, but it will get better. And we certainly do have time here. Simply by sharing it, you may have accelerated your healing process."

"How does sharing it help?" Sobbing blond girl asked.

"If the quake of a trauma fails to maul your spirit, the aftershocks might attempt to eat you alive. I recommend accepting it as a part of you instead of denying its existence."

"Will it ever go away?"

"Depends. Some allow it to consume them."

"What happens then?"

"Some of you have witnessed what happens to a lost-minded spirit."

A faint banshee wail shrieked from somewhere in the filing of Alex's mind. Her own scream erupted along with it. They harmonized like a horror ballad.

"Treatment centers exist for that purpose."

This got her attention. The screams ceased. "Treatment centers for banshees, too?"

Ellington nodded. "There are spirits who believe that broken minds can be pieced back together and that we should help them. But that's a subject for another day and another workshop. Anyone else have similar experiences, flashbacks, or reactions?"

Alex saw Gabe's comfort rise with the hands that rose into the air like flowers growing through the cracks of concrete. He wasn't alone.

Blond girl hiccupped. "I can't believe so many of us experience the same things. I thought it was only my friends."

Friends? Alex mentally scolded herself for being so surprised that this crybaby had friends. Only the "chokers," who wallowed over their deaths despite the inevitability of their situation, would allow someone so depressing into their circle.

Half the seats in the room shifted from rickety folding chairs to cushy armchairs. Alex's didn't. She never felt comfortable in therapy.

Ellington curled his feet under him, pleased. His chair was now a red, velvet loveseat with squishy arms and a throw blanket. "Once we accept that despite our differences we are all connected, weaved together in this blanket of civilization, we can truly be at peace."

"That's never happened," Carr Cadman said. He'd told the group he dreamed his whole life—all eighteen years—of being a marine. During his first deployment, he died within the week. Sometimes, a gaping hole would appear in his chest, right where his heart had been. Perhaps that explained his cynicism.

Ellington shifted the pillow under his elbow. "Unfortunately, greed, selfishness, and stubbornness are also human traits. Think about how different your lives were, and yet you are all feeling the same things now. You would never have known it if you didn't speak to one another."

Chase's chair was still as stiff and uncomfortable as Alex's. But when Ellington had asked who in the group experienced the flashbacks, he raised his hand. It hurt Alex's heart to think the memories might pain him.

She saw what he remembered: a lopsided world with shattered glass, yellow lines on the road, and a battered hand reaching forward. In a flash, it changed to the field at the Eskers, a sheer image like a hologram before her.

Sometimes I'm back in the car. Other times, I'm in the field, and I can't save you. Both times I can't move. I hate it.

She'd seen this before. She couldn't distinguish whose memories were whose anymore. Alex could be sitting in class and suddenly she'd feel like she was flying. Then, she'd feel herself hit the ground. Her body would shake with the impact even though she hadn't left her seat. She felt what Chase was feeling during a game at the ball fields, a jolting and difficult sensation to conceal without seeming crazy.

Someone would discover their secret, eventually, if they hadn't already. Every month since the attack, she and Chase were required to check in at Dianab Medical Center. Doctors stuck tubes to their heads and wrote on their clipboards, whispering to one another.

What's the matter? Chase asked. The strength of the invisible bridge between them reached across the circle and held her.

Nothing's the matter, she replied. *Nothing at all.*

Chase made a lemon-sour face as though he could taste the lie.

Chapter Three

Sigorny Liechtenstein had always been nosy. Her father called her inquisitive. Her mother called her a busybody. Her teachers called her obtrusive which she thought was a compliment until she was old enough to use a dictionary.

She was the eager girl who would tag along with the popular crowd even if they ridiculed her for it. Sure, she wanted to fit in, but her motivation was more so to appease her infatuation with the most intriguing people, to see what made these people tick. If she had discovered her love for journalism in life, she might have found an outlet. It might have saved her. She wouldn't have been so willing to be cool, to drink so much of that pungent Southern Comfort before following the homecoming queen into the ocean for a late night swim. After Sigorny died, she used to dream every single night of drowning in those harsh, black waters. She would burn as the water filled her lungs. She hated the silence of her scream. The water became gentle far under the surface, rocking her to eternal sleep. That sleep turned out to be anything but restful.

Ellington suggested she should write a literal diary of the dead to escape her nightmares. The more she wrote, the better she felt. So when she first met the Darwins, who were practically Eidolon royalty, instead of hounding them and following them around like a bad odor, she researched them instead. She wrote a piece on them. It began a pattern. A wonderful pattern! She wasn't so skilled at the writing itself, but she told newburies what they wanted to know. That mattered more. She mattered more! She practiced more and the better she became with the words. Her strength? She was great at pushing questions, at getting people to talk; she was great at being *obtrusive*.

Other newburies became interested in her writing because so many of them did not have the connections of the multigenerational, at least not the very old ones who called themselves the legacies. The dead considered knowledge to be a treasure, and like many objects of value, the knowledge often seemed to be kept secret, all to themselves. She wanted to change that. It wasn't until she wrote the article featuring Sephi Anovark that her recognition extended further than the Brigitta campus.

Success!

She would write about Sephi until people stopped reading. She didn't care if the Lasalles threatened her. Sticks and stones don't matter when there are no bones to break. If the Lasalles took notice of her, she felt victorious. Attention swarmed them like desire, and she inhaled it like a pheromone.

Ahhh, lovely.

She stood looking up at Kaleb Lasalle, and she focused on her knees so they wouldn't buckle. This was a difficult feat since she was also trying to win him over in wit, to persuade him to answer some of her prying questions. Kaleb was, in a word, *overwhelming*. He was exactly the type of boy she would have followed around in life to get a glimpse of him up close. She would have grazed him with her fingertips as she loaned him a spare pencil in school, to make sure he was real. Such a thing thrilled her. She would have made a great groupie.

"Sigorny L.?" a voice rang out, and she watched Kaleb's head jerk upright. He looked past her and grinned upon seeing to whom it belonged. "The so-called voice of Brigitta?"

Sigorny looked back to see Gabriel and Chase Lasalle approaching. She felt an odd sensation, the way the drop of an elevator feels in the stomach. Her knees would certainly give out now. Would Kaleb catch her if she fell? Oh, the thought was delicious. That was a better word for Kaleb: delicious.

Alex Ash followed at the boys' heels, tiny but formidable in her own way. Presence is stronger than size, especially when the mind rules the world.

Sigorny watched as Gabe opened his mouth, no doubt ready to object to this powwow, so she spoke calculatingly. "Perfect timing! I was just getting ready to ask your brother about the 'Eskers kids' as they have been nicknamed. How do you feel about their *release*?"

Her question warranted the desired effect. Each of their mouths flew open like toy nutcrackers. She absolutely loved the feeling of shocking people whose existence alone was usually shocking in itself. It made her think she could conquer the impossible.

She watched Chase's arm swing around little Alex's waist, a hook to a latch. As though the Eskers kids might spring from one of the bushes and try to attack her again. No one had ever cared for Sigorny like that. She wrapped her fingers even more tightly around her pen, clutching her livelihood.

"It's true? The mob that tried to kill us is going to walk?" Chase was composed, but Sigorny could see his jaw moving, gnawing at the inside of his cheek.

"We were warned," Kaleb reminded his brother.

"But it's been months."

Sigorny smiled. It felt like she was part of their conversation, their lives. She shook the welcome thought from her one-track mind. Back to business. "Alex, you little scream queen, did they diagnose you as a banshee yet?"

Everyone knew Alex fought off a banshee last year, but what everyone didn't know was that she'd screamed like one during the Eskers attack. She'd momentarily paralyzed every spirit in a thirty-foot radius. Sigorny couldn't scrounge enough proof to write an article about it because her witnesses, the Eskers kids, were detained. She could only drop hints.

"No comment," Alex replied.

Sigorny went on to her next questions. "How was therapy?

Any post-traumatic stress?"

Gabe stared at her. Glasses appeared over his hypnotic eyes. What was he trying to see? "Do you know anything else about the Eskers kids?"

"They should be headed back to campus right about," Sigorny glanced at her watch for dramatic effect, "*now*, in fact."

Kaleb held out a hand and pressed his palm against the world like a mime. Sigorny hadn't realized the air was trembling until he stopped it. "If the Broderick officials say they're innocent, something about the mind control has to be true."

Gabe shook his head. "Actually menticide is more about manipulation than control ..."

Here he goes. Sigorny tuned out Gabe's intellectual jargon, seizing the opportunity to scribble on her pad of paper. She could definitely twist Kaleb's quote into something juicier.

"... by stimulating the projection of where the prefrontal cortex of the brain would be."

Sigorny interrupted Gabe's tutorial. "Do you believe, Kaleb, that the writing in their notebooks could have that sort of power?"

"Mind control?"

"Thought reform," Gabe corrected.

Kaleb shrugged. "Whether or not they were manipulated, that wasn't my decision to make, was it?"

Choosing words was like choosing moves during a chess match. "It's only an opinion. In your *opinion*, can mere words have so much power over a person? Actually, that question can be for any of you."

Chase lifted his chin. "Of course words are influential. Isn't that the purpose of your column?"

"Well said." She beamed, batting her lashes at Chase. He called her influential. It was quite the high. "What I mean is, do you think words can sway someone to do something they don't want to do? Alex?"

Come on. Give me something good, Sigorny pleaded.

"I believe that someone can only be influenced if they want to be."

Boring.

"And what about Jonas?" Sigorny asked. The figurative dagger pierced each of them differently. Alex looked at Chase. Chase looked at Kaleb. Kaleb looked away. Gabe looked at Sigorny. Their reactions chilled the scene, and her mind recalled the sensation of feeling the hairs on her arms stand on end. None of them spoke. How about a nudge?

"How do you feel about his involvement in all this?"

Kaleb began to speak, but Gabe interjected. "We spoke to you about Jonas months ago. Nothing has changed."

Sure it has, she thought. This was so much fun!

"The ranks are still divided, I see. Gabe, you don't believe that your brother should have been sent to the interrogation levels of the Dual Tower with the rest of the Eskers kids?"

Gabe's mouth tightened, and Sigorny tried not to stare at the marks streaking his gorgeous face. It was a treat, really, that her questions provoked their emotions. It gave her time to observe them without seeming odd. The defined lines of their features consumed her, so crisp, so definite, like their personalities. She longed to reach out and touch the lines of their high cheekbones, their heart-shaped mouths, and their jaws that twitched whenever she asked a question they didn't want to answer.

"You are well aware, Sigorny, that Jonas left the Eviar group. His intention, unlike the others, was never to harm anyone."

"So you say."

Kaleb took an aggressive step forward. Oh goodness, he was even closer now. "They would have arrested him otherwise."

She held up her hands. If she outstretched them, they would be on Kaleb's chest. Adrenaline surged through her. "Okay, okay, I'm sorry." But she knew she didn't sound sorry at all. She was under their skin like a disease, and she was pleased to be there. It meant she had the power, and she could write about their reactions all she wanted!

"What specifically *did* Jonas tell you about his involvement?"

"None of your f—"

"Careful, Kaleb," Gabe said.

She tried so hard not to smile. "The only reason I ask is because I thought you might have researched your family history afterward."

"Why's that?"

"Because each of the Eskers kids is connected to a family

historically poisoned by greed or bitterness. Even Joey Rellingsworth. How do you think his great-great-grandmother hoarded all those stocks of pure copper? They weren't miners, those Rellingsworths; they were chemists. Rumor has it, they killed for their supplies."

Gabe ran a finger along his scars absently. "I read your article about the Rellingsworth family."

Sigorny's pride surged even higher. He read her work! He *remembered* her work! Oh, spirited brains remember everything. Still! "I'm just saying that Jonas doesn't seem to fit with the rest of the Eskers kids."

Kaleb snickered. She didn't understand why.

"I apologize if I've offended you. I'm only trying to help our peers understand the situation. I'm sure you know that people are still wary of your brother's connection and even his disconnection with the Eskers kids."

"I can't control how people think any more than you can."

She felt herself smiling but didn't respond to Kaleb. Hadn't they earlier established that she actually had that power? With words.

"Come on," urged Kaleb. "We need to get to the Grandiuse." The four of them turned to leave, but Sigorny raised her pen in the air. "One more thing, if I could. Alex?"

Chase and Alex regarded one another before Chase pressed his fist to his mouth, stifling his amusement. An inside joke? Peculiar didn't begin to describe those two.

"You have a pretty solid relationship with Professor Duvall, right?"

Alex humphed.

Oh, don't pretend you don't like this, Alex, Sigorny thought. She pestered enough people by now to know when they truly felt bothered by her. Alex Ash didn't mind it, which Sigorny found interesting considering the hostility of her friends.

"Has she ever mentioned anything about temperamental ink?"

"Why would she?"

"She is Eidolon's notorious witch. The ink found in the Eskers kids' notebooks is the product of witchcraft."

"I think spirits with knowledge as extensive as Professor Duvall's prefer to be called the gifted."

She smiled. "Thank you. I'll rephrase. The ink is the product of the gifted, correct?"

"I don't know. I'm not one of them."

That you know of, Sigorny thought. *Sephi sure was.*

Alex crossed her arms. "Spirits wouldn't be nearly as advanced as we are without the help of the gifted."

"That's debatable. There's a reason our societies choose to separate. You don't think Duvall is somehow involved?"

"Not at all."

"And why is that?"

Alex raised a palm, balancing an invisible tray. "Because if Duvall was going to send secret messages to students, I'm sure she wouldn't be sending them to Reuben Seyferr or the Bond twins."

"True. Duvall makes it no secret that she despises those students which is why I asked. If she were going to put students in an illegal situation, wouldn't she choose spirits she didn't favor? The Eskers kids are connected to the hunters who threaten her kind."

"I suppose that would make sense," Alex replied, and this caused Sigorny to look up in surprise. "That is if the students they were attacking didn't include someone with whom she, as you worded it, has a *pretty solid relationship*." She pointed a finger at her own chest.

Chase chuckled.

"Hm," Sigorny murmured. "Thanks. To all of you. I appreciate your time."

"Come on, we can't be late," Gabe said, ushering his crew away. "Sigorny, you probably don't want to be late either."

Her pride swelled. "Thanks for your concern."

She would get to the evening meeting. But not yet. She lowered herself to the ground where they had been standing, and she wrote furiously. The scent of ambition began to ricochet off the nearby trees. She loved it. It smelled a bit like new office furniture.

Chapter Four

Books wallpapered the looming tower of the Grandiuse, chattering louder than the children sitting among them. The stories lowered their voices as Alex passed, filling her with that adolescent insecurity that they were talking about her. She watched Skye touch their bindings, tilting her head. It wouldn't surprise Alex if Skye understood their language.

Alex once asked the two sisters who guarded the doors why the walls slouched instead of standing upright as if the structure buckled under the weight of the roof. The little girls, Maria and Elizabeth, ignored her like they ignored everyone because they were too busy writing stories about nineteenth century heroines.

Skye had replied by saying, "The walls are tired."

With all the whispering, they didn't seem that tired to Alex.

The interaction with Sigorny nearly made them late, and each table was too packed for them to sit together. A group of girls beckoned Kaleb to their group, but there was barely enough room for even him to fit, and he seemed to be looking for someone else.

Alex took a step closer to Chase. If their group was forced to split, she wanted to stay with him. He squeezed her hand, and his voice knocked on the door of her mind:

We'll sit on the floor if there isn't room somewhere else.

A redhead popped up. Skye flicked her finger in a few directions, and kids left her table to join other groups. She waved Alex over to her multigenerational table. Gabe cursed in a low voice, and Chase flattened his lips in distaste, but Skye, who was a Legacy herself, already tugged Kaleb's arm, pulling him down onto the bench. He looked pleased.

"Hello, Alex," Tess Darwin greeted her stiffly. "Chase."

Gabe plopped down opposite them. Linton Darwin opened his mouth to speak, but thankfully Professor Duvall breezed past them down the aisle. Linton's words were lost, as were everyone else's. Duvall held two smoking vials in her bony hands, and the puffs of purple smog stole their voices.

Madame Paleo stood at the front of the gathering hall. When she smiled, her nose widened, taking up most of her face. "Good evening, newburies. Tomorrow we will introduce several new workshops, so please remember to select your desired sessions. This evening's gathering will be a bit unconventional: an introduction to the new workshops led by another guest from the Dual Towers at Broderick Square. She can only be with us for a few minutes as her line of work has been rather trafficable these days, but she's been kind enough to find the time to teach the workshops and to greet you this evening." Her outstretched hand revealed a nearly translucent woman. "Please welcome Dr. Massin."

The woman quavered like poor television reception.

Alex felt motion sick. "What's wrong with her?"

"She's boring," Kaleb replied.

"Maybe she's been dead a long time," Chase guessed.

Funny, she didn't slouch like the walls.

"Or she's boring," Kaleb repeated a bit louder, curling his disinterested body over the table and resting his cheek on his fist. A table of girls giggled at him, and he winked to them in reply. "I could think of a much better way to pass the time."

He glanced at Skye to see her reaction, but she continued to face the front.

The wispy woman blinked through thick glasses, adjusted her fuzzy Muppet-blue sweater, and greeted them in an echo of a voice as nasally tight as the hair spiraled atop her head. "I'm honored to have been chosen as the sociology representative this session, and I'm pleased that my area of expertise is being taken so seriously, especially after last year's incidents."

Alex's angst rose higher with each person turning to find her in the crowd, and embarrassingly enough, her attire transformed. A loose-fitting sheer blouse slouched over her tank, and her hair twisted in a side braid with a wave of bangs to frame her face.

Chase elbowed her. "Nice shirt."

She shushed him.

"Sociology." Dr. Massin sang the word like a hymn, and Kaleb groaned loudly. "It is necessary in order to understand the society in which we live."

Alex's mind rummaged through its contents. Images danced like the flashing pages of a flipbook, each pertaining to the topic of sociology. Her tenth grade English teacher. The name Karl Marx. Opening a dictionary and seeing: *denoting social or society. French, from Latin, socius.* A history show and Mr. Lasalle watching from a leather recliner. The pictures continued as her memory attempted to sort through them, to make sense of them.

Somewhere in the back of her mind, underneath the *swishing* of flipping pages, she heard a voice ask Dr. Massin how this was so important.

Alex refocused on their guest speaker, who lifted a hand to her chest in offense. She must not work with newburies very often.

"Of course it's essential to understand how spirits interact not only with one another but with other forms of the living."

"Forms?" Madison Constance asked. She sat nearest to the podium, ever attentive. Her hair twisted into a ballerina bun, mimicking Dr. Massin.

"The bodied. The gifted. The broken. The lost."

Gifted? They were actually going to openly discuss the topic? Alex scanned the room looking for Professor Duvall, whom she found crouched against the far wall in a heap of shawls and jewelry. Several empty vials lay at her feet. Her expression didn't indicate any sort of surprise though she fiddled with a large stone.

"Wasn't that the point of the Intro workshop?" Linton Darwin spoke only loud enough for their table to hear.

"You'd think," Tess replied, hawk-eying the woman. "What is she *doing*?"

Dr. Massin stood still at the edge of the podium. Her face curled into a smirk. "Part of the social knowledge you carried into death will not change. Your judgment ..." Her tweed skirt, which hovered above her geriatric grandma shoes, began to shrink until it tightened against her curves. Her horrid blue sweater shifted to sky blue and thinned to silk.

"Um." Kaleb rubbed his eyes, and a smile played at his mouth. "Hello."

"Your stereotypes ..." Dr. Massin's height increased as her shoes shed their Velcro and turned to black pumps. The glasses disappeared from her face, and her black hair fell to her waist. "The way you initially *see* people doesn't change, nor does the way you categorize them. We all do it. Our minds have been geared that way by our bodied societies."

Skye huffed and flipped her hair over her shoulder. "Not all of us."

Despite Skye's disagreement, the Grandiuse became quiet. Dr. Massin had the full attention of the newburies, due to her tricks or due to her breathtaking—though still annoyingly blurry—projection. "Why is this subject important? Well. You need to learn the values, the norms, the rules of *this* society, a culture of people who live in their minds but carry the predetermined guidelines from the living."

"Massin?" Tess drew out the name as though trying to place it.

"Civil rights?" Linton asked her.

Tess nodded. "Anti."

"What civil rights?" Chase asked.

"If she's the Massin I've been warned about," Tess snarled, "she adamantly, and very vocally, opposed the advancement of the gifted during the Civil Rights Movement."

Dr. Massin vanished. She reappeared, hovering over Madison Constance. "The topic is always presented to those of you preparing for the Categorization. After all, we naturally categorize each other. You'd be lying if you told me you didn't have an opinion of me before I began to speak due to my style of dress and the way I spoke. Sociology is always a part of the newbury learning process, but due to certain events, the advisors ordered me to visit the entire congregation of the Grandiuse tonight to encourage you to begin your studies a bit earlier."

Xavier Darwin turned his critical gaze to Alex. Linton and Tess followed suit, and Alex flinched at the pinpricks of scrutiny. Their interest was as sharp as their noses.

"What?" Alex finally demanded of them.

Tess stretched over Skye's lap, the edges of her black hair grazing Alex's shoulder.

"I've been meaning to tell you, we came upon some information I think you'll find illuminating."

Tess quieted as Madame Paleo strode past their table in her

ugly power suit and joined Dr. Massin, who faded even more. "That's about all the time Dr. Massin has tonight. We need to allow her to return to her obligations at the Dual Tower." She faced the flickering projection of a woman. "We thank you, Doctor, for joining us for a few minutes. I know it was difficult."

"My pleasure." Dr. Massin smiled. "I'll see you guys soon."

Kaleb strained to watch her, so much that he had practically draped himself over the table. When she snapped out of sight, he flopped down, thumping his head against the table. "Damn."

A lectern appeared on the podium. Paleo petted it and sighed. "Being a spirit is more liberating than the confines of humanity. Long ago, spirits were free to do whatever they pleased. Then, as we've discussed in history, mankind expanded. Eidolon was created, but our settlement, the largest and most powerful in the western hemisphere, is only one of many. We choose to live the urban life. However, should your Categorization lead you elsewhere, you do have options."

"Categorization?" Alex asked. "What is that?"

Kaleb grabbed a sheet of paper from Gabe and began scribbling. "Newbury Categorization." He folded the paper into a note and slid it across the table to Skye. She opened it with a frightened expression but laughed upon reading whatever it said.

Alex tried to peek at it, but couldn't see what he'd written. "I have no idea what you're talking about."

"You won't need to worry about it," Tess intervened. "None of us will. We're not going anywhere."

That still didn't answer Alex's question. She turned to her

left to look at Chase. *Do you know about this?* she asked.

I've heard bits from other newburies. After a certain number of workshops, we are evaluated for our placements.

Why?

To know what we will do and where we will end up after the workshops are finished.

Alex didn't like the sound of this. *It's a choice?*

They choose for us.

This was news to her. Chase waved his hand as if to indicate she shouldn't worry about it and pointed to the podium, encouraging her to listen.

"There are many suburban settlements. They are smaller establishments that promote a simple afterlife with simple governments and representatives who act as liaisons. They are affectionately termed colonies, although some argue that the connotation of the word is demeaning. Our own city here in Eidolon is, of course, the most sought after home in the afterworld."

Tess must have decided this conversation was not of importance to them because she folded herself over Skye's lap to speak to Alex again. "We want to invite you to join us later this week."

"Where?"

"Legacy meeting."

Alex heard Chase snort beside her. She jabbed him, but he grabbed her elbow and tucked his arm under hers.

"This week is going to be overwhelming with the new workshops," Alex said. "Can't you just tell me now?"

Tess shook her head. "This isn't something I can tell you. I need to show you."

Alex glanced at Chase and then shrugged back to Tess. "I might have to wait for another meeting."

"Suit yourself. Just let me know."

Madame Paleo addressed a question about lingerers and wanderers and thoughts popped over her head like bubbles.

Tess put what looked like a formal invitation down on the table. She pressed her fingers over the golden cursive lettering and pushed it down the table toward Alex. "FYI, it's about your family history. These are directions to the room."

The air around Alex began to spark. Chase's shirt grew a hood, which he lifted as though the sparks might ignite his hair.

"I want to know now."

"Like I said, you need to see it."

What about her limited family history would have to be seen and not spoken? She glanced sideways at Tess's pointy profile, disliking her immensely and willing her to give in and confess what she knew, but Tess shook her head with an expression that read, *be patient*.

To Alex's surprise, Chase picked up the invite. "Tess, Paleo said this Massin lady is going to teach us how to treat one another. Do you think she's here because of Alex?"

The large doors of the Grandiuse creaked open. Funny, the doors did not make such noises when anyone else entered. They deliberately drew attention to the situation because the children who stepped through the threshold were not about to be given a warm welcome. A cold gust of wind rustled the hair of the sisters by the doorway, extinguishing their candles and weaving its way through the crowd in warning. It crawled up Alex's spine to tickle the nape of her neck.

The Eskers kids were back.

"Nope," Tess whispered to Chase. "I think she's here because of them."

The Eskers kids shuffled in slowly with their heads bowed, all except Jack Bond, who stared out into the crowd, unaware of the hatred they felt for him. Alex felt the bitterness, the disgust from newburies around her, saturating the room. Joey Rellingsworth looked ready to cry, but the last time Alex saw him, he was throwing copper stones at her, trying to kill her. A hat appeared over Hecker Smithson's large head, and he pulled it down as far as he could. Several of the other Eskers kids had sunglasses.

Alex watched the group move to the back of the room. They didn't even try to find a place among their peers. They were not equals anymore. They were outsiders, which ironically was the very last thing they'd wanted when the brotherhood found them. Ardor Westfall told Alex last spring, the only way those kids could have seen the writing in their notebooks was if they were looking for it, looking for a place to fit in and belong. They found a niche all right, but it dug them deep into a hole of isolation.

If Jack had truly meant to hurt her, to hurt Chase, and Jonas and Kaleb, he would be ashamed of himself. The others seemed ashamed but not Jack. He didn't look apologetic; he wasn't embarrassed. He snarled at her, looking positively furious.

Chapter Five

Jack Bond wasn't worth the energy to hate him. Chase knew this. He'd been wary of Jack from day one, and he ignored it. Stupid. Jack had hidden behind his freckles, his nerdy horse teeth, and Alex's pity. Chase should have known better than to trust Alex's expectations of people. He wished he had half as much faith in the human mind as she did, but he lived in reality, a colorful one. A truthful one. Where Alex saw smiles and listened to tone, Chase saw greed and ambition and pain.

His irritation pooled at his feet as they walked the streets, but the fog overpowered it. Gabe called the fog a ubiquitous force. His brother used words others didn't care to say in normal conversation even with genius brains. The strength of Chase's dead eyes allowed him to see the actual water droplets in the mist. They waded through the haze that crystallized a calm blue, a billowing baby blanket. Blue, he assumed, meant peace. Some days, he resented the colors dancing before him because it took the mystery out of people. He knew their mood and their intentions before they spoke. But nature was different, more honest, so he liked it better.

"Did you see how he looked at me?" Alex asked.

"Don't even think about Jack."

How dare Jack glare at her. How dare he look at her at all. Chase could still feel the heat of his anger blazing underneath his cheeks, but it didn't compare to the fire he felt at the Grandiuse. He'd launched himself from the bench and took aim at Jack, shoving the air so hard he accidentally knocked over Joey and Hecker too.

His brothers did nothing to stop him. In fact, Kaleb bolted forward with his fists raised, ready to finish what Chase started. It was the Darwins who held them back, calmed them and spoke sense. The *Darwins* playing peacemakers? How quickly things changed.

Why did Alex care about how Jack Bond looked at her? He watched her wave to Josepha and Johanna as they passed their store. Somewhere along the way, Alex had picked up a need for acceptance, and his acceptance alone wasn't enough anymore.

"What's wrong?" Alex murmured. "Why do you look like that?"

"You're making fun of my looks now?"

"I can feel it. Why are you worried?"

"One of us should be."

"Chase?" Alex lifted her head.

He kept his gaze above her head and felt his jaw clench in response.

Look at me.

"Or what?"

She stopped walking and turned to face him. He couldn't help himself, and he couldn't think of a reason to hold back. He tugged at the bottom of her shirt to make her fall into him. He heard her sigh as he buried his face in her neck. He didn't need to breathe but thank God he remembered how. She smelled like honeysuckle and sugar. He placed his hand gently around the base of her neck and lifted her chin to kiss her. She tasted like sugar, too. He could feel her grinning through the kiss, and it was contagious.

God, he loved her.

Truthfully, it frightened him. Vulnerability. No one wore it well, but Chase had never been one to care about how he appeared. Despite his fear, he gladly accepted it and with each kiss, with each turn of his head, he became more and more addicted. He opened his mouth wider to savor the cool sweetness that scorched his anger.

She was the one to pull away, and the space surrounding them sizzled. Her hair fell forward, grazing his face. "People are staring."

Her face was still so close to his that he could only stare at her pink lips as she spoke. He savored the marvelous sensation drumming through him. "So?"

He turned his head to kiss her again, but she retracted. He

hoped she'd change her mind, but she tugged at his hand to keep moving.

Damn it.

"Tell me about this Categorization," she said, wrapping herself around his forearm.

He groaned and continued slowly down Lazuli Street. "What about it?"

In his peripheral, he saw the space around Alex redden. It wasn't violent but rose-petal soft with an undertone of confusion. Alex's passion came in many shades.

"It sounds repressive to me," she replied with a huff— also red. "I mean, who are they to say someone doesn't have enough potential to do what they *choose* to do?"

"Not everyone is *meant* to do what they *want*." This was the very reason Chase resented the fact that the afterworld government knew about his colorful sight. He didn't want to read and report people for the rest of his existence. "I'm sure the process saves some spirits the time trying to figure out where they belong."

"Always the voice of reason."

They skipped over stray bricks littering Lazuli's crooked street of mossy walls and misshapen doorways. The ivy twisted around the legs of the lampposts like shy children. Two zigzagging gray lines lifted from the road and stretched over the rooftops like tracks in the dirt rising into the heavens. Chase wondered where the makeshift road led and how it got there.

"Look at the business owners," Chase suggested as they

passed the shops of various heights, sizes, and shapes. "They weren't chosen as Ardors or Movers or Meditators, and they seem to enjoy their afterlife just fine."

Death was easy for them, a party. Chase could see Kaleb and his lackadaisical attitude being content on Lazuli Street for the rest of his life. As long as he owned a substantial amount of attention.

"You're playing devil's advocate," Alex noted, and he didn't refute. "What good is living for a few additional centuries without purpose?"

She sounded like Ellington. Alex had always been impressionable, and Ellington imprinted his thoughts on others whenever he spoke. It was having an effect on her. What if their purpose was to enjoy the simple pleasures?

"I heard that."

He let go of her to massage his temples. Sometimes, it was a pain in the ass to have someone else in his mind. He didn't wander into her head too much because, with her eyes, he saw the world through a rose-colored lens. It gave him a headache, like wearing reading glasses without needing them.

Strolling next to her, wading through her passionate air, was it lame to think *this was* his purpose? To be hers. To protect her and love her?

Ellington would have a fit if Chase shared these thoughts with him. Complacency, that's what he'd label it, but Ellington didn't understand. Chase felt the weight of the world in these colors. The sorrow, regret, and disappointment seeping out into the universe from living beings, those poisons didn't rest on his shoulders, they weighed on his soul. There was so much sadness in the world, and he could feel it all. The only thing that made him feel better was the idea that he could be a protector. It made him think he had some sort of control over things.

Chase reached over and adjusted the messy side braid slung over Alex's shoulder. He bent to kiss her neck. "There's a fine line between the want for purpose and the want for recognition."

She lifted her fingers to touch the place on her neck where his lips had been. "You think recognition is bad?"

"I think too often the idea of purpose gets confused with attention."

"I don't think the Categorization is about attention."

"Isn't it?" he asked. "It singles us out."

"It's about scaring us into behaving and paying attention in class."

Chase snapped his fingers. "Paying what?"

"Attention." She realized what she'd said and smacked his arm. "Totally different. Why are you grinning like that?"

"Because I'm right."

"Whatever."

"Attention is better associated with except*ion* than accept*ance*."

"I'm not ready for such a deep conversation right now."

He grabbed her hand again and lifted it high to spin her around. "All I'm saying is that you shouldn't worry about the Categorization. You're not going anywhere."

"I'm not worried about me."

"They know what I can do," he said. Damn government.

"You sound like it's a horrible thing. I think it's amazing, and I can only see glimpses in your head. If it were me, I'd want everyone to know."

He stopped walking. "You say that even after all the Sephi Anovark hype?"

"It's not so bad."

She forced him to keep moving, but his restless mind wandered more quickly than his feet. During life, when Chase got into trouble his consequences were detention or being grounded. When he broke rules in Eidolon, he hadn't realized the severity of what he'd done. They took him into custody at the Dual Towers, but it wasn't solitary confinement. They figured out how to use him. They stuck him behind a two-way mirror and made him spend his detainment documenting colors during interviews.

He didn't worry so much about why they were using him but if they'd *remember* him. Use him again. They might not be so polite next time. This was the government, after all. Look at Ellington, stuck greeting generations of newburies outside a bunker in the woods. Of course, Chase's talents guaranteed him a seat in Brigitta's learning center for another few years. Ellington thought this was wonderful, but Chase didn't enjoy being a human lie detector.

On the other hand, he would be more than willing to ride the air of the opportunity and allow the breeze to carry him along with Alex. He wanted to be wherever she was. It reminded him of those gray lines leaving the ground and running parallel to one another into the sky and beyond. Eventually, they could go up no higher before falling, aiming for the ground.

They were nearing the end of Lazuli Street. If they didn't turn back, they would enter the hoopla of Broderick square. The idea of tourists caused him to tense, and Alex must have felt it because she placed a hand over his racing heart.

"By the way, since when do you hate attention? You're a Lasalle."

"I never asked for it."

"Spoken like a true attention hog."

"It's not the same as cracking jokes or winning a race. I don't want people to act differently around me."

"I never would."

"That's because you're stuck with me."

A cluster of spirits gathered ahead along the side of the road where Lazuli met the square. They chatted excitedly and watched, waiting for something.

"Is there a parade or a festival we didn't know about?" Alex asked.

He wondered what it would be like to be so blissfully innocent. She didn't realize they were waiting for her until the spirits began to buzz and the trajectory of their excitement landed on the crown of Alex's head. She waved, and Chase groaned. If he led her into Broderick Square, she would have a celebrity bull's-eye on her back. And whether she was willing to wear that bull's-eye like a prom dress, didn't matter. He wasn't willing to find out who might take aim.

She continued to smile at the onlookers, but he put his hands on her shoulders and steered her off the road. "Come on."

He shoved her through a door shaped like a large P. Stauffer's Pub. It was a sanctuary with its grungy wooden interior, coating of dust, and scarce crowds. Chase used to escape here a lot.

He and Alex went straight back to the corner, the best spot in the bar, nestled by a cracked, yellow window with age-warped glass. Alex slid onto the bar stool and steered her seat to face him. She placed her hands on his knees, situating herself between them.

He ordered them two drinks, which Stauffer deposited with a gruff nod. Alex took a sip of the mist and jolted back in her seat. She blinked several times and used her knuckles to wipe away invisible tears. "That's strong."

Her dark eyes were oversized, along with her hair and her idealism. He'd always been intrigued by the way the shape of her eyes turned down sadly at the edges. She allowed him to stare, and she did the same, as though some unspoken secret sat between them. Even in their minds, they didn't have to talk. Chase didn't need words to understand contentment.

He gave her a tug to encourage her to come closer, and she accepted, brushing her lips against his.

This time he was the one to pull back. "Why do you think spirits are so worried about purpose, Al?"

She thought about the question so intently that her brow folded, and he desperately wanted to smooth out the lines it created on her forehead. Her face wasn't meant to frown.

"We were given this amazing gift. Life. Time. I don't blame spirits for not wanting to waste it."

He twirled a loose curl along her temple. "And what about you? Why do you personally think *you*, in particular, were given this gift?"

"You're being very serious today."

"Is this too serious? We can change the subject if you want. How about that blue flower you've been carrying around. I'll bet Skye stuffed it in your pocket, didn't she?"

The corner of Alex's tiny, pink mouth lifted. "No, we don't have to change the subject. I think I was dealt a shady hand in life. This could be my repentance."

"Because you were sick?"

"No. Because of you. We didn't get a chance when we were alive. It wasn't fair."

His feelings for her swelled and threatened to burst from his projection. The electricity between them hummed, and the light on the bar beside them dimmed, brightened, and then died.

Chase took a sip from his drink and spoke without thinking. "Do you think spirits live here together?"

Whoa. Where did that come from? Once the words left his mouth, he pictured himself waking up each morning and finding her next to him, and he wanted it. They deserved that.

"Where? In the city?" She flattened her mouth. "I never thought about it, but I don't see why not. There are so many high rises in the government square."

"They say minds aren't meant to be shared, but it doesn't seem like we really have a choice. Commitment is a lot different when there is no …"

"'Til death do you part?" she finished for him, and he nodded. "Death already did us part. It didn't work."

Too close for comfort.

"You think you'll get sick of me?" she asked.

"In a world of infinite opportunities? No."

"What if we were in a more limited world?"

"No." The grin on his face felt stupidly wide, but he couldn't help it and he didn't care. "You keep life pretty interesting. And death, too."

She gritted her teeth. "Not intentionally. I can't believe you brought up living arrangements after Brigitta, and you haven't even let me see your room."

He liked the few moments of watching her sleep before she woke up and saw him. "I don't want you to get into any trouble."

"My record is clean. How's yours looking?" She rested an elbow on the bar, glancing behind it. "There might be a broom back there."

"Oh, I get it. You're going to clean my record. Did you forget that you're the reason it's such a mess in the first place?"

Alex's face became serious. At first, Chase thought he'd offended her, but he followed her gaze to the window where there was now a group of spirits outside gawking through the hazy glass. Some seemed angry, shaking their heads and sneering. Others were curious, swaying from side to side to sneak a better peek at Alex. Many of them held papers in their hands.

Stauffer's Pub never attracted more than a handful of barflies, but Chase was so engrossed in Alex and their conversation that he hadn't noticed the buzz. Each stool around the bar was filled. The tables crowded with spirits pretending to watch the prehistoric televisions mounted on the wall, but their attention crawled to the corner by the window, to them. How long until these barflies bit?

What could make one person so fascinating that people would stalk them? The heat of his anger returned.

"How did they know you were here?" he wondered aloud.

"Skye mentioned something about a map."

"A *what*?"

"Do you need another drink?" a man on the other side of Alex asked in an accented voice. He extended his hand, reaching out for her with tattooed fingers.

"Don't touch her," Chase warned.

"Chase."

He pulled Alex closer to him, pressing his hands on either side of her waist.

The guy held up his palms in defense. "No harm."

Even as he said it, he took a step closer, bringing his muddy colors with him. Muddy wasn't good. This guy couldn't decide what he wanted to do here.

Stauffer watched them while slowly scrubbing the bar with a rag. He turned to glare at the musty window where the dust rose like ashes and clouded the view.

"There's a back door, yeh know," he whispered. "Leads out to Gramble Street."

Alex looked from Stauffer to the window, and then back to Stauffer in surprise. "We don't have to leave."

A girl climbed off her barstool and hurried over to them, shoving an envelope in Alex's face. "I was wondering if you might be able to tell me about my grandchildren. Their pictures are here."

Alex stumbled over a response, visibly confused, but Chase understood. If people thought she was Sephi, she'd be able to give them answers to impossible questions.

Chase's heart pounded. Curious people were one thing, but curious was one step away from crazy. Alex reached out and placed her open palm over his heart once again to still his racing pulse, but her touch was more like a zap of electricity.

The window beside them exploded and shattered glass fell like rain. Chase worried that his panic had caused a reaction until a brick thudded on the ground at their feet. Chase cursed and pushed Alex into motion.

"Let's get out of here."

He kept her in his sight, trailing behind her as they walked to the back of the bar where Stauffer waited to show them out to safety. One word drifted around the room, spoken in different voices. Chase's mind shuffled like a deck of cards, as the word bounced from wall to wall, slamming itself against the confines of his memory. Havilah. That's what they were all talking about.

Havilah. It was a Parrish family.

Why the hell would they know that name here?

Chapter Six

September was loud. Alex assumed the reason was either the looming chaos of autumn festivities or the electricity of change. September whistled while it worked, carrying an array of opportunities in its briefcase, but the shifting of seasons did not affect tourism in Eidolon.

"Skye, how do you deal with it?"

"What?"

"People staring at you all the time."

Skye pointed at Alex's shoes as they thumped down the vestibule ramp. "Seriously, are you trying to make that much noise?"

"Sorry. I like the clicking sound."

"You're so weird. Anyway, is this because of the mob scene you created on Lazuli the other day? I hear spirits are actually asking for your autograph now."

And throwing bricks. "By the way, your steps are making as much noise as mine."

"I'm just trying to keep up." Skye dropped to her bottom and slid down the rest of the ramp into the vestibule. At the foot of the ramp, she jumped to her feet. "You don't strike me as a wallflower. I'm sure you had plenty of attention in life."

No. Any favor Alex had earned in life rode the emotion of sympathy. No one wanted to trade lives with the sick girl, even if her friends happened to be the Lasalles. Such renown didn't fall into the same desirable category as Gossamer charm. Skye complained about her hippie community, but she still went to school like everyone else, where Alex felt positive Skye was as desired then as she was now.

Alex was only getting attention for something she wasn't. She knew she was standing on Sephi Anovark's pedestal. Spirits took swings at her, but at such a height, the danger posed little threat and only meant more recognition. Since the publication of Sigorny's first article, spirits began to reach out their fingers to feel the energy of her projection. It frightened Chase, she knew, but she couldn't ignore the buzz of it, the high of fame. It was difficult to hate it.

Alex followed Skye into the courtyard. The day smelled of fresh earth, so another newbury might have arrived or the rain was simply making a statement. "Spirits bow to you when you steal their seat in class. You get the royal treatment wherever you go."

"I'm a Gossamer. Comes with the territory."

Alex kicked a rock. "They've never tried to remove you from school for it."

Skye stopped. "What are you talking about?"

Alex focused on the moss growing through the cracks of the stone walkway. "Romey had a meeting with me the other day to discuss my options. I guess there's been talk of keeping me away from everybody. Not forever. Just for a while until things die down."

They paused to watch a rowboat float by in the fog. When it disappeared into the trees, they began to walk again.

"What about your workshops?" Skye asked.

"I'd do them here at Brigitta or in the classroom alone."

Skye's mouth fell open. "Whoa. Really? What did you say?"

"I didn't have to say anything. *Westfall* stood up for me." She took in Skye's shocked expression. "I know, right? He said if we isolated me, people would treat me even more differently. He thinks the best thing to do is to act like I'm just another newbury. That's why I asked you how you deal with it."

"Did you not use that flower I gave you? Everything will work out. The world wouldn't have it any other way."

"I guess I'm still trying to figure out if this craze is good or bad."

Skye looked her up and down as they climbed the steps to the learning center. "You want to be like everyone else? She who likes to make noise when she walks?"

"Well, no."

"All right, then." The red in Skye's hair lightened. "I came to that conclusion a long time ago. Craze comes with the territory. You can't have it all. If you want to stand out, you are going to have to sacrifice a little bit of privacy, and if that means people stare at you while you and Chase make out in the street, then fine."

"We don't do that."

"Please. You're all over each other."

They entered Duvall's macabre classroom, wallpapered with vials of slime, frames of gray bones, and the moaning of rot. Above their heads, thousands of tiny glass tubes and flasks swayed and clanked together, harmonizing a symphony that sounded vaguely familiar. *Carnival of the Animals*, Alex's mind told her. The lopsided office door opened, and Duvall stuck out her head of raggedy hair. She grinned upward at the field of glass and jerked her arms around to direct the music.

Alex slid into a desk next to the aquarium, pretending she didn't feel left out when Skye and Duvall began their usual gossiping. Duvall never asked Alex for her observations, only Skye. How in the world did Skye know that the trees had a lousy night? How did she know that the fountain mist in the vestibule needed to be refreshed? How did she know that nothing out of the ordinary had occurred in the courtyard that morning?

Many times Alex attempted to interrupt their ridiculous conversations, but before she could form words, Duvall stomped her foot and Alex's thoughts flattened against the ground of her mind.

Duvall snapped her knobby fingers. "Alex, did Skye get a chance to look at Sephi's letters?"

Skye retracted and crinkled her nose. "Oh, I sure did."

"What's wrong?"

Skye shuddered. "The second I touched that devil box, it snapped at me like a guard dog."

Alex swore she heard the box snarl that day. "Skye cowered in the corner and cried."

"I don't like that thing. I think you should bury it and never look at it again."

"Cobwebs!" For Duvall, this was a curse word. She pushed up the sleeves of her layers of wool to reveal deathly skinny arms. "I'm not responsible for the personalities of my creations, but the box served its purpose. It kept Sephi's treasures safe."

Skye moaned. "Please tell me that what you have in mind for us this morning has nothing to do with those letters."

"You're in luck. The task I have for you is simple. Travel down the river and to the edge of our boundaries on the western side of the city. Remember the tree with the bark that coils and twists like ribbons?"

This didn't sound simple to Alex. The new workshops would begin in a few hours, and she didn't want to exert all of her energy playing go-fetch.

"You know which one I speak of?"

"Yes," Skye replied.

"I need some of the bark."

"How much?" Before Skye even finished the question, Duvall was handing her a burlap sack.

"Fill it, please." She handed another one to Alex.

"That's a big—"

Skye shushed her. "I've seen the tree before. The banana slugs love it. Are you making more Thymoserum?"

A box waited on the floor by their feet. Duvall used her mind to transfer multiple vials from the ceiling into the box. "It isn't for my own personal use. No matter the level of intelligence and study in the Broderick Division of Science, they still don't make Thymoserum as effectively as I do. They don't appreciate the diligence of doing something by hand nor do they understand the temperament of botanicals and the attitudes of minerals."

With that, she shooed them away.

Alex struggled to keep up with Skye. She felt frazzled, and it showed. No matter how hard she concentrated, she kept looking down at mismatched clothes, and her hair fell annoyingly in front of her eyes.

"What's wrong?" Skye asked. "Is it the Eskers kids?"

They would be there today. Alex couldn't avoid them during workshops.

"Stop worrying. You're making the air shake. There's nothing harmful about those kids except for overeagerness and botched ambition."

Alex wished she could believe that. She reminded herself that considering Skye's lack of consciousness during the Eskers battle and beating last spring, she didn't carry the same traumatic memories as Alex.

"Have you seen them since the Grandiuse?"

Alex shook her head.

They kept quiet until they reached a ramose creek, which divided like driveways in a cul-de-sac. Alex stopped, but Skye continued to tread along a path running parallel to the leftmost branch of the creek.

Alex concentrated on her feet so she wouldn't leave tracks in the mud. Or get it on her shoes. "Where do these creeks lead?"

"Coming up soon."

As they traveled, the water quieted until it became silent. They reached a lone pier, leading to a simple wooden cottage. As if finding this in the middle of the woods wasn't strange enough, the water whitened, frozen around the pier despite the heat. If she tried hard enough, Alex could hear the icy water screaming.

"Who lives here?"

Skye shrugged. "Not sure, but each part of the creek leads to a different house."

"Is the tree here?"

"Not far now." She ignored Alex's exaggerated sigh. "I don't think you realize how far we've gone so quickly."

"Where are we?"

"A few miles from campus."

"*Miles?*"

"You concentrated on following me. I concentrated on projecting us places."

No wonder Alex felt dizzy.

Skye shook her shoulders in a little dance. "That's why

I didn't tell you what I was doing. You question everything. Even right now. There's a question hanging off your lips. I can see it dangling there."

Alex wiped her mouth. "You projected us forward? Why didn't you do the same thing last spring in Parrish when we went looking for Chase and Jonas? Why did we run instead?"

"Because I was following *you* that day. I didn't know those woods. We can only project ourselves if we can see where we're going. And I couldn't really explain that to you then because we were in a hurry." She spun in a circle. "Isn't this cool? No one usually travels this far away from the buildings."

"I can see why." Alex glanced back at the mossy path behind them, wondering if she'd get too terribly lost trying to find her way home. Their company only included monstrous redwood tree trunks and the sounds of nature. Alex zeroed in on the squeaking of squirrel talk. They argued over which direction to travel. Alex wasn't sure how she knew their language, but she did. "I might go back. I want to get my things ready for the workshops."

"We have plenty of time."

Alex couldn't think of a legitimate excuse. Peeling the bark from a tree didn't sound stimulating, and a trek through the forest didn't help.

Skye's face brightened. "Want me to show you something?"

Not really.

"A secret."

Alex perked up. "Are you finally going to explain how you know so much?"

"Huh?" Skye stiffened. "No. It's something here."

Alex took in their surroundings: trees, bushes, plants, dirt, and pinecones. "No offense, but it looks the same as the rest of the forest."

"Wait." Skye lifted a finger to her lips and moved soundlessly through the brush.

"How do you find this tree without anything to mark where you are?"

Skye stopped. "This stays between us, but the first time Duvall sent me to find the bark she needed, I got lost."

Shocking.

"She didn't send me again until it was an emergency. And she gave me a landmark."

Alex glanced left to right. "I think you missed it."

"No one knows it's out here because they don't need to look for it, and likewise, I don't think it tries to be found. Come here." She waved a hand, urging Alex to follow. She used her other hand to push aside a few branches, revealing a misplaced, red-brick pathway. It began from nowhere but weaved through parallel aisles of large T-shaped, gray flowers. The flowers stood in rows, as still as gravestones but as loud as the dead.

The flower field rose into a hill, creating the illusion that it marched straight up to the sky. At the edge of the hill was a square entryway made of stone. It interrupted the beauty of gray crosses and stared at them with its sharp, black eye.

"How do you feel?" Skye asked.

"What?"

"Tell me what you feel when you look at them."

"The flowers?" Bemused, Alex turned back to the field. At first, her cynicism hindered her senses, but she focused on the symmetrical rows. The clouds lingered low, thought-bubbles of puffy white.

She sensed so many different things at one time, yanking her mind in so many directions. She felt the comfortable fatigue after finishing a task. She felt the gratification of winning first place. She felt the humility of accepting defeat gracefully without regret. She felt the dissatisfaction of a bittersweet ending and the promise of meeting someone new. She felt the heartbreak of losing someone special.

Skye watched her, nodding.

"I feel ..." Alex felt the emotions swirl around her, pulling her back and forth at her elbows, "... full."

"My sentiments exactly."

"What is this place?"

"I tried to ask Duvall about it once, but she told me that some things don't need to be discussed. When I'm walking through the woods, I wait until that feeling hits, and then I follow it. The tree we need is just past here."

Alex didn't want to leave. These sensations were fulfilling. "We don't have go yet, do we? What's in the cave?"

"No clue."

The gray flowers shone like light behind stained glass, glinting despite the overcast of redwood shadows. She crouched down next to them.

"Have you ever picked one?"

"No way. I don't know what they are!"

Alex gazed longingly at the T-shaped blooms, considering the risk.

"Come on," Skye said. "The tree is back here."

"Can't we stay a little longer?"

Skye grinned, exposing a line of perfect teeth. "Oh! I thought you wanted to head back and spend some time stacking your books and practicing your handwriting."

"Shut up."

Skye held up the sack. "Let's go. It might take a little while to peel this much bark."

Alex bid goodbye to the field and trudged slowly after Skye. "Is this going to take forever?"

"Stop complaining," Skye reprimanded, lifting her knees high to step through the plants. "You won't even remember all the hard labor."

"Don't be so sure." Alex swatted at tree branches.

"We're peeling the bark from a tree that makes the mind forget. Trust me, you won't remember."

Alex couldn't decide if that made the task better or worse. She knew Thymoserum tricked people into forgetting what they saw. It was how the spirited removed things they needed from the bodied world.

"We're almost at Eidolon's gate."

Alex could sense the border before they reached it. It pushed against her like walking into the wind, cautioning her. Finally, she saw the withered grandmother of a tree wilting near the perimeter, stretching its knobby branches in through the gate. Even its thin, frail leaves wrinkled with age.

Alex ran her hand along the bark, which broke away easily like brittle bones. She pitied the tree. It begged to come inside, reaching out to them. "Will it hurt the tree if we take too much of its bark?"

Skye sat on a root, like a child on a grandparent's knee. "I think she likes being needed. She wouldn't stretch through the gate otherwise. The rest of them aren't so willing."

"The rest?"

"These trees are all around the perimeter. I think they were planted there so if people happen to get too close, they won't remember."

"You always take the bark from this tree?"

"Her branches are the only ones I can reach without going outside the boundary."

The bars of the gate intertwined and zigzagged in a spider web pattern. Alex closed her fingers around a section of it, testing the durability. "Out of curiosity, do you know how to get through?"

Skye's voice dropped. "Why?"

"So we can take bark from some of the other branches. That way, this side won't be bare."

"Yeah, I know how."

"After I died, Ellington said he had to pull me through it or I couldn't do it."

"That's only because your brain was limited at the time. You wouldn't have believed you could cross through those bars even if he told you."

Alex ran her fingers along the tough, cold gate. The crooked "bars" extended high above them and felt as strong as steel.

"Any spirit can get through if they know how," Skye explained. "The gate has energy, like anything else, but you can feel the strength of it, right?"

"Is that to keep newburies from knowing how to go through it?"

Skye stuck her hand through the gate. "If that's the case, they failed. It's really easy to go in and out."

"Is it safe?"

"In my opinion, we're more at risk waltzing through that fishbowl of tourism in Broderick Square."

"Good call. You know," Alex cocked her head, "you kind of remind me of Jonas sometimes."

Skye scrunched her nose.

"It's a compliment," Alex murmured, breathing deeply as a breeze rustled the leaves.

Skye touched her hand to the tree and her face clouded.

"What?"

"Nothing. It's just a little tired."

"Who?"

"The tree."

"How do you *know* that?"

Skye shrugged, and Alex jutted her chin forward to show that she wanted a legitimate answer.

"I know how to listen. Stop looking at me like I'm insane." Skye stepped backward through the gate, watching Alex the entire time. She appeared on the other side, grinning like a goof.

If she wanted to change the subject, she'd succeeded. Alex's jaw dropped down into the moss below. "How did you do that?"

"I pictured myself walking through. And I did."

"But I didn't see you go through it. You appeared there."

"Didn't look the same in my mind. Walk through it, Alex. Sometimes you're like a brand new dead kid. If you don't believe half the things we do, and if you can't see it in your mind, how the heck do you expect it to happen?"

"Chase calls me naïve."

"You're naïve enough to think this isn't possible. Shift your mind enough to put you on the other side."

Alex blinked, and in that split second she pictured her projection as a chess piece, moving from one square to the next. She found herself on other side of the gate, on the outside looking in.

"Whoa!" She grinned at her friend. "Are you gifted, Skye?"

"No!" She let out a brisk cough of humor. "No way. Why do you ask?"

"I've wanted to ask you for a long time. You understand things, you know, kind of the way Professor Duvall explains them."

"Not at all. Not gifted. I grew up with a bunch of tree hugging drug addicts. They were *all* different there. If I had the abilities of the gifted, I would have used that power to turn the rapist who murdered me into a beetle."

Something fell at their feet. The impact was heavy, like bitterness. Skye had never given any details about her death.

"If I was magical, I wouldn't have died. He lived in our colony for three years, and no one saw him for what he was. They had other things on their minds and in their bloodstreams, distorting life." A branch lowered to her shoulder. She patted it. "There was nothing magical about my life."

"After something like that, how are you so *sweet* all the time?"

"Because death is so much better."

Skye's seriousness felt foreign. Alex wanted Skye to go back to preaching about the properties of flowers and herbs and stones. She wanted her to throw her hair over her shoulder and giggle at the boys trailing behind her.

"I'll tell you my secret if you tell me yours," Alex offered.

"No offense, but your secrets hover over the heads of the newburies in the vestibule every morning."

"Not all of them."

Skye considered this. "Fine." She spun on her heel.

Alex stared at Skye's back. "Why did you turn around?"

"I can't look at you while we do this."

"Why?"

"Just because. You go first. I'm not sure you have a secret to equal mine."

"I'd be offended by your lack of trust, but I know this will be worth your secret, so fine, I'll go first." Alex felt a knot forming in her mind, thoughts weaving under and over, through themselves, tightening in apprehension. "Chase and I can speak to each other in our minds."

"Like how?"

Alex threw her hands in the air. "I don't know how. We just can."

"When you're in the same room?"

"No. He could be across campus, and I can hear him. I can even see what he's seeing if I want to."

"I've never heard of that."

"No kidding. Why do you think we kept it a secret?"

Skye still didn't face Alex but reached out to peel some of the bark from the tree beside her. "You know, that explains some things, like why you guys sit and stare at each other, looking like you're in mid conversation."

Alex followed Skye's lead and picked at the tree. She hadn't realized she and Chase were so obvious. "Don't tell anyone, okay?"

"Agreed."

"Oh, this is silly, Skye. Turn around and look at me."

Skye twisted with a pout on her face. "My secret has to do with pictures. They haunt me."

"Pictures?"

"In my mind."

Alex leaned against the tree and crossed her arms. She didn't think this was worth spilling her guts. "Aren't we all *haunted* by snapshots when our minds remember things?"

"I don't see only the things my own thoughts have filed away. I see the things that objects have saved in their memories. See, you can rest against a tree and be at peace. When I touch something, usually whatever it is, the thing decides to speak to me."

Alex watched as Skye crouched down and stroked the petals of a bright red flower. "A gray fox passed by here not too long ago. No more than a few minutes because it's the first thing the flower decided to show me."

"The flower?"

Skye nodded. "Some things are too proud, but most are more than willing. In class, I'll sit in a chair and see the person who sat there before me, or I'll see the teacher or the lesson. I get a lot of answers right that way. If I try hard enough, I can shuffle through several memories, but it's tiring. Trees are the most willing to share. I think they get annoyed about not having an opinion. I couldn't do this during life though," she added. She lifted her palms up in defense. "I wasn't gifted."

"Have you talked to Duvall about this?"

"No. Considering the questions she asks me and the tasks she gives me, she knows though."

Duvall always preached that everything had an energy and life of its own. Skye's talent went hand in hand with such an idea.

"Does anyone else know?"

"Only you."

Something settled between them, clicking like a key in a lock. "Secret's safe with me."

"Likewise."

They stood regarding each other for several slow moments, and Alex enjoyed the feeling of solidarity.

"So trees speak the most, huh?"

Skye nodded. "Gossipers, yes."

Alex touched the grandmother tree. "What about this one? Looks like she could have some stories to tell."

Skye picked a piece of bark with her nails. "To tell you the truth, most of the time I'm scared to ask, but let's see."

She pressed her entire hand against the gray trunk. After a moment, she dropped her bag to the ground with a crunch.

"What?"

Skye spun around. "Don't move," she hissed.

"Very funny. Are you trying to scare me?"

Skye sucked in a large breath. "Shhhh. Do you smell that?"

Alex inhaled a lungful of ashes. It reeked of fire. Why? She saw nothing, felt no heat, sensed no danger.

Skye slapped her other hand to the trunk of the tree, muttering to herself. "How long ago was she here?"

"What do you see?" Alex insisted.

"A girl. Wiry hair. Ignited eyes. Energy around her. She's looking for something. Her intentions are desperate." Skye let out a loud curse. "She's still out here! Get back through the gate." She snatched Alex's hand. "Come on! What are you doing?"

But Alex couldn't move. Once as a child, Alex was so wrapped up in a game of capture the flag that she hadn't noticed a copperhead snake coiled three inches from her foot. Its thick, scaly body pulsated as it watched her. Fear struck her, freezing her mind and trickling ice down her spine.

The same sensation struck her now as she felt tiny hands clasp her shin. She shut her eyes tightly, hoping it would go away. Whatever it was, it let go momentarily before wrapping its whole arm around her leg, and its hair brushed against her.

Alex opened one eye. Then, another. *Look down*, she commanded to herself. A barefoot toddler clung to her. Her white cotton dress matched her white, silky hair, which rippled down her back until it ended in a crashing of curls like the break of a waterfall. Alex stared at the child who stared right back.

"Pick her up," Skye commanded.

"Why?" Alex cried.

"Because she's stuck to you, and we can't stay out here in the open."

"Is she bad?"

"No. Pick her up."

The child reached up, outstretching her short arms. Alex didn't know what else to do but obey.

"The bodied can't get through the barrier of the gate."

Alex scooped up the girl and cradled her like a baby. "Can she get through?"

"Of course she can," Skye spat. "Can't you distinguish the dead from the living? No breathing child looks like that!"

Once they were safely on the other side, Skye stopped and grabbed hold of the interweaving bars, peering into the unknown.

"Are you sure there was someone?"

"It was one of the gifted."

"Not her though?" Alex jutted her chin at the child.

"No. I already told you she's dead. And you can put her down."

Alex set the child on her feet.

Skye shivered violently, and her hair rippled like a curtain in the breeze. "I don't think my body will ever abandon old habits."

Alex didn't understand why the gifted should be so feared. She thought of her friend, Liv, and her endless supply of jokes. "I knew someone gifted growing up, and she was ordinary."

"Then you never saw her trying to do anything out of the ordinary."

That was true. "Can you touch the gate or anything else to see if it saw her?"

"Good idea."

While Skye played patty cake with nature, Alex surveyed the little girl in wonder, mesmerized. Pink cheeks glistened under a perfectly sculpted nose. With her tiny hands, she tugged at Alex forcing her to crouch down. The girl reached to cup Alex's face.

Skye ran her fingers through her hair. "Nothing. But the fog is rising, and that's not a good omen."

The girl nodded empathically.

"We'd better go talk to Duvall," Skye said.

But by the time they passed the field of gray crosses and reached the frozen creek, they couldn't remember what had frightened them. They knew they hadn't completed their task, but they didn't know what had scared them enough to make them leave. They scratched their heads and wracked their intelligent brains, but each time they opened the bag to see that it was only half full, the haze of forgetfulness deepened.

The child followed, shaking her head. Alex wondered why she kept peering past them into the woods beyond the gate.

Chapter Seven

When they were alive, Chase's brothers ridiculed him for being so optimistic. He knew they loved him for it. They said he could see the light in any situation. But then he died, and life's cruel intentions shaded his vision. He'd been forced to sit and watch Alex shrivel into nearly nothing before death decided she'd suffered enough. His lively, witty Alex was more of a ghost at the end of her life than she was now. The sight still haunted him enough to scare the optimism out of him. Death made him skeptical.

This tiny, ghost-child also made him skeptical. Not because of her colors. It took only a glance to see her purity. A white glow surrounded her. And she gazed at Alex in sparkling adoration. His apprehension derived from his fear about what Alex would do when this child left.

He tried to sound normal. "Duvall said she knew her?"

Alex nodded. Her fingers toyed with the girl's silky hair. "She said she comes in and out of the city sometimes."

"And you picked her up and brought her home?"

"Something scared us, so we needed to get out of there."

"Something?"

"We can't remember what it was."

He rubbed his jawline. "Something scared you, and you didn't consider that it might be the three-foot ghost crawling up your leg?"

"It wasn't her. We couldn't remember because we were dealing with the tree bark that goes into Thymoserum. Forget-me trees, Duvall said. They botch your memory."

Chase suspected there was more to the story. "What is she?"

"Skye called her a Lost One. Duvall called her Rae."

Rae stretched out her legs on Alex's bed, her bare feet overlapping one another. She clasped her hands on her lap. The more lovable she appeared, the more concerned Chase became. She had baggage with her, unhappy blue circles around her heart. She brought her pain and suffering, and it was ruining Alex's room.

"What the hell is a Lost One?"

Alex retracted in response to his tone. "Duvall said children this young are considered lost because they never stay in one place for very long."

"Didn't Ellington tell us that the little ones couldn't control their emotions?"

"Duvall said she's old. She's had plenty of time to tame her feelings."

"She's been here before?"

"Yeah. She wanders around the woods or sticks to the ABC room, but apparently she likes me. Are you okay if she stays here?"

No. "It isn't up to me."

"Of course it is."

"We're two different people, Alex."

"I want to know what you think."

"I think you'll get attached. And then she'll leave."

And I'll have to feel your heart break.

Maybe it stemmed from the way her father treated her when she was alive, but Alex took in strays like an old lady, the kind with five hundred cats. One time, a beagle puppy found its way into the Lasalles' yard, and when the owner came looking for it, Alex howled in agony and cried for an entire week. He didn't understand how someone could have so many tears. Through broken bones and dislocated joints, he rarely saw her cry. Her body must have kept all those tears bottled up inside, waiting for something ridiculous like this. Because of Alex's reaction, Chase's mother nearly broke down and bought Alex a dog—even though his mother was allergic—just because Alex was so inconsolable. What would happen when this child left?

"Do you have to take care of her?"

Alex fiddled with her fingers. "She usually lives on her own, Chase. She doesn't need anyone to care for her. She followed me. That's all."

He sat down in the armchair and hunched forward, resting his forearms on his thighs. "What else did Duvall tell you?"

He realized he was speaking in a very cautious tone, walking on eggshells, his mother used to say. Those eggshells crackled loudly enough for Alex to hear.

She took a step away from him and closer to the kid. "They're rare. Children this young don't usually end up here."

"In Eidolon?"

"In the afterworld. They pick the bright light instead."

Rae shifted to sit on her heels, her hands still clasped in her lap as though she was praying. The innocence of it made Chase wonder why the world would punish a child so young.

Alex gasped. "You think this is punishment? Being here?"

Damn, his thoughts must have filtered into her head. Chase held up his hands in defense. "See. That's why you need to stay out of my mind unless you're invited. Knock first. That's not what I meant at all. This life is obviously not a punishment for me."

Alex hugged her arms around her torso.

"You were given back to me. But a kid that young? Imagine how she felt. She couldn't have understood what happened when she died and showed up here."

Alex's face crumbled, and he felt her distress in his own heart. "Will she speak?" he asked.

"No. I guess Lost Ones don't talk."

"You want her to stay here?"

She nodded. "If she wants to."

The light around Rae glowed even more radiantly. She lifted herself to her knees and reached out to place a small hand on Chase's shoulder, her expression mature. This child was not the baby in the room.

"Is it okay with you?" Alex asked.

"Whatever makes you happy."

Rae scrambled off the bed and grabbed a book from the shelf. It levitated beside her as she toddled to the desk chair and climbed up. The gigantic book drifted down onto her legs. All that stuck out were her small, bare feet. The pages swished as she read. Chase did a double take as he glanced at the title: *Aerodynamics of the Afterlife.*

Geez, Chase thought, *get this kid a pop-up book or something.*

"I guess you don't have to take her with you to class today...?"

"Something tells me she's pretty self-sufficient." Alex gestured to the book.

Part of Chase was pleased that Rae wouldn't need the time and care necessary for a normal toddler. Alex wouldn't get so committed. At the same time, if Rae was so independent, so intelligent, and apparently so old, why did she want to stay on a newbury campus?

***

There was a blank note in Alex's memory, taunting her. She was forgetting something, and spirits don't forget. The note flapped and flew around in her head. She hated it. Fear seeped through her when she thought of the grandmother Forget-me tree and the gate, but she didn't know why. She only accepted her forgetfulness because Rae distracted her.

Chase, on the other hand, never accepted anything right away. His brothers behaved similarly. They didn't trust anyone. Kaleb's initial reaction to Rae was:

"What is that?"

Followed by:

"Does it need a leash?"

"Cut it out," Alex warned, watching Rae peer over the railing of the seventh-floor balcony. Alex tried to take her downstairs, but Rae refused, planting her feet at the landing and shaking her head.

"So what? It's going to live in your room like a pet?"

"Kaleb, knock it off," Gabe said. He tucked a book under his arm and unfolded the pamphlet he'd been using as a bookmark. "She's a person. It will be interesting to have her around. Lost Ones are brilliant. They have to be to make it here so young. She died with a youthful mind, so she's probably learned ten times as much as any other spirit who died the same year."

Kaleb regarded Gabe with incredulity. "Sometimes, I wonder if we're related." He jabbed a thumb in Rae's direction. "Does she do any tricks?"

"Chill out, Kaleb," Chase whispered.

His baby brother never asked for much. Kaleb held up his hands and surrendered.

"You don't have to stay up here with us," Alex said. "Go ahead and hang out in the vestibule."

Kaleb hooked his feet on the bottom railing, to stand taller and take in the scene. "I can't go down there right now. I'm avoiding someone."

"Whose heart did you break this time?"

He faked shock, slapping a hand over his chest. "It pains me that you think so lowly of me. I have a stalker. That new girl who sits with the Legacies."

"Legacies." Alex crinkled her nose.

"It's not like I had anything to do with it! I can't help how irresistibly handsome I am. She keeps popping up out of nowhere, and it's starting to freak me out."

Gabe folded the pamphlet and tucked it back into his book. It advertised something called a health center. "She's actually really cute."

"Skye doesn't like her," Kaleb said.

Alex laughed. "Skye doesn't like any girls. And since when do you follow the crowd?"

"She's jailbait. She's a newbury, and I think she's only sixteen or seventeen."

Alex fought off a grin. She wasn't used to seeing Kaleb so uncomfortable. It only increased when Rae moved closer to him, grasping the rungs of the railing and poking her head through it to look at the crowd. After a moment, she tugged at Kaleb's jersey and pointed downward.

He followed the path of her gesture, and then he looked back at Rae in surprise. "Thank you."

"What?"

"She found the girl I was talking about. How did she know?"

"Told you the Lost Ones are smart," Gabe said.

"She could come in handy." Kaleb patted her shoulder. "Gabe, I told you that my stalker would be waiting down there."

Alex wanted to get a glimpse. The girl's light brown hair matched her skin, and when she spoke to the person seated across from her, her bright white teeth rivaled Skye's. "Wow, she's hideous," Alex joked. "How exactly does she stalk you worse than the other girls around here?"

"That's the thing. She's not like the other girls. She shows up in every one of my workshops and sits next to me, *smiling*, and asking me to show her around."

"Sounds like a monster."

"It's annoying." Kaleb bolted upright before spinning around to crash to the ground. "She saw me."

Alex caught Chase's eye, and they both began to laugh.

Kaleb scowled. "Don't you guys have a workshop to go to?"

"Yep." Chase tried to stop smiling, biting his lips together, but it only made the humor more contagious.

Alex squatted down to Rae's level. "What do you want to do?"

Rae took one last look at the vestibule and turned to head back down the hall.

"Guess she's going to the room."

"This place gets stranger every day," Kaleb noted.

Alex couldn't agree more. Her brain was beginning to feel like an iPod shuffling after only playing five seconds of a song. Each time she wanted to focus on one thing, her mind would shift to the next before she felt ready. Additional workshops didn't help. If she considered one word, her unbound mind would keep sorting and sorting through the remnants of knowledge it contained, and then it would shift over to Chase's mind. From definitions to root words to Latin derivatives to movies, songs, and books; it was enough to drive her mad. Struggling to manage the reins of her thoughts exhausted her, but she worried if she let it go, her mind would take off and never come back to her again.

Today, through each of her workshops, her brain kept reverting back to one word. Legacy. It was like typing the term into Google; her brain would erupt with connections to the word like her own personal search engine.

A page with highlighted words: "A gift of property"

A Webster's Dictionary

The Lasalles discussing college sports recruiting

Keys

Another page with highlighted words: "Anything handed down"

And trees. There were thousands of images flashing through Alex's mind, but trees appeared with each one.

The clock ticked slowly leading up to the midday recess, but it was time to see what this legacy fuss was all about.

Tess's directions led her to a room nestled deep in the west corner of the learning center. When she found the green door shaped like a keyhole, it swung open before she could reach for the tree-shaped handle.

It was like stepping into the forest. Or a coloring book. Large trees, bonsai trees, painted trees, scribbled drawings of life-size trees—they all inhabited one strange room. Some existed as artwork on the walls or freestanding paper while others were rooted to the ground. The room couldn't decide what it wanted to be.

It felt like being stuck in the children's book, *Where the Wild Things Are.* For a moment, Alex pictured the monsters hiding in the trees, and an image of Jonas flashed across her mind. Sitting crisscross in the Lasalles' old living room, he crawled toward her with his mischievous grin, cackling, "I'll eat you up I love you so."

His words had new meaning now, and she missed him in spite of herself.

But this wasn't a children's book. It was real life. So, how in the "real" world could a scrawled, crayoned tree stand taller than a ten-foot pine?

Newburies rested among the undergrowth, waiting for the meeting to begin. Some talked, some read, others sprawled on the ground with their arms draped over their faces as though they were relaxing outside, not cooped up inside a meeting room. Others lounged in office chairs, their feet propped on a conference table sprouting from the shrubbery. She guessed with so many spirits depicting their own thoughts of this reality, the images were bound to be differentiated. Even if every person in the room thought "tree," it didn't mean they would picture the same thing. This was the result.

Ellington would be proud of her. Last year, she wouldn't have been willing to see half of this. She reminded herself to tell him later.

Tess Darwin sidestepped away from her two brothers, who stood at the head of the table, deep in conversation. As she made her way to Alex, her smug expression clearly stated, *I knew you'd come.*

"This is different." Alex's interest swooped around the room perfumed with cedar and emotion. The feelings here existed as living, breathing entities— kind of like Ellington's classroom.

Tess spun her finger in a circle. "Look closely."

"What?"

"At the trees. Then you'll understand."

Tess's kindness clashed with her stiff and robotic persona, and Alex wondered if the trees leaked a relaxant into the air. She wandered off through the "woods" but didn't see anything that would explain the purpose of the scenery or why this multigenerational group needed to meet here. It seemed like a waste of time she could be using to check on the three-year-old holed up in her room, but if she left now, she'd never know why she'd been invited. She recognized all the newburies, after all, it only took a glimpse for her mind to memorize a face, but she didn't call any of them friends. She wondered if their lineage was documented here.

Like a light bulb, she knew what she should be looking for. Her head whipped around to study the nearest tree, and there on the trunk a name was etched. Ondine.

Family trees. Oh, how clever.

The one marked Ondine stood proud as one of the largest. Beautiful and elegant, its large shell-like leaves sprang from branches and dripped with rain despite the dry ceiling. Names covered every inch of the bark. The thick boughs claimed larger names, and alongside them, smaller names etched the wood to indicate a marriage. More limbs stemmed from each couple, with more names. This family was huge.

"This is an Alder tree," said a smooth voice beside her.

Alex had never heard Xavier Darwin speak before. She didn't expect a boy with such hardened features to have a soft tone.

"Beautiful, isn't it?"

She waited for him to swallow his congeniality and shove her into the wall.

"The older families, they have the grandest trees."

Alex took in his jagged features. Sharp chin, sharp nose, which, for once, was not angled upward. "Why are some of the names brighter than others?"

"The brighter names are souls who made it here."

Against the contrast of the bark, those names shimmered. "There are so many."

He nodded. "It's hereditary. My relatives say we evolve like anything else, and this family has been around since the documented beginning."

Alex measured the crowd gathered in the room. "Everyone here has a name on one of these trees?" Xavier nodded, and Alex ran her fingertips along the etchings. "Why aren't the Bonds here, then?"

Xavier's stare cut the air between them. The mention of the Bonds acted as a grindstone, and his sharpness returned. "After everything they put you through, you're still concerned with them?" He didn't wait for her response. "They've wronged a good many people here. Generation after generation, they do nothing but make mistakes to the detriment of our society. Apples don't fall far from the tree."

"The *detriment* of our society." Alex scoffed. "That's extreme, don't you think?"

Xavier shook his head. He grabbed Alex's hand, and she gasped as a surge erupted up her arm, like an injection of winter itself. "Follow me," he ordered.

They zigzagged through the forest of names. Xavier stopped when they came upon a giant pine. Alex squinted at the names, but they were impossible to make out through the snow.

"Colorado Blue Spruce," Xavier announced proudly. "The Darwin family tree." He pushed aside a branch of thick needles, and there, like holiday lights, twinkled the letters of his name. Tess's and Linton's names clung to his.

When Alex stepped close enough, she heard crying. She ran her finger over their branch, names with identical death dates.

"You three died on the same day?"

Xavier nodded.

"An accident?"

He shook his head. "It isn't a pretty story."

"Death usually isn't," she said, watching Xavier pinch the bridge of his nose. "I'm sorry."

Xavier shooed off her apology. "It's fine. My father, he drank a lot."

"We have something in common."

He nodded with his jaw set tight but bowed his head in this moment of camaraderie. "I was the oldest. I should have protected my brother and sister."

"From what?"

He jutted his angular chin toward the tree. "Him." He showed her a toothed name over his own. Jesper Darwin, his father. A name that didn't glow. "I don't know how, but he knew about the afterworld. On the last night of my life, he staggered around our shoebox of a house, drunk and screaming about how he couldn't find something. He kept saying we would be better off if we went to a different place, a place he hadn't screwed up, a place where we would be royalty. I thought he was just drunk as usual, looking for a hidden bottle. He was a screwup, my dad. The rest of our family wasn't too proud of him. He realized that, though, because he said this was the greatest thing he ever did for us." Xavier's voice trembled. "Turns out, he wasn't looking for another drink, he was looking for his gun."

Alex raised a hand to cover her mouth.

"It's fine."

In that instant, colors rained down from his eyes to his cheekbones. His emotion painted a rainbow of tears over the white canvas of his face.

"The bastard shot himself after he realized what he'd done. He was right about this place. How he knew about it is a mystery, but he knew."

No wonder the Darwins took this world and this city so seriously. "I'm sorry."

"No pity for us, please. We all have our sob stories from life."

True. "You haven't explained why the Bonds aren't invited here."

"Oh." In a flash, Xavier's sharp cheekbones held no more stains. He picked up a nearby stick and lifted it to a branch near the middle of the tree. Some names appeared as they would be carved on a normal tree, names like Jesper Darwin. Dull and lightless, these were the ancestors who had lived a normal-bodied life. Some sparkled but with clouded brilliancy—the light behind the diamond had vanished.

"The ones who lost their light were killed before their minds expired here. Those names here ..." He tapped a cluster of cloudy Darwins. "Those are my ancestors who died because of the Bonds."

"What? How?"

"The Witch Wars during the 1800s. The Bond family directed the Interactions Department of the government, and they were openly anti-gifted. When the gifted retaliated and tried to fight back, the Bonds enlisted the help of a certain hunting family I'm sure you could guess."

"Seyferr?"

He nodded. "Their deal with the hunters made everything worse. Spirits against the gifted. The gifted against the hunters. Battles broke out and spirits tried to put out the flames to keep our secrecy. My family suffered because the Darwins have always worked to maintain Eidolon's secrecy. And we got stuck in the crossfire between the two worlds. Skye's family, too."

"Why isn't Skye here?"

Xavier's jagged, black bangs scraped his forehead. "Legacy rules permit absence so long as one member of a family attends."

Skye mentioned Gossamers in the city but not as young as newburies. Gossamers were difficult to miss, so when Xavier guided them back to the others, Alex searched for someone with a cloud of charm above them.

Pax Simone stood at the head of the conference table and called the meeting to order, beginning with an enthusiastic update on something called a Truce March. A celebration, she claimed, for one hundred years of peace due to the efforts of her family. She grinned. Girls with big noses always seemed to have take-charge personalities.

Xavier spoke over Alex's shoulder, close to her ear. "Pax's family took over the Interactions Department once the Bonds were demoted."

"What's the deal with this Truce March?" she whispered back to him.

"It's between the gifted and the spirited."

Pax demanded updates on the obligations of each Legacy family for the event. The room swelled thick with entitlement. *This is like a high society ass kissing,* Alex thought.

She swore she heard laughter back in the trees. Xavier turned to look over his shoulder at the sunlight shoving its way through the branches even though a solid ceiling contained the room.

"Is this all you do?" she asked.

"This is about preservation."

"What are you preserving? Status?"

"Respect." When the word escaped from his mouth, it appeared in the form of smoke, curling around them and escaping to the trees to pay homage. "For the names on those trees. For what they did for this world. For those of us that needed second chances."

Such would explain the personality of the room, but accompanying the entitlement were pleasant winds of esteem and flutters of admiration.

"Without remembrance," Xavier continued, "consequences have no meaning. Incidents like last year would become more frequent. If we preserve them, instead of preserving those who caused the damage, then we win."

"And how is the Eskers group different from yours?"

He snickered loudly. "You don't see us trying to hurt others."

"Didn't you torment those kids?"

"We knocked a few books from their hands. We didn't try

to kill them. We knew they were up to no good and tried to keep them in line. There's a difference."

Looking around, Alex couldn't help but think that those misfit Eskers kids longed for something like this, somewhere to belong. She didn't condone what they'd done, but a part of her understood their desperation. She stuck out like a sore thumb when she was alive.

"Your compassion will get you killed," he murmured.

"Excuse me?"

Xavier faced her, attempting to read her unwritten expression. "You shouldn't feel sorry for them. No matter the amount of influence, no one can make someone do something against their will. Some part of each of those kids wanted to harm you for their own personal gain. I hope you realize that."

She should agree. His words made sense. She didn't understand her mind's adamancy to swim against the current of this truth, and it confused her. She turned to meet his gaze, but her words got lost somewhere in her confusion.

The agenda of the meeting took a turn in their immediate direction.

"… with the return of the Eskers kids," Pax said. "I think we should delegate members to keep surveillance on the accused."

"Is that our responsibility?" someone argued. Alex followed the trajectory of the voice to the girl Kaleb was avoiding in the vestibule.

Linton appeared on the other side of Xavier. "Little Gossamer. She's bold for a young one. I dig it."

Gossamer? *That* was her? Kaleb's admirer. Alex wondered if Skye knew about this.

"Yes," Pax replied. "If we value our campus and our city. We need to set a good example. We need to promote peaceful living this year especially."

"She's right," Tess piped up. "The Eskers kids need to know that their actions last year aren't acceptable, and if—"

Pax held up a hand, and Tess stopped so abruptly that the sharp edges of her chin length hair flew forward. Tess never had a hair out of place. Her mind was a well-oiled machine. But for the first time, her hair began to frizz.

"No, Tess. I mean we need to show the Eskers kids some support."

"Wh—"

"We are the ones who lead."

Xavier clenched his teeth but didn't come to his sister's aid. Alex followed his glare to a barren, blackened tree behind Pax. She imagined it might have glimmered once, but its sleekness withered now, devoid of beauty. She didn't need to look at the name to know to whom it belonged.

She elbowed Xavier. "Why do the Bonds have a tree if they aren't here?"

"Spirits still think about the Bonds even if they don't like them. Instead of focusing on what we love, our minds focus on those we hate. It can't be hidden here."

When the meeting was adjourned, the members didn't leave right away. Some resumed their leisure on the ground and others propped open books or remained where the gathering took place to chat. Little Gossamer noticed Alex and beamed so brightly that Alex needed to lift her arms to block the light. Little began heading her way, but Pax cut her off.

"Alex Ash." She said the name with a tinge of annoyance. "I'm sure you're dying to know why you're here."

Alex really wanted to ask Pax about the abandonment of the Bond family tree after her mighty speech about leadership and support.

"Would you like to see your family?"

Alex's mouth fell open. In all the talk of families and legacies, she'd forgotten that there was a reason she'd been summoned here.

"Family." The word melted on her tongue like candy.

The sugary sweetness intensified when Pax stopped in front of the source. From several feet back, Alex could feel its power, even more so than the monstrosity of the Ondine family. She was afraid to step nearer, like traveling too close to the sun. She didn't need to be any closer to see the name, Havilah. It was carved in brilliantly artistic cursive on the gleaming trunk of the tree.

The Havilahs were spirits? She didn't need the flipbook of images in her mind to know that name.

"Congratulations," Pax said, patting her shoulder. "You're a descendant of a founding family."

Chapter Eight

A dozen years back ...
Parrish, Maryland

The girl beside Alex hummed a familiar nursery rhyme. The eerie tune always gave Alex the chills, but this time distraction overpowered her fear. She was busy watching large, tear-shaped globs of paint splotch her white art paper. Deep blue raindrops of imperfection fell one by one.

The camp counselor hovered over her, holding the lid that dripped like a melting ice cube. She didn't notice Alex's exasperation because she was reprimanding Jonas for using craft time to garnish himself in war paint. Alex could feel the heat of anxiety pressing against her throat. The paint tarnished her clean slate before she began, a metaphor for her very existence.

Her frustration followed the course of the counselor who hurried across the room, but when Alex went to glare down at her already ruined art project, she noticed that the paper was magically white once again. Chase sat opposite her, his arms folded over a blue speckled paper.

"Okay!" The disheveled counselor attempted to add pep to her directions. She lifted a dirty hand and used her wrist to sweep back her damp bangs. "Who knows what today is?"

"Blue Day!" The younger children answered in robotic unison. The older campers scoffed, knowing this day was much more significant.

"Yes, but does anyone know why we celebrate blue today?"

"Because it's Parrish Day," Kaleb grumbled, sulking in his seat. Flopping forward onto the table, he lifted his head to look at the counselor. "Which presents the question of why we're here if no one is working today?"

Their parents were working all right ... working on killing brain cells. On July eleventh, the adults in town would begin at the top of Main Street and stop in every bar on the way down like visiting relatives on Christmas. As the only adults in Parrish who were not already three sheets to the wind, the camp counselors grew antsier by the minute. Their work ethic perspired from them, dripping down their foreheads. By five o'clock, the legal drinkers in town would join the illegal drinkers at the beach. Parrish Day presented a yearly opportunity for the entire town to lose itself. Parents turned a blind eye toward their children just as the children turned a blind eye in return.

Alex's father was especially drunk on Parrish Day. He hated to be social, but on July eleventh his doomed marriage to Erin Ash, formerly Erin Havilah, forced him to be a public figure.

"That's right. It's Parrish Day, but you didn't answer my question. Why do we celebrate the color blue?"

The only response was another roar from the air-conditioning unit.

The counselor raised her voice. "Colonial Parrish kept its head above water with its abundant crop of indigo."

Kaleb shot up in his seat. "Indigo? What is that?"

"It's blue, dummy." Jonas scoffed.

"No kidding, moron, but the color blue doesn't exactly grow on trees, does it?"

The camp counselor seemed pleased that she managed to capture Kaleb's attention, so much that she ignored his disrespect toward his brother. She perched on a nearby table.

"No, it doesn't grow on trees; it grows from the ground. Indigo is found in plants. Parrish Day commemorates the founding of our little town, but we wear blue in honor of the crop."

The girl next to Alex began to sing the nursery rhyme again. Mackenzie. She shared a class with Kaleb.

"Please don't sing that," the counselor begged. The older campers began to chant in unison while the younger campers quivered in their seats:

On the nights when the breeze stinks of indigo
Shut your window tight on the sill.
The Havilahs dance in the shadows

Leaving fingerprints shaped like Anil.

You'll hear them calling for you.
They'll knock thrice at the door.
And you'll wake in the morning to find the adorning
Of blue footprints streaked 'cross the floor.

They come for you in silence
And whisper in voices so hushed
And on their breath is the scent of death
With traces of ashes and dust.

Jonas stood on the table, using his paintbrush to lead the group like an orchestra conductor, but it was hard to tell whether he orchestrated the singing or the crying. Gabe ignored it, dipping his fingertips into the paint and dabbing blue prints on his paper. Kaleb tapped his fingers on his chin like a piano, composing a song of mischief.

"You gave me an idea," he said to Gabe.

"Oh, joy."

Chase touched Alex's hand. He didn't need to speak. His expression told her that she needn't worry. This would be harmless fun.

Kaleb had already snatched the sidewalk chalk from a nearby bucket, and he hunched over, sketching out a schematic of Parrish. The town was shaped like two giant backward C's, one spooning the next. The outermost part of the circle represented the modern town, built as a fortress to protect the past. He shaded this larger C with peach chalk. The older, smaller C encircled the Esker woods that gave way to the Parrish Cove. At the highest part of the woods sat the old Frank house. Kaleb grabbed the blue chalk and drew this first. Their friend, Liv Frank, had a grandmother who lived in the cottage that had withstood its ground for centuries. Upon seeing the building, one might believe they'd entered a time warp if it weren't for the neon glow of an electric sign in the shape of an open hand that read: *Palm Readings.*

At the southernmost tip of the woods was the Havilah church. It had no modern purpose in the town besides being a historical landmark. At the curve of the C, Kaleb wrote one word, Jester. He shaded this in red. The Esker woods, inside of the C, nestled comfortably against the cove, shielded unless you entered through one of these means: the cove, the Jester's territory, the Frank house, or the Havilah church.

Kaleb's arm covered his map as he scanned the area, checking for spies. His voice became low and serious.

"We take this path." He tapped his paintbrush at the peach shaded area. He traced a square marked *Parrish Park*, their community. He traced the paintbrush along a road which snaked its way south. "Until we reach the church."

"That's dumb," Jonas hissed. "It will take us twice as long. Why don't we cut through the woods?"

Kaleb punched Jonas's arm. "Okay, fearless leader. Are you going to lead us through the Esker woods *on foot*? No one has done that since cars were invented. Judging by the look on your face, the answer is no."

Jonas scowled which only accentuated his trembling lower lip.

"Anyway, as I was saying, we get out of here at five, put in an appearance at the beach so Mom and Dad know Chase and Alex are accounted for. I'm guessing you two will want to come with us?"

Their little heads nodded in unison.

"We take the road around the woods past the school and to the old church. I've heard there are still Anil plants growing there."

"And what, oh what, are we going to do with Anil plants?" Gabe asked.

Kaleb clapped his hands. "We are going to scare the pants off this town! We are going to honor the spirit of 'ole Esker Havilah."

"Indigo," Gabe said flatly. "We're going to steal indigo from the Esker woods?"

"It isn't stealing if it doesn't belong to anyone. The Havilahs are dead. Well, with the exception of one person ..." Kaleb glanced at Alex, "...and she doesn't seem to mind."

Alex's mother and father once embraced their role in the small town. They rode in the parade, and they brought family heirlooms to be put on display at the museum on Main Street. When her mother died, Alex became the last of the Havilahs, the founders of Parrish. Alex's father hated the fame because he hated living outside his whiskey bottle. The elders in town always "tut-tutted" him because he didn't let Erin and Alex keep the Havilah name, but it wouldn't have mattered anyway.

"Exactly my point," Gabe warned. "The Havilahs are dead, so who's to say they aren't still lingering around their property? And I'm guessing your plan is to print the windowsills?"

Kaleb grinned. "Esker Havilah would be proud. He hated all this, what's the word, Gabe?"

"Sin?"

"No! The fun one."

"Frivolity."

Kaleb snapped his fingers. "That's it. I like that one. Chase and Alex will be lookouts."

Chase, always the brave one, spoke up. "Are we looking out for ghosts or drunks?"

"Both," Kaleb replied with satisfaction. "Although I doubt a drunk will stumble out so far from the watering hole if you know what I mean." He outlined Main Street. "We should have free reign of the area. It will be a ghost town."

And it was. They met no opposition. Every living soul in Parrish traveled downtown by early evening. The town was theirs for the taking! And take, they did. Kaleb climbed up to the termite-ridden pedestal on which Esker Havilah himself used to preach to his congregation of avid followers. Kaleb's voice came out low and eerie.

"We must rid this town from impending doom. We will mark windows with shades of blue."

"Clever." Gabe examined a book at the altar. "You're a poet, and you don't know it."

Jonas frowned. "That really didn't rhyme."

"Shut up, Jonas," Kaleb and Gabe said simultaneously.

Jonas made a face and disappeared into a confessional.

Gabe leaped onto the podium, intoxicated by the moment. "No dancing after dark!" he preached in a booming voice. "No unannounced gatherings!"

"No joking," Kaleb added. "No gaming. No drinking and no merriment. No fun allowed here in the town of Parrish!"

Alex and Chase used their elbows to army-crawl on their bellies under the dusty pews, but guilt caused Alex to pause. She plucked a spider web from her forehead and wondered if Esker Havilah was rolling over in his grave right now. The very essence of this day was the complete opposite of the ideals on which he had founded this town. And here she was, his descendant in his church, mocking it.

"On to our mission!" Kaleb leaped from pew to pew with deer-like agility. "We have to expose those who have broken the laws of the land."

"That's the whole town," Gabe pointed out.

"Then we will mark every house in town tonight!"

Gabe looked doubtful. This was a task of epic proportions, as likely as Santa visiting every house in the world in one night. Alex watched as Gabe bit his tongue and allowed his big brother to maintain his glory.

"Lookouts." Kaleb turned to Chase and Alex, speaking in a deepened voice of authority. "Establish yourselves out front. As much as it pains you, divide to cover more ground. We won't be gone long."

Kaleb snatched Jonas from the confessional and followed Gabe around to the back of the church en route to the Esker woods. Chase reached for Alex's hand.

"We can stay together if you want."

As if she had any other intention.

They sat thigh to thigh in the overgrown grass by the warped, wooden steps of the church, leaning on one another for support. In the woods, the day aged more quickly, carrying an air of dirt, graves, and death. It cheated the children of time and daylight. The three eldest Lasalles returned from their expedition unsuccessful and empty-handed, their spirits murky like disposed watercolor, as gray as the day. Only Alex and Chase were pleased that there was no cause for punishment from the other world. They had never wanted to steal the indigo in the first place.

Gabe suggested they use chalk to carry out their plan, but thunder rumbled in the distance, and chalk painted windowsills would not withstand the rain. The skies opened before they even reached Parrish Park, soaking them from head to toe. Alex and Chase parted ways at their side-by-side mailboxes, and Alex stumbled into her house and fell into bed, exhausted from the day.

When she woke in the morning, she tried to convince herself that the marks on her face were battle wounds. She tripped several times running home in the rain, and she bruised like a rotten banana. She couldn't deny that the blue marks on her face bore resemblance to the same striking blue as the prints she found on her windowsill that morning. An indigo handprint, palm across her chin, fingers framing her cheekbone, as though someone had been cradling her face with stained hands.

Chapter Nine

Whenever Alex had a high fever during life, the size of the world around her became distorted. Usually, she became larger. Or the world became smaller. Either way, she felt off-balance and out of place. Her doctor called it Alice in Wonderland Syndrome and claimed it was only a disruption of perception.

That was how she felt now. She was taking up too much space even though her projection was the size of a ten-year-old. It might have been her imagination, but it seemed like the newburies in the hallway cleared the way when they saw her coming, scurrying away from the big, fat feet of a giant. Her footsteps clunked as she reached the staircase, and she could have sworn she heard the banister creak under her weight.

The staircase arched and curled like waves, which made her feel like she was floating in a tide. It didn't help her current mindset, and to top things off, she remembered halfway down the steps that there was a new addition to her schedule.

Thank goodness Chase was waiting for her, saving her a seat at the middle tier of stadium rows, all the way off to the side where she wouldn't be noticed. He rested against the wall with his feet propped up on the chair next to him. When he spotted her, a dimple appeared on the right side of his cheek, and that alone was enough to make Alex feel better.

She dodged the hovering books, ducked under floating papers and hurried to him. Chase removed his shoes from her seat. "Who would've guessed the Havilahs would be a household name here, too?"

Alex dropped her belongings and collapsed down next to them. "You were eavesdropping, huh?"

"Do you blame me?" He kissed her hello. Pulses of orange energy brightened her mind. "No wonder you have super powers. You're old blood."

"Yeah, yeah."

What's your kryptonite, Supergirl?

She lifted her palms to the ceiling. *You.*

That doesn't sound very appealing. He reached for one of her outstretched hands and took it in his.

Her mind still remembered what it felt like for skin to prickle in an anticipatory way; her senses knew he was going to kiss her again before he did it. When he pulled back, she could see waviness in the small space between them like heat rising above the asphalt in the dead of summer. Her brain conjured images of cooking grills and the term *refraction* before she shook the slideshow from her head. The information rattled around. She had to be tired because she wasn't controlling her aching mind very well. The moment she thought about her fatigue, Chase grasped her hand, and she felt a small surge of energy as though he sacrificed some of his own, literally handed it to her.

Alex wasn't sure she needed energy for a course entitled "Meditari." She assumed meditation meant sleeping, but within the first few minutes of their new workshop, Dr. Banyan Philo argued that it was the very opposite.

"Focused attention," he called it, holding a vat of Ex nearly as tall as his small frame. He didn't drink it but instead hunched over every few seconds to inhale the mist. Between sighing amid the after effects of his Ex, he discussed the various ways for a spirit to train its mind in order to control its mental processes.

Alex felt neither calm nor focused. Her knee bounced and her hands shook. The fact that she descended from a founding family set her mind in motion on whirlwind speed. After seeing the name, Havilah, her brain shuffled through images like faces in the windows of a speeding train, and she couldn't keep up. No wonder she felt exhausted. She'd always been well aware of her family background in life; she never figured that history would follow her here in death. The loose ends of her life were going to strangle her sooner or later.

"Chase," she whispered. "Did I ever tell you what happened the night the Jester chased us away from the Esker woods?"

"You mean the night we've been reliving in your dreams

every other night? What else is there to know?"

"Back then I thought you'd think I was crazy if I said anything. That night when we got home, I got in the shower."

"I like where this is going."

"Shut up. I'm serious. Anyway, I was in the shower and I got this feeling that I wasn't alone. I remember I was shaking because I was sure someone was there, but the bathroom was empty."

"Great story."

Madison turned around and gave them a look of reprimand. Chase made a face at her.

I'm not done, Alex continued in Chase's mind. *The feeling didn't go away so finally I said aloud, "Why are you here? Couldn't you wait until I was out of the shower?" I actually said that to the empty room like a crazy person. I almost fainted when a boy's voice said, "You came to visit me without knocking. So I came to visit you without knocking."*

Chase leaned on his hand. *Are you serious right now?*

She lifted her palms. *I might have imagined it, but he kept talking. He told me that he came to see my face in the light and that* they *were going to find me eventually.*

Who are "they?"

He didn't specify. All he did after that was sing the rhyme about the Havilahs.

You think he was talking about the Havilahs finding you? They're dead.

Chase, I told you about the tree. They're a spirit family. This afterworld is probably crawling with them. But why would he be worried about them finding me? I lived a mile away from the woods. If Havilah spirits really lived in town, I'm sure they would have seen me before then.

Chase sighed. *I don't know.*

Alex shifted her attention to Dr. Philo, who waved his hand and an image of a face in the clouds appeared above him. "Recognize this man?"

Tousled bedhead. Wide chin. Bored face.

"Is that you, Doctor?" Madison asked.

"You may call me Banyan, and yes it is."

"How did you do that?"

Banyan stooped forward to snort up another whiff of Ex.

Alex elbowed Chase, who curled his nose at the man.

Banyan wiped his nose and raised his arms above his head in the direction of the photograph. "I think you'll be ever more impressed to know that as this was taken from the window of an airplane at an altitude of thirty thousand feet, I was in an auditorium, mid-lecture much like I am now. Hundreds witnessed the feat."

"That's all possible through meditation?" Jack Bond's voice intruded in the discussion.

A few newburies took the opportunity to turn and stare at Jack. Chase's hand balled into a fist.

"Yes, focused attention is a powerful thing." Banyan blinked upward, and the projection changed. In place of the clouds sat the outlined silhouette of a red person against a red wooden door. "It can take years to master, and before the mind is trained, our powerful minds often travel by accident.

Usually, the mind will take the person back home since that's where it is most at peace."

His soft words crept to the corner of the lecture hall and nudged Alex, awakening her attention. *The mind will take a person back home.*

"Usually when humans see apparitions, it's only spirits traveling in their minds. That's why many of the bodied believe spirits to be translucent. If their minds are open enough to see us like this," he circled his arm around the room, "we become visible like any other living person. Such is not the case with meditation."

Alex remembered Professor Massin during their first sociology introduction—her translucence wasn't due to her age but because she was in two places at once that day.

Alex elbowed Chase. *Do you think this is why my dreams are back to Parrish?*

Those are dreams. You aren't concentrating on anything when you're unconscious.

That's what I mean. If I'm a Havilah, it makes sense, right? They built the whole town. It might be natural for my subconscious to take me back there.

Chase's head shifted back and forth with Banyan, who began to pace on the podium. *I get what you're saying, but I don't think that has to do with meditation. I think that has to do with your mind being the director of your dreams.*

Alex twirled a finger through one of her tangled curls. She felt fairly certain she would regret sharing this. *I think it's more than a dream.*

Why would you think that?

I think Liv Frank can see us.

Right. You told me she could see spirits. It's not surprising at all, knowing her. He circled his finger around his ear to indicate Liv's craziness.

No, I mean she can see us in the dream.

Chase placed an elbow on the table and shifted in his seat to look at her.

Humor me. In my last dream, when we were walking along the beach she was staring right at us.

Oh, yeah?

She could tell he didn't believe her at all. *Fine. Next time it happens. Next time we're there, watch her. Okay?*

All right, Chase agreed. *I think you're forgetting that Banyan isn't talking about dreams. He is talking about real life.*

What if Liv did really see us that day, and we never knew it?

You mean when we were actually alive and sitting right next to her, you think she saw us walking on the beach as ghosts?

Could happen, right?

That's a whole new level of psychedelics.

Not if I'm projecting us there.

Back at the podium, Banyan stood stiff as a statue, his eyes shut, and his short arms dangling lifelessly at his sides.

What is he doing now?

The room was so silent they could hear Madison scribbling notes with her pencil.

I bet he passed out from all the Ex sniffing, Chase murmured in her thoughts. *Anyway, do you remember what we were taught about the Havilahs?*

Of course she remembered. There was an entire day dedicated to them every year in Parrish.

Do you remember why they built the town? Why they built the Eskers?

Yes, she knew. Esker Havilah's name was chiseled so flawlessly on that family tree. No mistakes. Disciplined, like him. He molded the town to obey and furthermore preach the behavior he thought was necessary.

Who would have thought those Havilah ghost rumors were real? When Pax Simone showed me my family tree, she said that it was one of the first ones. It was as old as Brigitta and Broderick Cinatri's tree. The Havilahs were friends with the founders of Eidolon.

SNAP.

Alex yelped as Banyan's face appeared in the space between her and Chase. She gawked at the luminous image, separating their conversation.

"What the …?" Chase shot back in his chair.

At the front of the room, the actual Banyan stood lifeless. The specter of the doctor grinned. "Just making sure you're paying attention."

Several newburies began to clap. Others had their hands over their mouths in shock as the fake doctor disappeared, and the actual Banyan awoke at the podium. He bowed. "One day we may not need to physically travel at all if we can figure out how to make it last. We could use meditation and abolish those burdensome wormholes. But that opens a whole new can of debatable worms."

Madison took her pencil from her mouth. "Is it safer to exist that way?"

"Our projections are nothing but memories. We meditate with our minds, but we exist in our minds as memories, and those can be stolen, captured, manipulated, destroyed. So no, it's not safer." Banyan tossed stacks of cards onto their tables. "On to the interactive part!"

He ordered the class to break into pairs with their cards. Alex saw this activity last year. One person held up the card with a picture facing away from the partner. The partner guessed the image by trying to envision themselves using the other person's eyes. It was a watered down version of meditation, but the hall buzzed with excitement.

Alex and Chase finished in two minutes. With access to each other's thoughts, the activity was ridiculously simple.

Chase reverted back to their conversation. *All the rules the Havilahs made. You remember, right?*

No drinking, dancing, any sort of fun. I know, I know, Alex thought to him. *It was all banned.* She also knew it was a scapegoat for what the Havilahs really hated. Back then, they called it devil worship.

Witches.

The gifted, Alex corrected. *If they were such good friends with Broderick and Brigitta, I wonder if they had anything to do with the way the dead treat the gifted.*

She didn't need to open the door between their minds to know he shared the same thought as she did. If the Havilahs created a town dedicated to impeding any action related to witchery, it only became all the more strange that Alex, their last living relative, was the spitting image of the sort of person they hated.

***

Alex regretted her neglect for the ghost girl. The day felt so long that it was difficult to believe it had only been a few hours since they found her. Alex rushed across the courtyard and into Brigitta Hall, walking too quickly for anyone to have a chance to stop her.

Rae did not seem to have missed her. Alex found her on the floor, sprawled on her stomach. Surrounding her were no less than twenty sketches and several pencils dulled down to the erasers. Rae sure did have a talent for the arts because with standard number two pencils she'd created several masterpieces of extensive dimension and depth, making the pictures seem real, like black and white photographs. Alex stood transfixed among the stepping-stones of papers littering her room.

Not knowing what exactly to do, she crisscrossed her ankles and wilted to the floor. With so many smudges on her arms and face, Rae looked as though she'd been rolling through soot, but she glanced over at Alex with a knowing smirk.

"You know you're good at this, huh?"

Rae lifted a finger to her lips and scanned her work. She selected one from the middle. She'd drawn a tunnel with chipped, gray edges, but anger emanated through the dark shading. Alex could feel red through the cloudiness. Rae didn't like this place. She examined Alex's reaction through the threads of her fine hair, and Alex stared back, wondering what Rae was trying to tell her. After a few minutes, Rae shook her head, selecting another sketch. This one was a mess of scribbles, but when Alex held it in her hands, the picture filled her with warmth and comfort. It told a story of safety. Love. And the strength of it overwhelmed her.

"Oh," she murmured. These weren't just sketches. Rae could somehow *draw* emotions. It wasn't until Alex set down the paper and saw it from a distance that she noticed an outline hidden in the scribbles. The spirals took form of two arms cradling the chaos. In realizing this, Alex felt two rings of warmth; one tightened around her shoulders and one around her abdomen as though there were arms holding her. She gasped.

Rae smiled.

Chapter Ten

Lucia Duvall had been alive a long time, long enough that things didn't surprise her anymore. But Rae surprised her, more specifically, the way Rae attached herself to Alex Ash. She drummed her fingers on her desk, scowling at her thin, bony fingers. It took so much effort, so much mind power, to keep up her appearance. Her mind kept aging and thus it fought to project her appearance accordingly. It wanted to hunch her shoulders, tighten her joints, and wrinkle her skin. If she didn't keep focus, she'd sag into an old hag. It became increasingly more difficult to remember how she felt during her youth. She always loved a challenge though. Her brilliant mind—with the help of secret herbs and minerals—always came through. She concentrated and watched her skin repair itself.

Now stay that way, she commanded. With creamy, smooth

fingers she held up a glass flask to inspect her tired reflection.

No stone was left unturned in her search for the link between Alex and Sephi. The conclusion, as she suspected, was that the Anovarks were extinguished. Those damn Havilahs had made sure of it. Bastards. That family harbored so much hatred for the gifted.

If there was one thing Duvall learned in all her years, it was that with as much love as there was in the world, there were equal parts hatred. Chalk it up to nature's annoying need to maintain balance. Sometimes one outweighed the other, good over bad, bad over good, but like an old brass balancing scale they always found their way back to neutral.

She glanced out the window. She could feel the presence of the gifted out there somewhere. Their dissension with the laws of the afterworld grew thicker by the day, and Alex's death had given them hope. They'd waited a long time.

Surely Duvall would know more if she had the courage to leave Brigitta, but with the exception of the haunted house and the occasional trip to the Dual Towers, she rarely left her office. She created the ABC club because it allowed her to gather the goods she needed without putting herself in the path of hatred, from both the spirited and the gifted. One could never be too careful.

She stretched across her desk and scooped up an aragonite stone, squeezing it in her hand and waited for something to happen. Few things in life and death were absolute, but minerals never failed. She sensed Rae before the child came trotting in like a pony. Alex strode at her side and not far behind followed her handsome friend. The Lasalle boy, the one who caused so much trouble last year.

This boy never accompanied Alex during her visits, but as they entered the room together, Duvall had to brace herself on her desk. She blinked several times and rubbed her eyes, which could see more than most because she embraced the odd and the impossible. These two had a visible energy undulating between them. Such a thing was rare. And dangerous.

"I think Rae wanted to visit you," Alex said, holding up a paper. "She kept showing this to me."

Alex presented Duvall with a sketch of the classroom. It included every miniscule detail, right down to the positioning of the flask Duvall set down and the stray pen on the table in the back right corner. Gray pencil lead streaked Rae's face, and she wiped the hair from her forehead with a dirty hand. The possibility existed that, yes, Rae wanted to see her, but more than likely she drew the picture because she knew she'd be coming to the room later. Her mind was an open door of possibility.

Rae wasn't the problem here. Duvall purposely walked in between Alex and the boy. As she suspected, she floated through a levitating pool of pleasant electricity causing her hair to stand on end. This was unfortunate.

"Here." She opened a drawer at the bottom of her desk where she kept a stash of charcoal pencils for Rae when she showed up.

Rae did a little dance as she took them before wrapping an arm around Duvall's leg. Duvall felt a tug in her chest where she once allowed a heart to beat.

Alex placed the classroom sketch on Duvall's desk. "Professor, why will Rae leave if she likes it here so much?"

"You're attached to her already?"

"It's hard not to be."

Duvall glanced down at the fair-haired angel. Rae appeared every few months or sometimes every few years. "She's too smart to stay. Spirits categorize Lost Ones with the gifted, and the gifted are outcasts in our society. Even if for some reason one of them was accepted, they would be put to use."

Like me. Duvall was a prisoner of this campus. She didn't know which was preferable. Moving every few weeks like the Lost Ones, or being stuck in one single setting forever. She couldn't complain about her treatment though. She knew of gifted spirits or Lost Ones living under horrific circumstances.

The vials above Alex's head clanked together. "What would they do to her?"

"You'll discuss this in sociology."

Duvall did her best to remain calm, but the energy between Alex and the Lasalle boy disrupted her thoughts. To test her theory, Duvall pretended to rearrange the jugs on the shelf but took the aragonite stone she still carried between her fingers and tossed it into the current as she passed between the two of them. Sure enough, the rock suspended like a secret between them.

She always thought the calm bubble of energy surrounding Alex felt like longing; she should have realized she tasted the same air when she had the Lasalle boy in class. Chase. That was his name. In three hundred years, she'd only seen energy like this once before. The electricity between this pair buzzed in a happier tone than the last two who carried such a burden between them. Sephi and Raive. That didn't necessarily mean it wouldn't change, however. Energy, like everything else, was temperamental.

Alex gathered Rae's hair in her hands and let it fall through her fingers like shiny tinsel. "Why are the gifted treated like outcasts?"

"It dates far enough back that the reason has been lost. People don't change. The Legacy families felt strongly about the separation between the spirited and the gifted."

Alex continued to comb her fingers through Rae's silky hair. "Why would they want to be separate from something like this?"

Being extraordinary is a double-edged sword. Even Duvall herself once wondered what it might be like to be on the other side of normal. Once upon a time, she left her life of gifts and tried to be a common human. And it killed her.

"Because that would be mixing the living and dead. The gifted can make things happen, manipulate reality. Losing the ability to distinguish what's real and what's not is terrifying. The gifted can be charming and lovely, but like everything and everyone else, they aren't always good spirited."

"What can they do?"

"It's all tricks of the mind. The gifted are people who are able to use the full extent of their minds even while the body protects it. Most are innocent, but some use their gifts to punish people or scare them by changing the appearance of things around them. Or make them think they're sick or dying."

She watched Alex shudder and tried to ignore the fact that a moment before it happened, Rae already placed her hand on Alex's arm to calm her. Rae died so young, but even back then she already had the weight of the world on her fragile shoulders.

Chase Lasalle cleared his throat. He stood off to the side like an onlooker.

"Professor, it seems to me that the spirited and gifted are more similar than different. Why the separation?"

"It's funny. People usually have difficulty getting along when the similarities are greater than the differences." She motioned to the space between Chase and the rest of them. "Why do you stand so far away from us, boy? With the pull between you two, you're likely to slingshot forward at any moment."

Chase Lasalle shared a look with Alex.

Yes, I can see your secret, Duvall answered. Appearance was not the only thing Alex and Sephi shared. They both shared their minds with their respective soul mates. Another rarity. Sephi claimed history would repeat itself, but Duvall hadn't realized how much.

The boy took a step forward, and she was then able to read his emotions. He carried his caution where most people carried their secrets, in his eyes. It wasn't because of her. Was it Rae? She inspected his projection, especially his baby blues.

Yes, her intuition answered for her. He wasn't scared of Rae herself but the effect Rae had on his Alex. He worried for her. He loved her.

Love. Duvall exhaled so heavily the vials rippled overhead. Love rarely turned out well when it was so strong. Mild emotions were much easier to control.

Chase must be the one who tried to read the letters. Duvall entranced that box too well. She attempted to keep a few letters last spring, separate them from the box to see if it would weaken their allegiance, but it did no good. Only the people who were meant to read the words on the page could see them. The stubborn, self-righteous box kept the words to itself because Alex hadn't known the rules. Duvall should have known better than to tamper with the emotions of things, even inanimate objects.

"I found something today about my family." Alex's tone lowered, buckling under a weight of importance. "Actually the Darwins found it."

Duvall perked up. "Why didn't you come to me sooner?"

"I didn't really know what to say. But Rae kept waving around that sketch of your classroom." Alex snatched a handful of her hair and twisted it into a coil. "I *am* connected to a Legacy family. You were right about that."

Duvall had to reach out a hand to steady the vibrating waves of energy around her. "Which one?"

"Pax said a founding family. The Darwins even showed me the tree."

Where had this information been hiding? She drained every single one of her resources trying to find a link to Sephi and … "The Kindalls?"

Alex shook her head. "The Havilahs."

The name struck a horrific chord, a triad of three notes: anger, confusion, and disappointment. The chord floated throughout the room, traveling toward her, stretching into a horizontal line before tightening itself around Duvall's neck.

"... you know them, right?"

Duvall clawed at her neck but found no release. How could this girl be related to the hunters who made it their mission to eradicate the gifted? When Alex said she was from Parrish, Duvall assumed she was a prisoner there.

Duvall bent at the waist, nose to nose with Rae. *Answers!* she demanded, but the child offered none. Blank. After mention of the Havilahs! The reason Rae was dead!

Duvall tried to scream, but only a choking noise escaped her throat. She scurried over to the wall shelves and tipped over a large brown vase. Mullein leaves fluttered to the floor. She snatched up a few and rubbed them on her neck.

This explained the mystery of the letters. Alex had not studied her family tree very well or she wouldn't be smiling about it. Perhaps certain names had been removed considering the events of the past. Family ties could be severed as easily as sawing off the branch of a tree.

"Yes," Duvall finally croaked, sinking her nails into her own arm to keep from shrieking. "I know that family."

She didn't dare say the name again.

Her mind couldn't focus enough to telekinetically extract what she wanted from the topmost shelf of her wall. Her trembling hands reached for the rolling ladder. When she grabbed the spray bottle and crawled down, she moved about the room like a tornado, cleansing her scared space.

Chase watched the air around her as she moved.

Rae held her gaze and shook her head, lifting a shoulder as if to say, *It is what it is.*

The aragonite stone shattered.

Chapter Eleven

Alex felt stupid. She should have wondered why the other legacies—in particular, the Darwins, who were so fond of ABC—hadn't already told Duvall about the Havilah family tree. No one wanted to detonate a bomb. After Duvall spritzed the entire classroom with foul-smelling drops of green goo, she overturned the bottle to douse herself. She whimpered as she escaped into her office and slammed the door without another word. The misshapen doorway trembled long after her departure. Rae took Alex's arm, patted it, and led her away with a look that read, *I expected this.*

Since death, Alex never had trouble sleeping, but that night she tossed and turned, sweating under the blanket of her own anguish. It made her feel feverishly ill, which, of course, made her feel distorted. Alice in Wonderland syndrome. She worried that she would break her bed.

When she woke to find darkness, she wondered if she even slept at all. Her fatigue continued to pound its fists against the walls of her aching mind. The whispers returned. This time, they merged into one single voice and began to sing. The harmony smiled, curling its edges into recognition like seeing an old friend, and it eased the heat in her head. It was the kind of sound Alex wanted to reach out and grab because she knew each cool, somber note would not last long. The singing faded, replaced by the sound of staccato *whishing*.

She turned to find Chase asleep on top of the blankets. He faced her with one of his arms draped over the comforter and still wore the jeans and T-shirt from earlier that day.

The brusque strokes of pencil to paper changed tempo. Alex sat up, holding Chase's arm in place so he wouldn't move, and leaned over the edge of her bed. She found Rae sprawled on the floor, knees bent and the soles of her tiny feet upward, dancing on air. Rae's distraught face hovered above her drawing, which was emitting a cloud of frenetic distress. Or it's possible she sketched quickly enough to produce an exhaust. No picture popped from the mess of shadows she created on the page, but undeclared meaning hid in the chaos like innuendos, none of which felt positive.

Alex observed Rae long enough for the day to announce itself, and the world began to lighten. And as Rae continued her frenzy, the shadows on the paper took the shape of two downturned eyes. The impact of the image grew until Alex could physically feel the pain resonating from them. It was sadness and loss. The hairs on her arms stood on end, or at least her mind made it seem that way.

Rae sighed and flicked the pencil to the floor, finished with her latest masterpiece. She collapsed into a sudden slumber, her white hair fanning out as her head lobbed to the floor. Despondence rose from the page next to her in rings, polluting the room.

Chase scrunched his face in his sleep, and Alex slid down to face him, pressing her lips to the lines on his forehead. Chase tilted his chin upward and brushed her mouth. A current of light waved around them. It killed the air of despondency Rae created. Grief couldn't withstand happiness; Alex knew this all too well.

He opened his eyes, two jewels that could see so many colors. Did he realize that they were the most incredible color of all? Was that why he could see so much?

She lifted the blankets. A silent offer. He slipped in next to her, reaching for her waist. She couldn't get close enough. The more she pressed herself against him, the more the energy buzzed, and the more alive she felt. He said something that sounded like "you," but it was lost as she pulled his lips to hers. She no longer remembered skin-on-skin contact. She was too aware that their bodies no longer existed, but it was so much better to be blanketed in the electricity they created. Chase cradled his hand around the back of Alex's head, turning it to move perfectly with the cadence of the kiss. She pressed her hands into his back and felt the light surrounding them like their own personal sun. He kissed her harder, and the light brightened. Every piece of her reenergized.

She never wanted it to end, so she gripped him even harder. She rolled on top of him to keep it going, and they fell to the floor without breaking the kiss. They climbed back up, heads still turning, mouths smiling into one another.

When Alex couldn't take the brightening of the light any longer, she pulled back. And the room was free of negative emotions.

Chase lifted her up to adjust the pillow under her head.

"When did you come in last night?"

"I don't know. I hate clocks." He rested on his elbows and admired the sketches. "Did you see the new one?"

Rae had sketched Alex's bedroom in Parrish, but how did she know what it looked like? Alex touched the drawing and felt the smooth lacquer of the wood on the sketched bedframe. It made her feel cold and empty like her room had during life. At the drawn window, snow fell thick as sugar cubes, sticking to the eyelashes of the boy crouched on the tree branch outside. A ten-year-old Chase held out a cinnamon bun, dripping with icing.

The sketch was as clear as her memory of a snow day filled with sleds, snowballs, forts, and cocoa. She loved that day, even the part when Chase carried her home because she dislocated her shoulder.

"How did Rae see that?"

"When I came in, she was sitting on the floor next to your bed, holding your hand."

"Really?"

"Yeah. I almost left, but she jumped up and waved me over. I kind of felt like she was waiting for me so she could hurry over to the corner and begin drawing."

"You think she saw my dreams?"

"Were you dreaming about that?"

"Yes, actually," she said, watching Rae. Alex decided to pick her up and put her on the bed, charcoal and all.

Chase got up and headed toward the French doors of the balcony. "See you downstairs."

Alex gathered her things for the day, listening to Rae's snores. She noticed that the eyes of the drawing—which now appeared more curious than sad—followed Rae to the bed, watching over her in a fiercely protective gaze.

She tried not to disturb Rae as she exited. Even so early, dozens of newburies already congested the vestibule. They gathered around the fountain and conversed by the blue flames, but most of them rested at the tables, poking the air with their pointer fingers, engrossed in the morning news. One would never guess they lived without the news tickers only months ago.

Alex fought the urge to glance upward, struggling to ignore the campus news, especially Sigorny L.'s large name over the popular editorial. She scoured the area, wondering if the others would consider her egotistical for obsessing over articles about herself. The harder she fought it, the more it antagonized her. She grabbed a seat and gave in, pulling the feed from the scroll with a rubber band *snap*. She promised herself she would only read a few lines.

By now you've seen them yourselves, but yes, the twenty-five supposedly brainwashed newburies have returned to your halls, your workshops, and (run for) your lives. No wonder The Dual Tower sent a representative from the Interactions Department to ~~spy on~~ *teach us. Dr. Massin has a long history of exploring sociology, as she's been employed in the department for over two hundred years. Only someone who specializes in social aspects would strive to remain so current in pop culture. Did anyone else notice her in the hallway the other day when the lyrics of the top forty songs of the week were spilling into the air from her thoughts? Who knew someone so old would like so many boy bands?*

In life, I always considered sociology to be one of those Easy-A subjects. In death, if you break a sociology rule, you might find yourself in one of the underground facilities we are too proper to call 'prisons.' In fact, one of Dr. Massin's great, great uncles ran off and pretended to be one of the bodied at the beginning of the twentieth century. Scandalous. And illegal. He was later found and sent away. He nearly soiled the family name. Perhaps the Interactions Department itself is cursed.

Underground facilities, like the prison she'd learned about last year from Raive's letters. Paradise. The term tugged at her whenever she thought of it. The ink on the paper of the letters flooded her mind. Paradise. Paradise. Paradise.

"Hey, gorgeous."

She snapped back to reality.

Chase kissed her forehead, slipping into the seat beside her. "Sorry it took me so long. My brothers wanted me to meet with them to talk."

"About what?"

"What else?" He huffed. "Jonas."

His name created a veil of angst between them. Alex swatted at it, but it stuck to her hand like a spider web.

"Anything new?"

"I really don't want to talk about it," Chase muttered, rubbing his forehead. "So, my dreams were rather loud last night."

"Are you talking about Rae?"

"No. I mean all the singing. I assume it was coming from your mind, not mine."

Definitely not.

"Do you recognize the voice?"

Alex assumed the voice belonged to Danya, his mother. Chase was the one who had grown up with a mom to soothe him, but Alex knew better than to mention Danya's name. Chase would never admit to it for the sake of tact; after all, he had seventeen years longer with his mother than Alex had with hers, but he missed Danya, and Alex knew it. She felt it.

"Never heard that voice before last night," Chase said. "Couldn't be Rae, could it?"

"Rae doesn't talk."

"That you know of." He intertwined his fingers with hers.

Alex shook her head. "That voice didn't belong to a child."

Besides, Rae wasn't calm enough to sing in such a soft

voice. Alex was beginning to wonder if Rae woke so frequently because of night terrors. She'd seen it happen several times. Rae would leap up, flailing and scrounging around for her charcoal. She'd panic until snatching a sheet of paper and delving into her own little world.

Rae only left the room to venture through the woods inside the city. She didn't allow many other spirits to see her. Skipping through the trees, she could have been any other happy toddler, and afterward, Rae sat with paper on her lap and created something beautiful. Her way of saying thanks.

"Did you see the article about the gifted?"

"No." Alex straightened. "What article?"

"Don't worry; it had nothing to do with Rae. Relax."

Alex tapped at the air, searching the news feed. "Where is it?"

She felt Chase shrug next to her. "It isn't that illuminating of an article, but a few of them have been spotted close to town. And by close, I mean miles away."

Alex wondered why the image of a gray tree crossed her mind.

"The government won't do anything about it. At least not until the Truce March, according to Sigorny."

"We're supposed to be separate, right?" Alex pushed her hands apart, dividing an invisible barrier. She noticed gray smudges all over her palms and fingers. Rae really had been holding her hands.

"I quote, 'The gifted are considered more bodied than spirited, so they are expected to remain at a distance for the betterment of both civilizations.' End quote."

Imagine the tourism if the gifted had access into the city. How many more people would be lining the streets to catch a peek of her?

Chase glanced upward at the railings above the vestibule. "I could totally blow off this day and go back to bed."

"Whose bed?"

"Doesn't matter. As long as you come with me."

Her mind remembered what it felt like for her stomach to flutter. As much as she didn't want to, she stood up. "Tempting, but you need to stay out of trouble. I'm only looking out for your best interest."

"Yeah, right." He grabbed his things and slung an arm around her shoulders. They made their way to the sociology workshop, which Alex dreaded, not because of the class but because of Jack Bond, who had taken to staring a hole into her profile. Whether he was trying to get her attention or annoy her, he was succeeding in both.

Dr. Massin's physique appeared solid in form today. It was easier to pay attention to her this way, but the boys in the room enjoyed Massin's projection because she strutted around in tight-fitting dress pants and a nearly see-through blouse.

Alex copied notes for the objectives: *Explain why people/ spirits behave the way they do. Explain impulses in terms of interaction and group participation.*

For half the session, Massin discussed why people feel the need to belong. Alex watched the Eskers kids sink lower and lower in their seats. Between her notes, Alex doodled in the margins of her notebook. She liked drawing cinquefoils, the kind etched all along the siding of the Dual Tower building. She began to zone out, and when she realized she was sketching pictures of hourglasses, not cinquefoils, she threw down her pencil. It ricocheted off the desk and clunked onto the notebook of the boy beside her.

"Sorry," she whispered.

Carr Cadman used one hand to pass back the pencil while the other rose into the air. "Do you think our confinement encourages spirits to act a certain way?"

Dr. Massin swayed her head, and her hair made a swishing sound. Every male in the class gravitated toward her as she took a seat on her desk and propped herself back on her hands. "Living in the city isn't mandatory."

"For newburies though."

"Still not mandatory, but very much necessary and encouraged. We used to own a great deal more territory before the Westward Expansion."

Words, thoughts, and question marks hovered above Madison's head. "Sounds like American Indians."

"Actually, it's a relevant comparison. We lived in peace with the bodied before new settlers discovered our land. American Indians were open to the idea of us and therefore willing to share their world with us and vice versa."

Alex flipped over the artwork on her paper. "I thought the bodied couldn't see us unless we wanted them to."

Dr. Massin paused to stare at Alex; then, she shook her head and sat up straighter. "*And* unless they're open-minded enough to see us in return. For the living to see the dead, they would have to be looking for us in the exact place, at the exact moment that we were there. And we would need to be looking for them, too. You guys have experienced enough meditation this session to know that sometimes our minds project us somewhere without our knowing it, a translucent version of ourselves. Many Native Americans could see these apparitions. Some could only feel us or at least feel our emotions, but we lived in peace together."

A few of the thought bubbles above Madison's head popped. "Is that considered gifted?"

"The term isn't quite so universal. Simply being able to see, hear, or feel a spirit is not so extraordinary. Those are mediums, and even *they* are rare now. The bodied aren't programmed to accept us anymore— just to fear us or hunt us. We don't worry about the bodied so much as we worry about the gifted, the ones who can do the things we can do with our minds even when they're living."

A know-it-all Bond voice squeaked from the front right corner of the classroom. "For a civilization as intelligent as ours, one would imagine a refined level of acceptance. Yet, discrimination prevails, strong as ever."

The way Jack said the word "discrimination" was so full of disgust that it sent a ripple over the heads of the newburies. The room began to stink like a garbage can.

Dr. Massin walked in Jack's direction. Alex had never seen anyone look at him without cringing. "There are basic causes for prejudice and discrimination. It's unfortunate." She tut-tutted.

Linton was positioned two rows over from Jack, and he shifted to sit on his knees, facing Jack and wrinkling his nose. "That's an odd question coming from you, Bond."

Jack lifted a scrawny arm and elbowed Joey, who had his head down on the table. Joey sat up but didn't dare face the class. "I'm wondering," Jack said. "Why all the hatred?"

"When you act in a way to warrant hatred, it's necessary," Linton remarked.

Alex never thought she'd be thankful for a Darwin. Her gratitude emanated from her, stretching forward over the heads of the newburies between her and Linton. He must have felt it because he lifted his hand to touch his head before looking back to find Alex. He nodded at her. "Jack, you can't sit here and judge us. Your family wrote out the laws for the separation you're sneering about right now."

Dr. Massin let out a tsk. "Lawmakers work to appease the masses. It isn't their personal beliefs that become law. It's the agreement made by the community."

Pax gave one huge nod of approval. Linton stopped grinding his teeth long enough to mutter, "Birds of a feather ..."

Jack used the situation to his advantage. "Dr. Massin," he said in a velvet tone. "Do you think that because hatred and discrimination are tolerated in regards to others, spirits are prone to hating differences in each other?"

"I do—"

"If you're comparing yourself to the gifted," Linton interrupted. "Some would call that karma, considering your family started the Witch Wars."

Dr. Massin ignored him, keeping her focus on the table of Eskers kids. "Hatred. Discrimination. They're behaviors. The spirited and the gifted have a long history. In the eighteenth century, spirits constructed many cities, including Eidolon, as a safeguard because of the growing population of the bodied. Even after the continent began to crowd, the gifted and the spirited had always been civil—not friendly by any means, but civil enough that they helped us to build our defenses around the structures of our cities. Somewhere along the way, the gifted were given the impression that the 'separate but equal' mentality no longer existed, that the cities would be for them as well."

Madison's remaining thought bubbles melded together. "You mean that the gifted, even if they were alive, would live here, too?"

Dr. Massin nodded. "The gifted claimed they were cheated of their rights, even though they were given their own land. They resented the fact that most of them had to hide their identities or live in small communities outside of society, both our society and that of the bodied."

Misfits. Like Jack. Like Reuben. And yet, the Seyferrs hunted the gifted and the Bonds went along with it. Was it a double standard, or was it a hierarchy? Alex considered the fact that Duvall might be right. *It's the similarities that drive a wedge between two types of people. But even if a wedge is removed, the splinters remain.*

"What the gifted failed to understand was that they have their own set of norms and rules. They have their own group, their own society. They are safer among themselves."

"Can't we all just get along?" someone whined.

Jack snickered, and Alex watched as Carr lifted his chin to get a better look at him. "Yeah right," Carr said. "The living don't get along any better. I died fighting because I thought I could change that."

"We are safer," Dr. Massin said, "when we know where we fit. The gifted were, of course, denied access to Eidolon. Broderick and Brigitta Cinatri originally constructed our city, and as our city thrived, the gifted became more and more resentful. The Witch Wars during the 1800s began after territory and rights negotiations. Too many losses occurred to be civil after that war. No interaction exists between us now."

Alex tapped her pencil on her notebook. She could still see the hourglass even though her paper was flipped over.

"Then why is a gifted sighting newsworthy?" Madison asked.

Dr. Massin found Alex. The weight of her gaze acted as a wind, pushing Alex backward in her seat.

"There are laws that we've agreed upon, and the Centennial celebrates the length of time we've lived without problems because of those laws. We can't enter their territories, and they can't enter ours, even if they're curious."

"How do we know one of the gifted when we see one?" Madison asked.

"You'll know. Like they know when they see you. And they can hurt you as much as you could hurt them. Their strengths are much like ours, a manipulation of the mind. If you see something warped, something that isn't right or out of place, trust your instincts. The gifted are not friendly by nature; they've seen too much adversity. Hence the warnings in the media."

"You said they weren't a threat."

"I don't believe they are. But my advice? If you see one," she paused to cup one hand to the side of her mouth, "run away."

***

Alex weaved through the crowded hallway feeling like a mouse in a maze, but no matter how quickly she moved, she could still feel Jack's glare on her back.

"It really is true what they say …" His threatening tone collided into her, causing her to stumble.

Since when did he become so bold? What happened to the quivering nerd with the idealistic thoughts? She'd liked that kid.

He cracked. That was the reason she felt afraid of him. He ridiculed his bullies last year, but now he played their game, antagonizing her.

She wished Chase was here, but he was in therapy. She reminded herself that Jack wouldn't hurt her in a clustered hallway with so many witnesses, and even if he wanted to, he could only do extraordinary things when he was around his twin sister. Twin minds make their abilities more powerful, but only when they share the same space and energy.

She stopped, took a deep breath, and faced her tormentor. He wasn't alone. Joey lingered behind, but Reuben stood shoulder to shoulder with him.

Jack squished up his face, causing his freckles to blend together. "History sure does repeat itself."

Alex crossed her arms. "You're going to have to be more specific."

He stood regarding her, with his mousy hair puffed like a lion's mane. He'd transformed from the scrawny outcast she'd befriended last year. She used to like the way Jack sauntered through the criticism with kindness still on his face, how high he held his cards even with such a poorly dealt hand. Now, his presence carried the bitter saltiness of hostility.

"Did you join another cult?" she asked.

"A cult? Please. You sound ignorant. I knew what I was getting into last year."

"Isn't that pleading your guilt? How did the Revealers see past that?"

"I can honestly say I never *wanted* to hurt anyone. But there was something I know now that I didn't know then. It might have changed things."

Alex sighed. "And what is that, Jack?"

"You're a damn Havilah."

People were rubbernecking as they walked by, and some stopped to observe the crash scene. Alex noticed kids watching Jack with interest, newburies who'd once ridiculed him, who'd elbowed him or slapped his books from his hands. They said and did nothing against him now.

Alex knew he wanted more than that though. When they were friends, he said he wanted acceptance, no, more than that; he wanted *prestige*. He had a long way to go. Fear was only a slighter higher step than ridicule.

"Why does my family mean anything to you?"

Jack's horse-like mouth hung open as he shook his head. "You're a hunter, no better than Reuben, and you're treated like some sort of second coming while his family is criticized and mine is blasphemed. See what's right in front of you."

"I know the history of the Havilahs. They never hunted."

Jack raised a fist. "No. What your family did was worse."

Reuben scratched at his cheek and nodded to confirm the validity of the statement. The newburies surrounding them began to whisper.

Alex's mind didn't forget certain things about her former body and confrontation. Clammy hands. Racing heart. Rush of adrenaline. "How?"

Jack snickered. "You don't know. What else is new? That doe-eyed Bambi look is starting to get old. That's how the Havilahs always avoid punishment. They play the innocent card and let others play the scapegoat."

Alex didn't even need to wrack her brain for a good retaliation. "Scapegoat? Who did the attacking last year? If I remember right, I was on the receiving end of the blows."

"Just like a typical Havilah to cry innocence. You were never in any danger."

"For being a genius I would have thought you would

discover my family ties before anybody else."

Jack waved a hand in front of her face. "Conveniently you hid behind that little disguise of yours. With that face, the Havilahs are the last place anyone thought they'd find you."

What was left of Alex's body began to tremble. "You know how much information I *don't* have about myself. By the way, animosity doesn't look good on you, Jack."

She felt proud of herself for saying it. She wished Chase had been around to hear it.

"I have a right to be bitter. They set us up. They wanted you because you're a Havilah, and whoever was in charge of that Eviar group, Eskers group, whatever, used us to get to you."

"Yeah, they really twisted your arm. How do you know it had anything to do with me?"

Jack's volume rose. "Haven't you wondered about the location?"

"My hometown."

"You're so stupid."

She didn't understand him. Was he jealous? Because instead of wanting her dead, as she'd assumed, for being connected to Sephi, they wanted her alive, for being connected to the Havilahs?

"I don't know why you're acting this way."

"Because something needs to change! Bonds have been paddling along, accepting ridicule. I'm not going to do it anymore! That much about history will be different."

Jack began to move forward, and Alex tensed. Little

Gossamer stepped out of the crowd and stood in between them. "I think that's enough," her singsong voice advised.

Reuben recoiled and twisted his nose at Little. Alex recognized that reaction. He usually only reserved it for her, at least when he thought she was Sephi.

"You know what?" Jack hissed at Alex. "For once, go figure out things yourself." And with that, he turned his heel and stalked down the hallway like a spoiled child. Reuben ambled along beside him with Joey trailing.

"Are you okay?" Little asked.

Alex nodded, but her mind began to ache. She never enjoyed confrontation, and all the words she hadn't thought to say, and all the wonderful comebacks flashed through her mind.

She shoved her hands into her pockets. Dodging stares, she noticed that a hood appeared on the back of her shirt. She ducked her head and shielded herself until she escaped through the hulking wooden doors. It was then that her fingers brushed against something in her pocket. She clasped her hand around a piece of paper, and before she opened the note, she knew what she would find.

She stood paralyzed on the steps of the grand building, staring at the sketch of an hourglass once again. A sketch that hadn't been there ten minutes ago.

Chapter Twelve

"I don't understand why they would release Jack," Alex complained to Ellington.

For once, she was happy to be in therapy. What she didn't understand was the way the room accessorized itself. Large, mirrored squares hung from the ceiling, dangling like Christmas ornaments on an invisible tree.

"I don't have an answer for you."

"Aren't you his therapist, too? What goes on inside that crazy mind of his?"

"Even if I was allowed to break confidentiality—"

"Wait," Alex interrupted. "I thought the objective of these therapy sessions was that you could report back to the government. Doesn't that kind of kill the idea of confidentiality?"

Ellington's face twitched. "It's twofold. Anyway, even if I could share my findings about other newburies, I wouldn't have much information for you. Jack isn't exactly social, even here. Even with me. That's part of the problem."

"How could the government think his friends were harmless after what they did?"

"The system in place for evaluation is relatively foolproof," Ellington said. "If Revealers say they're innocent, they're innocent. Secondly, the Patrol witnessed most of the fight in Parrish. I know you don't want to hear that, but they were curious as to how far the Eskers kids would go, and between you and me, I think they wanted to see what *you* could do. They didn't think the Eskers kids were trying to hurt you so much as they were trying to save themselves."

"Yeah, they didn't try to hurt me at all." Alex slouched in her seat. "I was only blacked out for a month."

"It went a bit too far."

"You think?" Alex asked sarcastically. "After all that, their actions can be ignored?"

"Not necessarily. They were acting under orders, and well, the government likes to see that."

The ornaments above their heads started to spin. Alex wondered if it would hurt if they fell on her. "That's sick."

"Our world is peaceful and progressive because of order. You know this. That's why newburies stay here for several years after their deaths. The theory is that if we can get to you while you're young, we can give you a role and, therefore, maintain the status quo."

"You mean program us to think a certain way."

Ellington cringed. "Stop letting Chase into your head. That's something he would say."

Alex choked and turned it into a cough.

"I don't blame you for saying it, but consider the alternative. This is what sparked the Restructuring. An afterworld without order became chaotic. It's best for children to fall into the pre-established order. Not try to create a new one. What we do and what we have works."

"Then why is Jack so angry?"

Ellington straightened the collar of his shirt. "If nothing around here changes, neither will Jack's fate, and, unfortunately, the Bonds tread on the same treacherous path generation after generation. Jack thought that since he was smarter than everyone else, this would change, but intelligence has nothing to do with it. He refuses to listen to my reasoning."

"How can you say that about intelligence? Isn't this world about the mind?"

"The progression of the world is mental. But existence? No."

Alex groaned. "You've gone over my head. Again."

"Their souls are cursed, not their minds. The gifted who cursed them knew better than that. A soul gives a person a life, but a soul doesn't *keep* a body alive, nor does it keep a mind alive in the afterworld. Intelligence and emotions, those are the fruits of the mind. That's where you find your strength here. Calla Bond understood that last year; Jack did not."

"Where is Calla? I haven't seen her with the others."

"Calla needed some time."

"That's vague."

"I'm not allowed to discuss it, Alex."

"She attacked me, Ellington. I think I've earned the right to know where she is, at least."

Ellington's bowtie had unraveled. It rested over his shoulders. "She needs treatment. Her mind cracked."

Alex knew all too well what it was like to feel outside of one's sanity. "Committed, you mean."

"Something like that."

"Is she still in the city?"

"She's not." Ellington flipped through his notes. "You were a resident of the Eskers Rehabilitation Center. Were you coherent there?"

"No. And you can say mental hospital, you know. What does my craziness have to do with Calla?"

"I'm sorry," Ellington said. "I thought you knew."

"Knew what?"

"The Eskers offers mental rehabilitation for both the living *and* the dead."

"Gabe had a book last year that mentioned lingerers and wanderers checking in to the Eskers, but the book made it seem like they only needed a break. Not that they were crazy."

"That's the case with some. Others need extensive treatment."

Alex was afraid she already knew the answer to her next question. "Who treats them?"

"Your family, of course. The Havilahs have always

maintained the treatment facility."

"Yeah, but they're dead. I didn't know they were still hanging around the treatment center!"

"Do you remember anything about your time there?"

"No. Is that why Jack is so angry? He mentioned the Havilahs."

"I figured he'd be furious at you."

Alex shifted in her seat. "Over what though? The Havilahs never hunted the gifted, right?"

"Usually the most vocal of opponents hire others to do their dirty work. That's something that doesn't seem to change in death. Those in charge spend their time speaking and designate others to accomplish the 'doing.' The Havilahs found benefit in targeting the gifted, especially after the Cinatris decided they wanted the gifted away from Eidolon.

"I'm sure after your encounter last year with the Eskers kids, you've heard or read—" he paused to peer upward as though the news projections might be hovering there—"about the families of the accused?"

"Jack said they were associated with hunters. So, he's mad because it's the Havilahs' fault? They encouraged others to hunt the gifted?"

Ellington twirled his pen. "It was a Bond who held the head position at the Dual Tower responsible for equal rights. The blame for the horrific treatment of the gifted falls on them. Jack is angry, but anger only causes insult to injury. Acceptance eases the swelling of hatred, but the pain must be endured. The Bonds have never been very patient."

Alex couldn't ignore the spinning bulbs anymore. "Why are those mirrors spinning so fast?"

Ellington followed their movements. "They're inhaling your energy. I got tired of you making my walls freak out and pulsate. A decorator suggested this." He shifted in his seat. "I'm not so sure how they're making me feel, however."

She watched the mirrors spin and reflect a million images of her face. "What do I do about all this?"

"Learn to harness your energy."

"No." Alex shook her head. "Not the bulbs. What do I do about this Havilah situation?"

"Oh. Embrace who you are. That's all any of us can do. There is nothing you can do to change it. But brace yourself, too. Once this leaks out, which I'm sure it already has, the attention surrounding you will only multiply. Unfortunately, you stand on both sides of the line."

The bulbs came to a stop.

"You are both the hunter and hunted. And anything unclear makes people nervous."

Chapter Thirteen

The ocean composed music. It didn't have a voice like the trees or the rain. It was more like the somber notes of a piano. The tune was as blue as the sky behind it, but it was inspiring, powerful, and addictive. No wonder the rivers flowed so eagerly to join it.

Alex spread her arms wide and laid back. Being in the waves was like swimming in a concerto.

"Why is Skye afraid of the water?" Kaleb's voice interrupted her trance.

Past the view of her toes and the tip of the surfboard, in the distance Alex saw Skye hugging her knees, sitting on a rock. The power of Skye's glare skipped across the waves like a pebble until it splashed them.

"She says it's too much."

Ever the attention hog, Kaleb had entertained a swarm of newburies all morning, but now that his company only consisted of his family, he dropped his act and gazed toward the beach.

"She's sitting pretty close to the edge. What do you think she'd do if a sneaker wave snatched her and pulled her in?"

"She'd probably blame her survival on some flower or stone she had in her pocket."

"I think Rae would save her," Chase said, running his hands along the surface of the water beside Alex.

Rae danced along the edge of the beach picking up shells and twirling like a top. It was strange to see her in public. It was even stranger to see her acting like a three-year-old.

Kaleb chuckled, falling forward on his board. He rested his chin on it and tapped his fingers against the surface of the water. If Alex listened closely enough, she could hear the *pings* of sound it added to the song of the ocean, like strums of a guitar. It was mindboggling that one person could have such an effect on something so vast.

"I thought Rae didn't like crowds," he said.

"This is hardly a crowded beach," Chase noted. "Maybe she needed a holiday as much as we did."

Every year before the chaos of autumn activities, the newburies got a mandatory holiday, a chance to unwind before the chaos of the season kicked off with the Autumn Mask and continued until All Soul's Day in November. When news spread that the holiday could be postponed this year, Alex wasn't disappointed because she felt comfortable inside the confines of Brigitta's campus. She would only venture to the more crowded areas of the city if Chase accompanied her. She made the mistake of saying this aloud, and Gabe labeled her institutionalized. She agreed to go to Moribund to prove Gabe wrong ... and because the Lasalles would be surrounding her.

They had always been the four crutches holding her up. Without Jonas, they were only three; they teetered but still held.

Kaleb's voice was muffled by his board. "There are more chaperones than usual."

"Chaperones?" Alex asked. "Where?"

"All over the place because of the hocus pocus witch hullabaloo. I think if Halloween wasn't around the corner Eidolon wouldn't be so hyped up about those gifted sightings. Everyone likes a good scare this time of year."

"Dr. Massin told us it wasn't a big deal," Chase said.

Kaleb flattened his mouth. "Massin was sent from Broderick Square. They don't want us to panic."

Alex felt a headache coming on.

"But you know, I think people like the panic," Kaleb added.

"You mean, *you* like it."

"It's entertaining."

Excitement had an energy and life of its own, no matter how positive or negative the source. In life, when a hurricane would set course for Parrish or a rare snowstorm would dump a few feet on the town, people moaned and complained, but they welcomed the thrill of it all. The exhilaration pumped life into the tedium of everyday existence.

Gabe paddled back in their direction, grinning. Athletics interested him the least out of his brothers, but he caught the most waves—he told Alex that surfing was all about physics. When they entered Moribund that morning and announced their plans to go out into the Pacific, Alex's mouth formed an O, large enough for Chase to reach out to close it. Surfing seemed like such a bodied thing to do, but the boys assured her that the thrill was worth it, the art of feeling out the waves and becoming one with a force of energy greater than them.

The quiet town of Moribund consisted of one main street of shops. Every few feet, the sidewalk broke to reveal side streets leading to small communities of large stone and stucco homes.

"How are we supposed to rent the boards?" she asked Chase.

He stopped to hold the door for an elderly lady leaving the market. Alex did a double take when the woman thanked him.

"She can see us?"

Kaleb led them to a building with a window shaped like a wave. "They can all see us here. The town is in on our secret."

Alex couldn't believe it. Imagine thinking it was normal to spot a ghost while you went out to buy milk.

"They keep quiet about us, and in exchange we give them all the money from the haunted house every year. They make bank on the fall tourism and live comfortably because of us."

They thought themselves into wetsuits and rented boards from a tanned, muscular man that spoke to them in surf jargon Alex didn't understand. The boys bobbed their heads in agreement to whatever he said, but Alex remained shell-shocked by the whole ordeal. The guy asked her if her name was Judith, and when Kaleb scolded him, he slapped his knee and called her Bunny instead.

When his brothers trotted out to the ocean, Chase gave Alex a quick lesson. The instructions jumbled in her head, but she knew they'd remain in her memory until she could smooth them out. Like magic, when she needed to paddle, she remembered to crawl stroke. The terms "pearling" and "corking" presented themselves as reminders that despite her weightlessness, she needed to pretend to act like one of the bodied. When she waited for waves, her mind shuffled through the etiquette; but, the chill of the ocean water drained her energy much like the effects of cold weather. Alex would rather lounge on the board recharging under the beams of the sun, like a human battery pack.

She wondered how this experience would have felt if they were alive. She and Chase grew up spending their summers on boats, but while the Lasalles learned to wakeboard and Jet Ski, Alex kept her crippled body in the boat. It was something she complained about but didn't mind because she was afraid of anything she couldn't see. It was impossible to see anything more than a foot under the murky waters of the Chesapeake Bay.

"You want the next one, Alex?" Kaleb asked.

"No, thanks."

"Sure? I would've thought you'd be eating these waves."

She liked the idea of it all. The freedom. But she didn't

want to move right now.

"Alex, do you know what's going on over there with Skye?" Gabe asked.

Alex didn't open her eyes. "She's afraid of the water."

"No. I mean, why she's talking to Pax."

Alex lifted her head and squinted through the sun. "Is she with Kaleb's stalker, too? Skye's distant cousin?"

Kaleb came to Skye's defense. "She said they're barely related. Her last name wasn't even Gossamer in life. She changed it when she got here so everyone would know her family." He continued to stare at the scene on the beach. "You said Pax is the legacy leader? She's kind of cute."

"I'm more interested in what she *knows*," Gabe said.

"Yes, she does kind of have a big nose," Kaleb joked.

"I'm serious. Skye told me that someone had news about Jonas."

Alex sat up on her board. "Xavier Darwin said Pax's family runs the Interactions Department."

"Interacting with people he shouldn't be? That sounds like something our darling brother would do, doesn't it?" Gabe asked.

Kaleb flopped to his stomach and began paddling in frenzied strokes to get to the beach. Gabe thought practically and projected himself to shore.

Chase didn't budge. "Let them go."

Alex slouched on her board and lifted her palms as if to say, *Really?* "Are you ever going to forgive him?"

"That depends. Are you ever going to blame him?"

She didn't know. She watched her board bob up and down.

"I'm sorry. I don't know what I feel. He set us up. He set *me* up at least."

"He's still your brother."

"I don't need to be reminded of that. I held his hand when we crashed in that car. I watched him slip out of life, and it *ripped* me apart. But he didn't hesitate to put me in harm's way. That's not a brother. That's not love." He splashed the water and held the droplets in midair with his mind, merging them together and letting them fall. "Not love for me or for you, no matter what he might have said to you."

Jonas never said those words to her unless it was part of a joke. Come to think of it, she never heard Jonas say he loved anyone.

She rocked up and down with the water, thinking about the concept of it all. "What do you think love is?"

Love. The word hung in the air, twinkling, lightening the bitterness of the previous topic.

"It definitely isn't selfish. So I'm not sure if it's something Jonas will ever truly choose to experience."

Alex leaned back to stare at the sky. "Oh, I don't think it's something you choose."

Chase rolled off his board and made no sound when he fell into the water. "Whoops," he said when he emerged. "I wasn't concentrating on that."

"No one is paying attention to us," Alex noted with a careless wave of her hand. "If they already know what we are, does it matter anyway?"

"I think this is like a practice arena for the real world. We should be trying to be normal when we're here whether it matters or not."

Chase remained in the water but rested his forearms on the side of Alex's board. Water droplets sparkled on his long eyelashes, and he glistened under the light from the sun. She couldn't help but reach out and touch him. Make sure for the millionth time that he was real. Her fingertips touched his energy, and his warmth was more powerful than the light from the sun.

She lifted her head to meet his lips, and he wrapped an arm over her, accepting, and through her lips he answered, "That is love."

He kissed her again, sliding his hand underneath her head to raise her closer to him. "That energy. That pulse." He turned his head in the other direction. "I know you can feel it. I always could. Since the moment we were born. Maybe before then. And now I can even see it."

A small piece of her could see it, too, through the colors in Chase's mind. His hand lowered to her abdomen and whatever heartbeat was left in him transferred straight to her belly.

That song of the ocean, it wasn't so sad anymore. It was louder, faster, as though they had the power to alter its mood. It fed off of them.

Chase straightened, breaking their kiss. "Whoa."

Little Gossamer perched on a board beside them. She lifted her sunglasses and placed them on her head. "Hi, I'm Gretchen."

"Nice timing," said Chase.

"Sorry."

"You don't look sorry."

Her jovial expression didn't falter.

"I thought your name was *Little*," Chase said. "That's what my brother calls you."

"Kaleb?" she squealed. "He does? Call me Little, then. I like that."

Alex thought the name suited her better anyway. "Did you project yourself out here?"

She waved it off. "Yeah."

Chase tightened his grasp on Alex's board, bobbing up and down in the waves.

"Is she with you?" Little gestured to the beach where Rae was turning cartwheels. Kaleb and Gabe were gone, and Skye's rock was also vacant.

Alex sat up. "Our friends were down there with her. I don't know where they went."

"I'm not judging." Her cheer was musical. "She's beautiful. Lost Ones don't usually cling to spirits though. I wanted to introduce myself the other day, Alex, but Pax stole you away. I've heard all about you."

Alex propped up on her elbows. "Yeah, I got into some trouble last year."

"No, I mean I knew about you before I died. You're famous."

"Huh?"

"I grew up gifted."

Chase let go of Alex's board and projected himself onto his own. "You're gifted? And they let you in?" He seemed to realize what he said. "I'm sorry. That didn't sound right."

She grasped her board with both hands as a wave pushed them back. "It's okay. I didn't live in one of the isolated gifted towns. Those witches know better than to choose the afterlife. They never do. Except Duvall, I guess. She was pretty excited to meet me, but I think I disappointed her because I don't know anything about the gifted life. My parents wanted me to have a normal childhood, but they still told me the stories."

Good thing she didn't need to breathe because the girl rambled in one long breath.

Chase ran his fingers along the edge of the water. "You're so young. I thought the gifted lived longer than most of the bodied."

She shrugged. "Being gifted doesn't save you from cancer."

For a second, her projection withered, her hair vanished, and her face sunk in. In a flash, she was back to being beautiful.

"If you're gifted," Chase said, "it's kind of weird that you're best friends with the biggest advocate for the Interactions Department."

"Pax was so nice to me the first day I died. She wants me to help with the Truce March."

There it was again. The idea of a Truce March gave Alex a funny feeling. "I always heard that the gifted and the spirited weren't friendly."

Little laughed and small pings lifted from the water like fish jumping. "It depends on who you ask."

Chase cleared his throat. "She gathered her information from the Bonds."

"That explains it. That family is nuts. My parents always said the spirited don't bother the gifted, and the gifted don't bother the spirits. Those are the rules."

Chase ran his hands along the surface of the water. "Then why did your parents keep you away from the others?"

"I didn't know there were others, or that there were colonies, until I died."

"You knew about Alex though?"

She wagged her finger. "I knew about Sephi Anovark. My parents told me bedtime stories about the revolutionary who made the world a better place."

"Why are the gifted celebrating Alex's death, then? If everything is so perfect already?"

"Wouldn't you celebrate if someone who made the world better returned? Do you have any clue what it used to be like? How the gifted were treated? Sephi gave us what we have today. She's the reason for our freedom." Several uncomfortable seconds passed. Little bent toward Alex as if waiting for her to say something. "Do you really know nothing about life before Sephi Anovark?"

"Something Sigorny L. hasn't already shared with the world?"

Little's eyes lit up. "I'm heading to Main Street in a little bit. There's this guy who has a shop with all sorts of cool stuff: antiques, trinkets, valuables. It might explain some things for you. If you want to know how the gifted used to be treated,

I think you'll want to come see this place. It's right by the surf shop, and you'll need to go there to return your boards anyway."

Chase glanced at Alex, who shrugged as if to say *Why not?* She didn't think it was possible to find out anything she hadn't already heard or suspected.

She should have realized by now that there's always more.

Chapter Fourteen

Moribund felt staged to Alex. Like the set of a movie town, it was real but not. The locals on the sidewalks treated them like any other bodied children, and the shops waited with open doors and waving flags.

Chase slowed his pace. "Little said it was right by the board shop. There's nothing else on this street."

Rae kept walking, even after the sidewalk ended, treading down an overgrown path that snaked to the right and led to a slump of interconnected stores, supporting one another lest they might crumble. Alex wondered why they wouldn't give these abandoned stores a facelift to match the rest of the town. A rickety sign dangled over a hunched building called Walt's Plastics.

"Maybe we're not looking at it right." Chase bent down

next to Rae. "You know, don't you?"

Rae shimmied her tiny shoulders and her cheeks grew pink.

Chase held out a hand as he straightened, gesturing to the line of shops. "What is a plastics store? Sounds to me like no one would ever go in there, and if they wanted to, how would they get in? There's no entrance!"

His words were like magic, opening their minds. Alex focused all her attention to the shops, this time looking through willing eyes, and in place of Walt's Plastics was a sign that read: *Maori's*.

Alex took Rae's hand. "There's still no door."

Chase walked forward. "Will you ever get used to being dead?"

As if this was an easy feat. She placed her other hand over his to absorb the shock of stepping through the glass, the pins and needles that stabbed her being as she crossed through anything solid. Alex worried about Rae, but the transition didn't seem to bother her. Rae ran the width of the entryway, breathing deeply.

The store smelled musty and dank. There were three archways, each protected by a curtain of dangling stones and bones. Behind the noosed objects, clusters of lights greeted them; it was like a vineyard of fireflies.

Rae let go of Alex's hand and eagerly pushed her way through the closest curtain, trotting down the center aisle with her windblown hair and wrinkled, sandy dress.

"Don't get lost," Alex warned, and Rae poked her head

back through the curtain with a childish smirk that read, *Yeah right*.

"Hoarders, eat your heart out," Chase joked. "I'll check out the far wall."

Alex started toward the left, and then she understood Chase's comment. The "fireflies" were actually tiny spotlights illuminating millions of trinkets for sale. The objects could have belonged in Duvall's classroom: rusty jars and distorted minerals. Alex came to a stop midway down the aisle and read the caption glowing behind a black rock: *Bloodstone 100%; Value 5/10; Origin: India.* From vials to masks to jewelry, everything had a bright, hanging caption with a rating of its worth and its origin. The brightest light in the aisle spotlighted a red shield.

Authentic coral from the Witch Wars; Value 9/10; Origin: Astor, Oregon.

"Hi, there."

Alex jumped in surprise, and a few of the lights flickered.

"Al?" Chase's voice was muffled, hidden by the maze of walls in the store.

"I'm fine," she called as she stared into the pretty face of Little Gossamer.

"Sorry to scare you."

Clattering disrupted the silence. Above the tips of the shelves, brass chimes swayed from the rafters.

Alex felt Chase appear behind her, and she reached back for him. For a moment, everything flashed to black and white. Alex had to blink several times before color returned to her vision.

"So, is that guy here?" Chase asked.

"I haven't seen him yet. Isn't this place cool though? Maori gets his hands on the rarest items."

Looks like a garage sale, Chase thought to Alex.

Little tilted her head to the side. "What?"

"Nothing," Alex replied. "This place doesn't exactly look like Tiffany's."

Little's attention lowered to Alex's feet.

Alex didn't realize Rae had found her until she slung a protective arm around Alex's thigh. "Oh. This is Rae."

The room tinted yellow and orange when Rae dipped her head and her hair fell over her face.

Are your eyes playing tricks on you? Chase asked.

With colors? Yes. I thought that was you.

Definitely not me.

Little's head shook back and forth between Alex and Chase as they spoke to one another. "Whatever you're doing right now, stop. It's weird. You guys have strange energy."

"Sorry," Chase said without a hint of remorse, "but colorblindness doesn't exactly make me feel comfortable."

Little's hands went to her cheeks. "Oh. I'm sorry. I might be doing that. Duvall says it's a gifted thing. I get kind of excited when I'm in here because all of these items are trying to tell me something. They have so many stories."

Skye would get along grand with this girl, Alex thought to Chase.

They're built from the same weird mold.

Little stretched her hand between them.

"What?" Chase asked.

"There was another weird sizzle of electricity between you guys. Did you feel anything?"

"No," Alex lied. Chase shook his head.

Little squinted at them.

Alex felt a tug at her shorts. Rae shook her finger at the door. Professor Darby stood outside on the other end of the glass. Madison hurried down the street to join him, and Tess followed.

"We're going to be late for curfew. What is it that you wanted us to see?"

Little slapped her hand to her head. "I almost forgot!" She hurried to the front of the store. "I saw it the first time my parents brought me here. It's why they chose to live away from the gifted society."

Little stopped beside a document, thick and yellowed. The caption read:

Official offer from representatives from the Union Army. Currency offered for Josephine "Sephi" Anovark. Sale completed.

Signed by:

Arthur Havilah, witness, and Edwin Stanton, United States Secretary of War.

Value: 10/10.

Origin: Parrish, Maryland.

For several moments, they each stood silently staring at the old paper. "Does currency mean what I think it means?" Chase asked.

Alex stepped even closer. "Money for Sephi?" She inwardly begged that this document had no others like it.

"This used to happen all the time. That's why I was so surprised you didn't know. Before the Truce, the gifted were traded like property. They were servants sold to the highest bidder."

"Who would buy them?"

"Whoever had enough money. The gifted were used, abused, and then slaughtered like magical cattle."

Alex didn't know what was worse: seeing Sephi's name on the paper or seeing the name of her family and her hometown right next to it.

"They were slaves."

Alex knew her family's reputation to be strict and unforgiving, but Parrish treated the Havilahs like royalty. If anything, they were monsters.

Chase shuffled back down the aisle, and with each step documents illuminated from both sides. There had to be hundreds of them, none as bright as Sephi's. Alex couldn't bear to look at the rest.

"This is what the Havilahs did. This is what Jack was talking about."

Little's nose pressed against the glass, reading the paper. "Sephi was sold to the Union. No wonder they won the Civil War. They had a prophet on their side."

"You're gifted," Alex blurted out. "Little, why don't you hate me?"

She angled her head forward. "*You* didn't sell people.

Besides, I can't possibly look at your face and hate you. It was that face that ended this mess."

Alex crouched down and buried her head in her hands. Which was she? Anovark or Havilah? When she finally wiped her face and straightened up, Chase had returned. He lifted a finger and placed it over a part of the glass.

"You notice this part, Al?"

Of course she saw it. Although she wished she hadn't. She wished they hadn't come into this store at all.

The mediator listed for the trade was a woman named Abigail *Frank*.

Chapter Fifteen

During the next few days, Alex couldn't think of anything without Sephi's contract invading her mind. The more she tried not to think about it, the more it tortured her. Alex's projection suffered: her hair tangled like a rat's nest and her mismatched clothes hung loose and sloppy.

Sale completed. Currency offered. *Sale*. Sephi was bartered, and the Havilahs were to blame. And the Franks. Liv's family. Alex's life continued to haunt her in death, the coincidences piling up like a stack of teetering books ready to topple at the slightest nudge.

Alex rested her chin on the railing of the seventh floor. She observed the crowd in the vestibule below; most spirits had already left for Lazuli Street. She could hear the ruckus beginning outside. The festival was in full swing.

"Happy birthday." A square, wooden box appeared in front of her. Next to it, Chase set down a large Ex cup with a candle balanced on top.

"It's not my birthday."

"Death day, I guess." He kissed the top of her head before sitting down opposite her.

"I didn't even think about it."

"The beginning of the festival leading up to All Soul's Day. A celebration of death. You couldn't have timed that any better." He sat back in his chair and studied her.

"What?"

"Nothing."

She wanted to know what he saw when he looked at her. She tried to jump into his mind, but he blanked out his thoughts.

"Make a wish."

The only thing she'd ever wished for was right in front of her. She tried to blow out the flame, but no amount of effort worked. She pouted. "Is that why you're grinning at me like that?"

"I wasn't quite sure what would happen. I'm thinking you probably have to use your head."

"Right. I'll smash the flame with my forehead. Happy death day to me."

The corner of his lips curled. "That's not what I meant."

She flicked her gaze to the flame and thought about it extinguishing. It disappeared in a flash, rising into a ribbon of winding smoke, twisting its way toward the very object of her wish.

"Bravo."

The only thing she wanted was for him to always look at her in such a way. A combination of intrigue and humor with a dash of adoration.

"You got me a gift?"

"Nothing crazy," he warned. "It isn't much."

She lifted the lid of the box, and the paper curled like the petals of a blooming flower to reveal a mask framed in white, fluffy feathers. The glass glistened like black ice, and long silver eyelashes stretched at least a foot high. Her attention gravitated to a jagged crack. The imperfection was no mistake; it zigzagged deliberately from left eyebrow to right chin.

"It's beautiful."

"You like it?"

"I might never take it off."

"Let's not get carried away." Chase clasped his hand around hers, bringing her to her feet. He lifted the mask from the box and fastened it around her head.

She bent to gather her things, and when she rose again, Chase's face was hidden behind porcelain. The black lips of the mask curled into a fitting smirk, and there were wise crow's feet painted around the outer edges. Attached to the top was a lopsided fedora. Even though it covered most of his face, the white of the mask and the markings around the eyes accentuated the brilliant blue shining behind them. Chase always looked good in costume. He looked good in anything.

One year for Halloween, Alex had her fragile heart set on Dorothy from the *Wizard of Oz*. It was the same year she became a regular at the hospital, and Danya struck a deal with her in August. If Alex remained injury-free for two months, she had free reign to select the boys' costumes. It was the ultimate prize. Somehow, she managed it, eight weeks with no dislocations or breaks and barely any bruises ... even after Jonas attempted to shove her off the monkey bars in a last-ditch effort to save his hide. Because of his interference, Alex forced him to dress up as the wicked witch. Even through the dark green paint, everyone could see his blush of embarrassment. Kaleb picked the Tin Man, Gabe picked the lion, and Chase was the scarecrow. It was her favorite Halloween.

On the day she died—exactly a year ago—she felt very much like becoming Dorothy again. When she left Miss Petra's classroom and stepped into her new world, it was like watching the movie switching from black and white to vibrant colors. She never thought she would ever again see something as fascinating as those colors upon first sight. She was wrong. They changed every day. They brightened, shifted, and sometimes bled into one another.

Now, a year after her death, weaving through the crowds of the Autumn Mask, she realized how weak her eyes had been even then. She could see merriment suspended above the dancing crowd in the form of a bubble; it hung like nostalgia, pulsing in the energy that fed it. Lazuli Street was ramose, something that had taken her months to realize. It was only the trunk to the other roads that branched off of it, roads that had been invisible to her until she was looking for them. Tonight, from those interconnected streets she could tell from a mile away which music was playing where. The classical pieces rose into the night as physical notes, tranquilly taking their time. The jazzy music shot bursts of jovial, energetic orange lightning. The jumpy dance music shook the stars overhead. Some notes were hyper enough to jump and others drooped with sadness; it depended on the piece.

Last year it frightened her. The people, the chaos, and the masks. The simple and beautiful, feathery and light costumes were swallowed by the darkness of the skulls, the flames, and the distortion. Alex remembered clinging to Jonas because he was something familiar in this hallucinatory setting. The vendors lined the streets eagerly promoting inventions, games, and refreshments. Josepha and Johanna twirled in hoop skirts outside their fashion agency. They yelled in French and passed out mouthfuls of wavy-looking steam cake. Across the street at the stairway to the Lazuli gardens, the florist stood on the steps lifting flowers into the air like lanterns. The flower shop itself was even in costume, wearing a pouty mask and a crooked hat on its angled roof.

The Ex distributors offered steaming cups of vapory emotion, and spirits sipped or inhaled. Comfort tasted like coffee, insight like honeysuckle, and energy like wine. Dancers, gamers, and storytellers intermixed with the partygoers.

She hadn't been ready to see certain aspects of the world then, and she suspected she still wasn't ready for the reality of the things her mind prevented her from seeing now. Through wigs of dancing ribbons and wings of spider webs, spirits clutched strings in their hands, attached to clouds suspended above their heads. Some of the clouds released rain, others released sunlight. Some of the walkways and stairways led to tableaus or light shows. Spirits ogled at the art or added their own touches; some rearranged their own features and limbs to make themselves the art. Hair grew from shoulders, arms became legs, and fingers stretched like yardsticks. A girl with pillar candles dripping wax down her face and shoulders spread red on an invisible canvas. Her art stuck to the night. Alex and Chase found Kaleb and Gabe standing in a crooked doorway, painting extra hands to a shattered clock.

Alex wrapped herself around Chase's arm and used her free hand to reach out for the bubbles of colorful energy floating over them. Each time she popped one, it released emotion. Her favorites were the yellow ones that drenched her in happy sunlight.

Kaleb managed to balance the bubbles on his fingers, taming them like butterflies. He'd offer them to the girls they passed, who giggled or kissed him in return.

They reached Gramble Street where the center of travel, Gramble Station, was dressed like a harlequin. A black and white checked skirt fluffed at the base of the building and the giant red mask around it had a beauty mark at the lip. A motorcycle raceway originated outside of Gramble and twisted around the walls of the city and through the trees, which were dressed like the night sky, twinkling with millions of lights. The Lasalles spent half the night trying their hands at beating the course without crashing, but they had no success. They returned their bikes in shambles.

The costumes intensified as the night wore on. Some spirits were aflame. A singing girl holding a raining cloud stood beside one torched spirit to put out the fire. Next to her, a girl somberly sang from underneath a cage of wires. The creepiest faces lacked costumes. Like smeared artwork, distorted light or misshapen features, they danced about in the kaleidoscope of a crowd.

Alex tensed when they reached the area for storytellers and aura readers. Last year, Jonas told her not to trust them, not to even travel into this section of the festival, but Kaleb wasn't afraid of anything and needed to be a part of everything. He had Pax Simone slung over his shoulder, and Little followed behind them, hanging off Kaleb's trail of energy, even though Linton Darwin was desperately trying to get her attention. Skye rolled her eyes and scooted away from them.

One deep-voiced storyteller wore a gorgeous headdress of a half-moon in sparkling gold. His nose and lips were made of stars, and constellations rotated around him. He was talking about the haunting of the Sallie House in Kansas, and Gabe perked up, leading their group to a vacant area to the left of the moon man. There, sandwiched in between so many mesmerized spirits, Alex felt comfortable because she was hidden behind a mask.

The next story began, entitled: *Paradise*. Alex gasped, and Chase reached out to snatch the blue mist, to catch the breath of surprise before the storyteller saw it.

"My stories," he began in a worn out voice, "they come to me in pieces, battered and torn, so sometimes they do not mend cleanly. One story may be comprised from ten different spirits over the course of a lifetime before finally fitting into place. This one took the longest to assemble because the pieces were so delicate.

"Some souls are larger than life, and their spirits are visible even while trapped in a body. Many of you sitting here were probably described in such a way. Spirited. Special. These are the people who become stories, the legends.

"Long ago, a man and his wife created three such spirits in three consecutive years. The children ran rampant through the town, aging their parents with their antics. Sneaky and wild but harmless in their fun."

Alex smiled. Sneaky and wild but harmless. They sounded like her friends.

"Their parents were doctors and gone often, making the three Cinatri children dependent upon one another. Brigitta, the oldest, took care of her siblings and tended to the house. Broderick, the only brother, taught the girls to fight. Balin, the youngest, she taught them how to love. When illness plagued the town and claimed Broderick and Brigitta, they passed into the afterlife with ease. Balin felt lost without her brother and sister. She mourned them endlessly and ignored the power in her mind until one day her sadness turned to rage, and she inadvertently ignited the home. Her parents feared her 'gift,' but more so they feared her punishment. They lived in a time when such talents were called witchcraft and were punishable by death. Thus, they used the fire to script her death and kept her hidden in the cellar."

Pity struck Alex's heart. She remembered how she felt after the Lasalles died. She mourned and she cried, but more than anything she was furious, enough to even set a house on fire if her mind was gifted enough to do so. Instead, she took out her rage on herself, but like Balin's parents, her father sent her away. Not under the ground in a cellar but close enough.

"On the day her spirited brother and sister came to her again, Balin was so used to darkness that she distrusted the light. Brigitta told her they were building a city for others like them. They called it Eidolon, a name that meant *phantom* but also *an ideal*. It would be their ideal world. They said Balin could come along, but Balin couldn't travel as they could, and she couldn't leave the darkness to which she'd become accustomed.

"Brigitta Cinatri, unwilling to allow her baby sister to rot away for however long her mind would last, traveled to Salem, Massachusetts, where she'd heard rumors of similar 'gifts.' To avoid the perils and persecution of 'witchcraft,' she encouraged the gifted to migrate west where they could build a town under the ground. A paradise of safety would give Balin a life again. Safe in the darkness, it would create a life for her sister. And so it was. But Balin missed her siblings. One day, she battled her fears and ventured up into the light and traveled to the town her sister and brother had built. But she couldn't get in. Her body prevented it. As did the town."

Alex felt a strong sensation of déjà vu. She pictured someone trying to get through the gates of Eidolon, but her mind kept inserting Skye and Rae and the gray Forget-me tree with the peeling bark.

"Brigitta begged for them to let in their sister, but Broderick refused. He was the voice of his people. The town had unanimously opposed offering sanctuary to the bodied, and that included the gifted. The hidden town of gifted souls cried foul, tired of living under the ground, they claimed that they had been promised safety if so desired. They chose violence. Lives were lost with no resolution, and the Cinatris put up even more walls around our city. At the end of the pointless fighting the world was no different, but never the same. The gifted attacked spirits and the spirits imprisoned the gifted. Balin Cinatri retreated to the darkness of Paradise where she eventually died. They could have reunited after the Cinatris passed on from this afterworld. But that is a piece of the story I've never found."

When he finished, his audience didn't stir. If they were anything like Alex, they were hoping he might keep going or begin a new story. Instead, he stood, with the planets revolving around his head. When he left, the stars left traces behind like contrails after a plane. Similarly, his voice lingered and hummed in his wake.

Alex continued to think of the story as she and Chase explored the rest of the festival. Spirits tossed around bulbs of light like balloons. The golden flashes stretched to the sky only to plummet again to the crowd below, unable to reach the stars they resembled. When one of them landed in Chase's arms, the light from the bulb illuminated his face and his icy blue eyes. He used two hands to push the bulb high into the outstretched arms of the spirits reaching over the rails of the balconies.

It never occurred to Alex that Brigitta Cinatri was a real person with real problems. She was someone who created a beautifully macabre world—in part for her sister—but failed in her ultimate goal. The story didn't explain how Paradise became a prison.

Chase took a seat on the grassy hill, watching his brothers sprint down to the playing fields. "What are you thinking about?"

Alex watched him pat the ground and sat down next to him. The earth was cold, and she felt tired and sluggish. "Did you ever notice that the ground in Parrish was always warm?"

"No."

"I never thought of that before."

"You might notice it now because cold air sucks the life out of us."

"Hm." She sat for several minutes, plucking grass from the ground and tying it together into knots. "I don't get how we're supposed to be so much smarter than everyone else, but we can't figure out a way to coexist."

"Are you talking about that story? If you think about it, really think about it, it's probably better this way. I mean, can you imagine what the physical world would do if they knew ghosts existed? Half of them would be frightened out of their minds. And the other half, the ones who would choose to acknowledge us, would figure out how much we know. Even the smartest of the bodied would suddenly be inferior. It would be like aliens taking over the world. People aren't ready for us.

They wouldn't understand. They would hate us."

"What about Moribund?"

"A town of a whopping fifty people is much easier to control."

A blade of grass snapped as Alex tried to stretch it too far. "So you think it's the right decision?" She plucked a dandelion from the ground and began to wrap the blades of grass around the strong stem. It needed something different to keep it from breaking. "Keeping the gifted away?"

"I guess I see the benefits of both. I can't imagine being alive and knowing about all of this."

That meant Ellington was right. People weren't ready for things until they discovered it for themselves.

"People would go out of their minds."

Out of their minds. The thought twisted itself around in her head until it formed a wonderful idea. Out of her mind. She could leave her mind.

Why hadn't she thought of that before?

***

Banyan taught them that meditation was a manner of consciousness. In other words, Alex needed to let her brain leave reality but guide it in the right direction. After the festival, she pulled one of Rae's drawings from the wall, a pathway under a canopy of trees. It was damp to the touch.

Alex knew the dirt path well and recognized the smell of earth and childhood. It had been so often imprinted with the footprints of five children, Alex being one of them. They never feared this northern area of the Parrish woods so close to Liv's grandmother. It was far away from the tormented cove and far away from the ghosts of the Eskers.

Rae had to be pulling scenes from Alex's dreams. She'd drawn the scene on the beach where Alex and Chase walked hand in hand by the light of the moon and the bonfire, except in the picture, she'd inserted herself sitting among the dunes. She hugged her knees and lifted her chin to watch them through the beach grass. Since the sketches depicted Parrish, Alex hoped they would help her. She crisscrossed her legs and tried to relax her shoulders, concentrating on the drawing of the pathway so intensely that her vision blurred.

"Alex!" Chase's voice sliced her concentration.

She put a hand over her heart. "You scared me."

"Sorry," Chase said. "I brought you Happy Death Day cake."

"Yeah, right."

"I'm serious." He held out a box. "Josepha and Johanna are always eating it. They gave it to me."

She hid the sketch behind her back. "You're kidding, right?"

Chase chuckled. "I can't image it tastes much more solid than Ex since we're dead and all, but it's the thought that counts."

"Is this the stuff you breathe in?"

"I used to watch you devour your cupcakes every birthday. You've always inhaled chocolate, so what's the difference?"

She reached out a hand to push his shoulder, but he caught that hand and didn't let go. He used his free hand to trace the enjoyment forming on her lips, but when he reached around to touch her back, he grasped the sketch.

He yanked it from behind her. "What's this? Is that Parrish?"

"I think so."

With a dumbfounded expression, Chase sat. "Look. You can even see our tree." The "treasure tree," as they called it, was engraved with each of their initials. In the sketch, it was small because of the distance, but it was there.

"If you try, you can feel the edges of our names."

"And why were you sitting with your nose in front of it when I walked in?"

"I'm trying to channel my inner Banyan Philo."

"You're meditating?"

She grimaced. "I'm trying. It's not working very well."

"Why?"

"I've never done it before."

"No." He laughed. "Why are you trying to meditate? And why are you using a drawing?"

"Because it's Parrish. And I think there's a lot we don't know about our little hometown. About the Havilahs. The gifted. Sephi."

He reached out to tuck her hair behind her ear. "You know, if I'd thought of that last year—meditating, I mean—I wouldn't have gotten into so much trouble for trying to see you."

"That's not your fault. You hadn't started any meditation workshops."

"Still."

She met his gaze. "You regret it?"

"Of course not. Some things are worth breaking rules for. Some things are worth crossing lines."

For a fleeting moment, he stared at her, zeroing in on her mouth. Kiss me, she begged.

Not now. We have work to do.

Get out of my head! You weren't supposed to hear that.

He turned his head and bent to kiss her. "There." He removed a pillow from behind his back. "Do you want to lay down or sit up?"

"What?" She choked out the word.

"Weren't you paying attention in class? You have to be comfortable to channel enough energy for something strenuous like this. In fact, you might want to take off that coat." There was humor in his tone, and the corners of his mouth twitched.

She hurled a pillow at him. "Why are you talking that way?"

He fell back into the comforter, tucking a white throw pillow under his arm. His shirt rode up enough to expose his stomach. She began to wonder how he projected himself to be so tan, but she became distracted by the way his hips rose and fell.

"Come on, Alex. There's so much tension right now that I'm surprised the glass in the windows hasn't busted yet."

He felt it, too? Embarrassing.

"This probably won't work," she said. "I wasn't getting anywhere before."

"Two heads are better than one. Banyan said it was like exercising; you have to do a little at a time to build up the stamina."

"Are we talking about the same thing now?"

"Get your mind out of the gutter." He smirked.

"You started it."

"True." He opened an arm to her. "We have to believe in what we're doing to channel the energy."

"Okay." Alex stretched out next to him.

"Close your eyes and focus on one thing."

Alex furrowed her brow and opened one eye. She stared at his profile, the perfect slant of his nose and the long length of his eyelashes. "How am I supposed to focus on an object when my eyes are closed?"

"We should both stare at the same tree in the sketch, and then close our eyes."

"No. Focus on the path."

"Whatever you say."

Alex adjusted her position to get more comfortable and nodded. "Okay."

"Ready. Set. Stare."

She bit her lip, but after less than a minute, she couldn't hold it in anymore.

"Al! This was your idea!"

"Okay, okay."

She couldn't free her mind of the thought of Chase so close to her though, breathing deeply. She peeked at him one last time before surrendering to the experiment. He was positioned like she was with his head back and his chin high in the air. Behind the curtain of her eyelids, the image of the pathway danced for a while, but it was replaced by Chase's face, the outline of his lips.

She tried to blank him out, but his outline remained, like the shadow profiles they used to draw in elementary school. Something flashed and she wondered if one of the lights in her room had gone out. Or if her consciousness was altered. Maybe she'd fallen asleep.

"Really, Al?"

She heard Chase, but she couldn't see him. Her vision wavered, like standing over the bay looking at a painting floating a few inches under the polluted water. Distorted. She could tell it was there, but she didn't know what it was. She could tell *she* was there, but she didn't know what or where she was.

"You didn't focus," she accused.

"Guess not."

Alex tried to sigh, but it didn't work. It caught in her throat like a forced apology. "This sucks."

He chuckled.

"Can you see me?"

"Not really."

"Okay, good. I'm not going blind."

"No," Chase said. "We're just not very good at this."

She felt his hand find hers, but it wasn't normal. It wasn't flesh; she hadn't felt mortal in a long time, but usually even as spirits there was compression, warmth, and energy between two people. Now his touch felt more like holding her hand out of the car window. She felt his lips press against her cheek and the same sensation followed. It traveled down like she'd dived right into that murky water of the painting or jumped out of the car window and into the breeze.

"I missed," he said, kissing her nose, her hair, and her neck before finding her lips. She didn't think those were mistakes. "You aren't so uptight anymore."

The sensation intensified as though wind billowed against the water. His hands pressed against her shoulders, her back, her head, everywhere. It was hard to explain where she was because she didn't feel as though she was standing up, but she wasn't sitting or lying down. She was nowhere; she was everywhere. But he was everywhere with her.

"What object were you focusing on?" she asked. Her voice curled around them like a smoke ring.

"You."

They were too similar. No wonder their brains had a bridge between them.

"You did the same thing, didn't you?"

She nodded but realized he couldn't see her.

"No clue where we are," he said.

In a flash—a gust of wind and a splash of water—it was over. Alex returned to real life with a loud *snap*, and she was stretched out on her bed, next to Chase.

He draped an arm over his forehead. "Why did you do that?"

The return of her sight made her shy. "I don't know what happened ..."

"Al?"

"It felt too much like when we were knocked out last spring."

Chase lifted his arm. "In the field?"

"And then after." They didn't wake up for weeks following the attack.

"I guess," he replied, propping himself on his elbows. His eyes began to widen.

"What?"

At her feet, the box of Syrus Raive's letters was now poised at the foot of her bed. She screamed and kicked the box. It tumbled sideways with a thud like dropping a bowling ball. The lid to the box moved back into place but not before the letters shuffled themselves.

It sounded like laughter.

Chapter Sixteen

Attention, like any other drug, was addictive. Tolerance built, and the monotony of everyday interest became humdrum. Alex's name in the news no longer fazed her; she expected crowds to follow her down Lazuli Street. Addiction, like any desire, required higher doses to reach the fix of the high.

When Alex received orders to stay inbounds during the autumn festivities, at first she panicked. She'd miss the haunted house! She'd miss the beach parties in Moribund! But she discovered that the attention from those around her multiplied because she'd been singled out. Some newburies pitied her, patting her on the back or offering kind words of condolence about the importance of her safety, while other newburies crossed their arms and questioned why she didn't have to work the Mansion of Morgues.

On the evening of the haunted house dress rehearsal, Alex followed Chase and his brothers outside of campus and into the city. The newburies were allowed to travel to Moribund through Gramble Station, and Alex tried to ignore the stabs of envy as girls giggled, flirted, and danced around Kaleb and Gabe on their way down Lazuli Street. It was also obvious that while Pax spoke to the Lasalles, she kept her attention on Chase. Alex tried her best not to show anger, and sunglasses appeared, shading half her face. Chase reassured her that she wouldn't be missing anything besides fake spider webs and excessive headaches from all the screaming.

Ardor Westfall promised the time would pass quickly. He'd arranged a comprehensive schedule, including extra therapy sessions to her annoyance, but also special history lessons with Madame Paleo, some bonus language lessons, and personal training at some place called the Patientiam Center.

She followed her friends as far as she could off Lazuli Street toward Gramble Station where Alex noticed that the street post had either produced new signs or she'd never been willing to see them before. Several arrows extended from the thin post, one of which was labeled *Patientiam Center*, but they veered off in another direction.

"Where do you think you're going?" a booming voice erupted.

Ardor Westfall stood among the redwoods, sturdy as ever, with his customary expression of derision. He'd swapped his military duds for jeans and a t-shirt but kept his combat boots.

"No-nowhere," Alex replied. "I wanted to see Gramble

Station. I've never been inside."

Westfall curled his lip. "There's another time for that. We have a schedule."

Her friends called goodbye to her, and she watched over her shoulder as they disappeared through Gramble's rotating door. Chase stood outside and waved her on, but he stayed rooted to the spot until she turned the corner, shivering in Westfall's shadow.

She kept up, watching him beside her and twirling strands of her hair through her fingers. He wasn't one for small talk, and even if she didn't realize this, he formed some sort of barricade between them. She pressed a palm against it. Silence felt like memory foam. He probably sensed her questions and decided to mute her.

They came upon a building, plain in comparison to its neighbors. It lacked the quaint historic feel of Lazuli, the dark beauty of Brigitta's stonework, or the powerful formidability of Broderick Square. The boring exterior of the warehouse offered no apologies, no bells or whistles, yet let off an atmosphere of pride as spirits entered and exited. It reminded Alex of Jack Bond, with its nose in the air despite its inadequate appearance.

As they neared the door to what was labeled The PC, a guy sat stretching his long legs on the bench outside. Everyone stopped to greet him. They offered hellos, and handshakes, and pats on the back. He might be the only spirit who received more attention than she did.

"Who is that?"

Westfall's copper hair tidied itself, gathering into a ponytail. "That's old Yazzie. He's been around since the city was built. He comes here to workout at least once a day. Not bad for someone who's been dead for four hundred years." Westfall's heavy gaze weighed down on Alex's shoulders. "Don't look so shocked. You wear your emotions like badges. Anyone ever tell you that?"

This came from a man who wore nothing but contempt.

Yazzie's tan skin pulsed between smooth and wrinkled, and his black hair flashed to gray. Westfall greeted him with a nod and a handshake, but the man's stormy eyes went straight to Alex. "The banshee girl."

Westfall crossed his arms. "Her screams haven't needed further analyzing."

Thank goodness. Along with her monthly brain screening at Dianab, Alex also had to report for her big mouth. They worried she was half banshee considering her scream at the Eskers rattled the earth and immobilized everyone within a fifty-foot radius. The scientists at Dianab forced her to wail into machines, but she'd held back for obvious reasons. They canceled her last appointment.

Yazzie fixed his posture. "You don't recognize me, do you?"

Should she?

"I suppose my cosmos costume was a little too good the other night."

"You're the storyteller?"

"You didn't try to see beyond my mask." He flicked the air,

and Westfall's shoulder flinched. "She's still pretty narrow-minded."

Westfall extended his chin at the building behind Yazzie. "Hence, our setting today."

She had no clue how this building, this 'health center,' could loosen the girth around her mind.

"I saw beyond your mask though." Yazzie's hair flashed to gray again. "I always loved the way Sephi used to shine. You do, too."

Alex didn't know this man, but she already liked him. Comfort swam around him like a friend she didn't know she'd been missing.

Westfall tapped his wrist, and a watch appeared. "Let's go."

They reached the revolving door and Westfall muttered, "Shine, he says?" Then he snickered. "Spirits see what they believe in, no matter how crazy."

She couldn't help herself. "So if Yazzie thought I was a bird, I'd take off flying?"

Westfall lowered only one eyebrow in a scowl that Alex doubted few could master. "Of course not. He couldn't actually believe that. He'd know it wasn't possible."

Westfall stomped through a wall-to-wall waterfall of vertically rushing air. Alex scanned the entry, but there wasn't any way around the world's largest hand dryer.

"What is that?" she yelled, hesitant to step through it.

"A filter," he bellowed through the blast of air. "To open your mind."

"How?"

"If you want answers to all these questions you ask, this is the best place you could be," he yelled. "You won't accomplish anything unless you *step through the filter!*"

"What's in it?"

"Just do it!" He spat at her through the filter.

She stepped through, feeling no different on the other side of the air curtain, but she didn't voice it to Westfall.

Her feet squeaked on the floor, and she didn't understand why. Dead girl shoes don't squeak. Was she making that happen? Did she somehow expect it? She squeaked all the way to a railing, beyond that was a crowded training area, far larger than the appearance of the building outside.

Westfall held up a hand to silence her, but for the first time in forever, she had no questions. She only wanted to watch. In the section directly below them hovered digital squares. The first had formulas for relativity and titles like *fundamentals* and *phenomena*. There were clusters of spirits below, some with pencils in hand, some reading and holding their heads in their hands. Alex recognized Kender Federive from the Ardors. She wiped her forehead with a towel and waved to them.

On one digital square, Alex read about the introduction to space-time and the concepts of wormholes. That tiny amount of new knowledge settled in her mind and spread through her like sunshine. She felt lighter.

Westfall rested his forearms on the railing. "Exercise is different now. This is how you'll live to be as old as Yazzie."

In different areas of the health center, Alex saw word

problems or "group fitness" where spirits discussed concepts like physics or trigonometry, political science or astronomy.

"We aren't required to do any of this?"

Westfall rested his chin on his fist. "It's voluntary. In Brigitta, you're learning to survive, and the staff learns your strengths and decides where you might belong."

There it was again. The Categorization.

"Don't tell me you disagree?" Curiosity brightened his being.

"Would that be shocking?"

He fought a smile; it was weird on his stern face. "Because your identical twin fought so hard to make this world what it is today."

"Sephi did?"

He nodded. "Many of things she fought for died along with her, but the Categorization was something she created."

"Why would she want spirits to be singled out like she was?"

"Think about what you said. Singled out like *she* was. It's a brilliant tactic! She figured out a way for everyone to be treated like her. If she hadn't died, I have no doubt the bodied would be down there working out with us."

Federive's blond ponytail swung side to side as she headed to a room with an open roof. Inside, tables of chessboards rose from the floor like wild mushrooms, and spirits crowded around them like gambling tables. Beyond them, stone archways formed a semicircle. Each of them was a different color door of varying shapes and sizes.

"What are those doors back there?"

"Past the gaming? That's where people can learn to play sports. Basketball, tennis, croquet, handball, and they can play alone. The ballparks exist for recreation, but the games include mind-strengthening tactics. The newburies who flock to the fields don't understand how much their minds are growing when they learn new plays for football or learn new skateboarding tricks. It makes them stronger. Some spirits don't want to be watched at the field, but that doesn't mean they shouldn't get the chance to play. Here they can play against computer animated opponents."

"Like a video game?"

He dipped his head to the left. "Video games are over in that corner, but those rooms are like being inside the system. Gaming is still learning, and learning is how you strengthen your mind."

It might be the coolest thing Alex had ever heard. She felt fortunate to be there, to be who she was, and have access to such things, such knowledge and understanding. She felt fortunate to be trapped between alive and dead.

"Liberating, isn't it? Don't you feel better already?"

"Yes," she admitted. "When do we start?"

His forehead smoothed. "Right now."

***

Alex figured she would spend the whole day at the Patientiam Center, but she couldn't go full throttle for more than an hour. Her mind throbbed in a satisfying way. The trainers assured her that she'd build up stamina the more she visited the PC, as they called it.

She couldn't wait to show this to Chase. And Gabe! He would love it. She jumped through the filter and left the PC, surprised to find that the building was now made of glass. Her reflection blinked back at her.

Yazzie still rested outside on the bench. His feet were propped on one armrest while his head rested on the other.

"Hey there, little bird." He grinned.

No one else was around. He had to be speaking to her.

"Don't mind the PC. It has identity issues, although it hasn't been glass in a really long time. It must be feeling vulnerable." He chuckled. "I heard what you said to the Ardor earlier. And if it means anything to you, I really do think you could fly if you wanted to."

She believed him, but she had a feeling that once she went away, the optimism wouldn't last.

"It's not merely your face that resembles her, you know. It's everything about you."

"Sephi?"

"Your mother, too."

Mother. The word burned. "Maybe one day I'll find out."

"She's gone," he said, sitting up. "I'm sure you knew."

The last childish piece of her, the distant memory harboring smells of baby blankets and the tone of love in a lullaby, finally broke away from the rest of her. "No one has ever given me a definite answer about that. How would you know?"

He slouched. "Because I buried some of her memories."

Confusion mixed with sorrow smelled a lot like that damn baby blanket. She blinked, and she was sitting on the bench next to him.

He tucked his tangled hair behind his ears. "I own the memory mine at the edge of the gates. I know you've seen it. You left your presence all over the place."

Questions. There they were again, each flashing in front of the other like pop-up ads on a computer screen.

"You can ask what you'd like. You have a curious mind."

"What's a memory mine?"

"Exactly what it sounds like." He looked up at the sky. "When a body dies, whether the soul comes here or not, the energy has to go somewhere. Think about how strongly you love something, or how strongly you hate something. That doesn't disappear when you die. The energy travels until it finds something to latch onto. When the bodied rushed to California for gold, the spirited rushed here for the memory stones. But my people, living and dead, we always knew the land better than anyone. We were here long before the others."

"Is that why Eidolon was built here?"

Alex followed his line of sight up to the redwoods stretching so high they were like several paths converging into one location.

"There are many things about this particular area that draw us. The mine is one, for certain. The arrival is another. After all we've learned and discovered with these radical minds of ours, we still have no clue what makes the spirited in this area of the world show up in these woods after they die. Blame it on the pull of the universe; our world likes to make some decisions on its own, doesn't it?"

"What do you do with the stones?"

He straightened his head in surprise. "Didn't you see the field? I bury them. It wouldn't be right to sell them."

"I only saw a field of flowers."

"The flowers sprout from the ground where the memory is buried."

Alex frowned. "But you said they were valuable."

"The stone begins like a cloudy diamond. When a memory finds its way to a piece of the stone, it turns black, and I chisel it away to bury it. Once the memories latch on to the stone, they aren't as valuable. Would you want to walk around with a random stranger's love for their dog around your neck? Or the sorrow of lost children? Or the greed of misers? However," he said and held up a finger, "the empty memory stones are a different story. If a stranger died in front of you, a piece of their mind would latch on to the stone. One particular group of people used these stones as trophies."

Alex's knee bounced and she twirled a strand of hair.

"During that time of change when the cities were built, it was kill or be killed. The Havilahs ruled the living, and the Cinatris ruled the dead. Neither liked my kind. I traded the entire mine in exchange for the freedom of my people. The trade was worth it to keep my people safe. We had so many tribes indigenous to this area, and the hunters were forced to leave us all alone even during the gold rush when so many others were slaughtered."

Alex hung her head. "I'm a Havilah, you know."

"Yes."

"Why are there so many coincidences between my life and my death?"

"I wouldn't call it coincidence. You're a Havilah, and Havilahs die young. Havilahs are also hereditarily spirited, so it isn't unusual that you found yourself dead or that you found yourself here."

A group of spirits exited the gym and gawked at Alex when they passed. A man with wild hair stopped to pat Yazzie's back, and Alex recognized him from the banshee attack last year. He was one of the Patrol.

"Now your appearance." Yazzie drew circles around her head and the shape remained in a silvery light. "That's another story."

"You think that's coincidence?"

"Not at all." He smudged the silver light until it disappeared. "I'd call that irony. Or karma." His chin jerked upward. "Or fate."

Chapter Seventeen

Memories were whack. They weren't something Jonas valued because they reminded him of failure. Jonas never really liked himself. He'd come to terms with that a long time ago. So why should he even try? He wasn't the youngest of his four brothers, but he still placed last in all categories. Likeability. Athleticism. Intelligence. Compared to the rest of the population, he was above the curve, but in his own family, he finished dead last no matter how hard he ran the race. Screw them.

When he learned that he could live after death, he'd been in that room alone, no brothers in attendance to cast their shadows over him. He clutched onto the opportunity and decided to continue being the person he'd hated for eighteen years because finally it was his chance to change, his chance to shine. How stupid of him to think death would be different.

He'd ended up in a fool's paradise, once again encumbered by the expectations of being a Lasalle.

Jonas plopped down on a park bench and took in the sights, wondering what the hell he was doing here. It seemed like a typical small town, nothing special: general store, bumpy sidewalks, oak trees, annoying children, and gray-haired bench dwellers.

A flustered-looking mother ambled to a stop beside him. Jonas lifted his feet and let out a loud curse when she nearly hit him with her double stroller. Of course she couldn't see him. It took a ton of effort on both ends for the living to see the dead.

"Excuse me," she said.

Jonas checked the grassy space behind him, but no one was there. She had spoken to him. He figured he should act normal, but the woman wasn't paying attention to him anymore. She was busy digging into her bag and telling the kids to cool their jets.

He moved aside on the bench and tried to figure out which direction to take next. His instructions were vague, but his determination remained steady. He needed to find the importance of this place.

The mother threw her bag on the ground and crouched down to find whatever it was that she was missing. Her toddler whined, her baby cried, and her preschooler clutched hold of the side of the stroller. Three boys. Three. If his parents had stopped at three, he would have been the baby. It was wishful thinking to believe that if it had been the case in his family, his brothers might have loved him more. They would have protected him like they protected Chase. But if Chase hadn't been in the picture, it's possible that Alex wouldn't have been either. A life without Alex didn't seem right. Who would he pick on?

He'd been searching all his life for friends who didn't worship his brothers, companions who didn't overshadow him yet were still cool. Surrounding himself with duds would be too easy. Enter the brotherhood last year. Eviar had promised him exactly what he wanted. What a crock of shit that was. Jack Bond? Really? Reuben Seyferr? No wonder their identities were kept secret; they were the crap of the crop.

This time was different. His brothers would be categorized somewhere desirable, but Jonas would come out on top when this was all said and done. He consoled himself, saying his path might be unconventional, but what he was doing now was better than anything he could do in Eidolon. He had become a part of something major, something Brigitta workshops couldn't give him. He was going to change the world. So what if he had to pretend like he sacrificed his family? After Gabe's attack, he knew Eviar wasn't what he hoped, and the very next day before he could back out of Eviar this group of spirits found him and offered him something better.

His brothers hated him, but he consoled himself by remembering something his mother used to tell him. Hate and love were the two most passionate emotions. If you take the time to hate something, it meant you secretly cared about it. No wonder he treated Alex like crap. If he beheaded her dolls or shoved her off a swing, it would make her hate him. And if she couldn't love him, at least she could hate him.

What would she think about what he was doing now?

She'd get a thrill out of this, his subconscious answered. Even when she was frail and sick, that girl held more life than her pygmy hands could hold. Her body couldn't handle it, didn't know what to do with it.

Beside Jonas, the mother with the stroller straightened up, clutched her back, and hung her bag from the handlebar of the stroller. The oldest boy, the one walking alongside, kicked his Batman shoe into the dirt. Jonas chuckled.

The boy gazed at him, causing Jonas to retract. No way. He lifted a hand and waved. The little boy waved back. *He* could see Jonas, too?

His mother grabbed his hand. "Come on, honey. We're late."

The boy twisted his body to catch one more peek at Jonas as his mother shuffled him past a sign that read, *Welcome to Astor, Oregon, est. 1839.*

The group that recruited him gave him no instructions except to travel here; he had to figure out the rest on his own. This felt like less of a mission and more of a test, as if throwing his brothers under the bus hadn't been enough.

What would his brothers say about this?

Didn't you learn your lesson the first time? They always hounded him. If his brothers knew whom he was working with, they wouldn't question his path or his footsteps. *They'd be jealous.* They'd want to follow, and that was why he couldn't tell them. He didn't want to share it.

He rested his elbows on the back of the bench and inspected the town sign. The sensation of familiarity crept closer, choking him in comfort as though he should feel at ease here.

He'd never traveled to this Podunk Oregon town before, so how could it feel like he'd been here? Streets of shops and restaurants ahead, a school to the left, neighborhoods to the right, and behind him was a building with pillars like a courthouse, but no traffic moved in or out. A town museum, he assumed but how the heck would he know that?

Because that's what it was in Parrish.

He gasped. Everything situated around this center square of land, right down to the sign proclaiming its name, was a replica of his hometown! What would Astor, Oregon have to do with Parrish, Maryland?

At home, the museum was stuffed with old Parrish artifacts. Alex's mother, being related to the town's founders, donated a ton of them. He drummed his fingers against his chin as a man came out with a stack of books. It was too good to be true. A library?

He stood up and dusted off his hands, hoping he could find what he didn't even know he was looking for.

Wasn't that how most journeys began?

He lifted a hand with the sudden urge to slap away such an idealistic thought. Jonas was many things, but idealistic was not one of them.

***

Sun streamed through the window of the library, highlighting dust particles. Jonas placed his back to the window and the distraction of the Parrish wannabe town.

Why me? he'd asked the spirits who sent him.

Because we need a newbury. And because you're the one for the job.

He held a stack of weathered books with cracks along the spines and nodded to the librarian staring at him. He figured he'd better act like one of the bodied and pretend to strain as he lowered the books to a table. Something about her felt familiar to Jonas, but everything about this place felt that way. *Twilight Zone*, his parents used to say, whatever that meant.

Jonas lifted the first book from the pile, beginning with the town's history. *Westward expansion*, it read. He was surprised how strong the pages were. In comparison to the busted binding, it was misleading, and it reminded him of Alex, broken on the outside and strong on the inside. A lot of things reminded him of Alex.

He shook away his thoughts. Jonas had mastered the art of letting things go. The stack of books swayed, but he caught them just in time. If he was alive, he would need to skim; it would take him days to get through this information. With a mind free of his body, he should be able to get through these in an hour or so.

Between the snoring chapters about the western movement, government formation, and legislation, he found a few needles in the haystack of books. On the day of its founding, the town had an instant population of ninety-six people, but there weren't any facts about their migration and very few facts about its creator, a man named Astor. One author mentioned Astor's birth to a prestigious family that founded their own self-righteous cult on the east coast of the Chesapeake. As a young man, Astor left to escape his family burdens, creating an identical town, but he built it to "right the wrongdoings of a condemnatory family whom he despised."

Bingo. Astor was a Havilah.

During the thirty minutes it took Jonas to find these crucial pieces of information, someone followed his every move. The librarian had flipped over the sign at the front door, and he heard the click of a lock.

Jonas sighed. "I promise. I'm only here for information," he said. What an idiot she was. He was a spirit. He could go right through that door whether it was locked or not.

An elderly woman stepped out from behind a bookshelf. "I don't have to ask if you're dead or alive considering the way you read."

Jonas tried to hide his surprise. "How do you know I'm not *gifted?*"

She put a hand over her heart. "If you were *gifted*, you'd know where you are. Besides, even the gifted can't read like that."

What did she mean by *where he was?* He put up his guard. "You would know, wouldn't you? I don't have to ask if you're gifted or not since you can see me."

"Seeing the spirited doesn't make one gifted. You must be young. That might save you, considering the law you've broken."

"What law?"

"The spirited aren't allowed to enter a gifted territory."

He shut the book in front of him, and a chill washed over him. Gifted territory? He knew little about the afterworld outside of Eidolon.

"What am I going to do with you?"

He zeroed in on her name tab. "Ms. Portiere, am I supposed to understand what you mean?"

She tapped her feet on the floor, but Jonas saw nothing but cheap carpet. Then, he felt something shift beneath his feet. An invisible force yanked at him trying to pull him down. His mind iced in panic and he scrambled to lift his feet to the chair.

The woman searched the space around him, dissecting something he couldn't see. "What is your interest with Astor? My family has cared for Astor's records since its founding." She jutted her chin as though expecting him to know what this meant.

He didn't.

"The *original* founding."

Was there any other kind? He cursed in his head, looking around the library and then back at her.

"Tell me why you're here."

"Because of a friend."

It wasn't quite a lie. Could Alex be the reason he was sent here? The thought made him remember he had a heart; it even struck a beat or two. Or that was his fear affecting him because the ground was trying to suck him down.

"Are you a Havilah?"

"Thank goodness, no." He knew enough about his hometown history to understand that the Havilahs were either unlucky or plain cursed.

"Are you from the Eskers?"

This woman sure did know a lot about Parrish. "Why, do I seem like a lunatic?" He looked like one, grasping the table in front of him to prevent himself from being pulled down onto the ugly carpet. The force coming from the ground acted like a vacuum.

She spread her arms wide. "To enter a gifted territory, yes, you might be mad. And is that what they're saying the Eskers facility is for now? The mentally challenged?"

"I was born in Parrish. I grew up there. I died there. That's all I got."

His voice remained calm but inside his mind raced. A gifted territory. What would happen to him? Why was he sent here? He worried less about the repercussions of breaking a supposed law and more about what he'd do if the spirits he trusted had set him up. If he did not have this group to fall back on, this so-called alliance of revolutionaries, where would he go? What would he do? He'd never go back to Eidolon. He'd put his eggs in one risky basket, and now that basket dangled over a cliff. Damn it. He wouldn't allow his brothers to be right about him.

He couldn't stand it any longer. He let go of the table, and he fell forward. He smacked his face on the table before crumbling down to his knees.

Ms. Portiere perched on the edge of a table promoting a

tween book club. "How did you come to find yourself here?"

"I wandered into town about an hour ago."

"Coincidence?"

"I guess so." But he didn't even sound like he believed that.

"This friend you mentioned, talk about her again."

"Why?"

"Because the only thing stopping me from sounding the horns is my curiosity." Ms. Portiere straightened her glasses and squinted at him.

The magnetic pull sucked his stomach to the floor. He rested his cheek on the ground to respond. "She's a newbury, too."

"What does this place have to do with her?"

"I'm not sure. That's why I wanted to know more about the history."

"There's more. You aren't telling me everything." Ms. Portiere raised her brows so high they disappeared under her gray bangs.

Jonas couldn't share who sent him, but when it came to Alex, he could go on for days.

"My friend, we grew up together. She's gotten loads of attention since she died because she looks like someone named Sephi Anovark."

Ms. Portiere pressed her hands together like a prayer. "It's true, then? The resemblance is strong? I wish I could travel to see it for myself."

"You know who Sephi is?"

"You're asking that of one of the gifted? She is our greatest treasure."

He tried to shake his head, but the suction from the floor yanked him too hard. "I don't know much about people like you."

"People like me," she repeated. "They pollute your mind early in death, don't they?"

He saw the opportunity, and he grabbed it with shaking hands, preparing his questions. He never liked jigsaw puzzles or word problems, and this task felt too much like both. The Havilahs were hunters. If Astor was gifted, of course he'd need to run away. End of story. What's the big mystery?

"What's the connection with Parrish? Why did the founder of this town leave when he could have inherited Parrish?"

"Astor came to us for help. He was a Havilah and he hated it. That godforsaken family couldn't see past their fears. Astor Havilah had no special talents, but his daughter did. She was taken from him, Havilah or not, because she showed early signs of being gifted. His family imprisoned his daughter, one of their own, with the intent to sell her into servitude. Astor and his wife left Parrish so when they had more children, they would be safe, and to bring some retribution to his family."

"Why are you willing to tell me all of this?"

"Because your friend needs to know. Eidolon is probably trying to poison her mind against us."

Ms. Portiere stood and curled her finger, gesturing for Jonas to follow. He groaned with the effort it took to snake-crawl, dragging his knees and twisting his torso down a long passageway of dank smelling books labeled: Mystery A-F.

"My family descends from a gifted builder who began his work by constructing catacombs. We fled here from New England when the Cinatri family paid us to build a world for the gifted, to live with Balin Cinatri underground. My ancestor never forgave himself for encouraging us to bury ourselves, for deciding to hide instead of fighting for our rights. He sentenced himself and all the Portiere family after him to be guardians over what he'd built. History isn't something you can run away from. Astor Havilah didn't understand that."

At the end of Mystery A-F, they entered an unmarked aisle, or Jonas couldn't see the label from down on his belly. The deeper they traveled, the darker it became. These books were different. They snarled and snapped at him.

He craned his head to peer at them. "What's wrong with these books?"

Ms. Portiere stroked the bindings with a wrinkled finger. "This is our history before the founding of Astor when we lived ..." She peered downward. "Astor knew where we were located long before 1839 because of his hunting ties. It was his idea to bring us out of the ground. A Havilah, of all people, brought the gifted into the light. To right the wrongs of his witch-hating family, he created something to protect them."

Ms. Portiere bent down to look at Jonas. "When you mentioned your friend who looks like Sephi Anovark, your mentality shifted. Did you realize? I did. I've always had a knack for reading between the lines, or between the waves."

"The waves?"

"Some members of my family are blessed with the gift of seeing the mental state of others around us. Don't look so surprised; there isn't much to it. If you've ever seen an EEG machine, it's very much the same. Our minds use electricity to communicate, and I see the signals producing that activity. That's how I knew you weren't here to harm anyone. You were here searching for knowledge. I saw the gamma waves."

"No offense, but that's weird."

"In my family, it isn't. Such a small thing classifies us as *gifted*. I have always seen the waves more vibrantly than anyone else," she said, straightening up and puffing out her chest. "When you mentioned your friend, your waves decreased to alpha. Close your eyes."

He would do whatever she asked as long as she would turn off the vacuum hiding in her basement.

"Like that. When people close their eyes, the waves change to alpha, and yours changed the same way when mentioning the girl. Because you genuinely care for her, I will escort you out of town unscathed. I consider anyone looking out for the Anovark girl to be on our side."

Jonas's eyes snapped open. Alex wasn't an Anovark. He didn't dare share this with Ms. Portiere, not if it would threaten his safety. The pull from the ground eased, and Jonas could lift his head.

Ms. Portiere came to a stop by a black door. Jonas took a crawl back, feeling paranoid. He worried she was about to shove him into whatever waited behind it and leave him there. The door had a nasty energy.

Ms. Portiere stood over him and twisted the knob. Jonas felt his heart in his throat. She opened the door a crack, only enough for a sliver of light to seep through, and she waited, glaring at the space between Jonas and the doorframe. He slithered closer. The door swung open and the breath of the whispering books chilled the air so he stopped breathing to prevent inhaling it. It took concentration to resist something he was used to doing. He inched forward and peered into the opening, noticing a spiral of downward, twisting stairs.

"This leads to your old town? The one from the 1600s?"

"Now it's a cemetery of sorts."

"I'm afraid to ask …"

"The dead reside there, but they are very much alive. Just detained."

Detained. A fancy word for imprisoned. He was about to end up in spirit jail for all eternity, he knew it. The worst part would be when his brothers found out. He pictured Kaleb's smirk and Jonas's fingers tightened their grip, clawing at the rotting wood of the doorway.

"Astor founded the most foolproof underground prison for any of the spirited that came into our territories or broke our laws."

"That's awful."

"Why? You don't think spirits have their own prisons for us?"

I never really sat around and thought about it, you crazy witch.

"Now you know why I was shocked to look up and find

you sitting twenty feet away from the doorway."

Jonas felt his mind shuffling through its contents, trying to remember the names of the underground cities his professors mentioned in Eidolon. He cursed himself for not paying more attention. Even with a brilliant mind, he couldn't remember what he didn't hear.

"Down there is where you'll find our former *haven*," she said, curling her nose. "Down there is where you'll find Paradise."

Chapter Eighteen

Alex found it funny how her mind dictated her weather. The temperature in the redwoods didn't shift much, but during the fall season she walked through the California trees and shivered with the chill from an east coast autumn because that's what her mind remembered. In Maryland, autumn smelled like chimneys, apple spice, and cinnamon, and such scents flooded her senses as she hid among the crowd on Lazuli Street. She wondered what everyone else smelled.

Alex's friends were still working in Moribund, so there wasn't anyone she wanted to see. Her desire to be inconspicuous caused her mind to dress her in a wide-brimmed hat and sunglasses. She would fit right in at the floral shop that always projected sunlight.

Last year she hadn't seen the floral shop—she hadn't

seen a lot of things—but in the spring, she followed a mossy stairway off Lazuli Street labeled: Olfactory Pathway. It led to the small building with a wooden sign: Olfactory Cottage. It was like any ordinary flower store, but each time she visited, something new and spectacular added itself. She'd been there over two dozen times, and now the shop could only be described as magical. Massive waterfalls crashed down from the sky to land in ponds with lily pads that hummed music. Mazes of rosebushes weaved through the yard with benches soft as pillows. Flowers sprang up in clusters varying in shapes, size, smell, movement, and emotion. The gardens stretched for miles. Balloons of rainclouds nourished the land, leaving trails of rainbows, except by the pine trees where snow clouds suspended overhead like white-gray umbrellas.

Alex already finished her requirements for the day. Her activities at the health center left her exhausted before attending Paleo's one-on-one session though Alex questioned why she needed extra lessons about the history of afterlife science labs. The day left her tired and cold, so a trip to the sunlight was exactly what she needed.

It was a shame she couldn't relax. Paranoia kept nudging her between the shoulder blades. Someone was watching her, but when she turned no one was there. The softness of the pressure made her wonder who would be looking at her in such a way while she journeyed through a field of pansies.

"Nice hat," a sardonic voice teased.

She spun around, and Jonas leaped back to avoid the smack. She felt anger boiling in her stomach. "How dare you!"

"What? You look like a beekeeper."

"That's not what I mean," she shrieked.

He raised a finger to his lips. Quiet. "You don't know what you're saying."

"Your brothers have been looking for you." She didn't care about her volume. If someone saw Jonas here, so what? That was his problem.

Jonas's mouth had a natural curl to the edges, and it bothered Alex more than ever.

"Sweet Alex. We both know you'll forgive me."

She tried to ignore the fact that he seemed so happy. Whatever he was up to, he was enjoying it. "Don't bet on it."

"I'm not the betting kind. I prefer to make my own luck."

"And you don't care who you step on to get there."

"Believe what you want, but I'm here to help you." He grabbed her elbow and led her to a nearby bench bordered by white tulips.

"Are you allowed to be here?"

"It's a city like any other."

She sat down on a bench, and for the first time it was uncomfortable. "You aren't in trouble after last year?"

He shook his head and the sunlight accentuated stubble along his jaw. She'd never once seen him with facial hair. "I'm a free spirit."

"You don't miss it?"

"Hours of workshops every day? Hell, no. I found something much better."

"I don't want to ask."

"Good. Because I can't tell you about it."

"Then why are you here?" When he reached for her arm, she snatched it away. "To visit your brothers, I hope. They're in Moribund."

He crinkled his nose. "I know where they are. I tried to find you there first. I thought you might go to the butterfly tree." He softened his tone. "And no, I didn't go see them. They'd probably tie me up and force me to stay."

"They love you."

"No, they love the idea of having a punching bag. They want everything to stay the same because they were happy that way. I wasn't."

"But you're happy now? Why?"

"I'm doing something real. And the last place I expected it to take me was right here, but Alex ..." He raked his fingers through his hair which was longer and lighter than usual. "You have no idea how much you're tied into this world. Sit down. This is going to take a while."

***

Chase and Gabe sat on top of a maze of walls in the basement of the Mansion of Morgues. Dust, whispers, and screaming filled the death-black room, and even though Chase helped build the maze this year, it scared him. Duvall taught them about the chemicals used in the house, and his job was to perch over the guests who walked below in the maze and sprinkle chemicals down to amplify their fright. He knew his fears were a reaction to the fumes, but when he breathed them in, his hands shook, and his chest tightened. He didn't like losing control of himself.

"Gabe?" Chase whispered.

"I'm here."

"Do you feel something funny?"

"This whole place makes me feel things I'm not supposed to."

Chase waved his hand in front of his face. Despite his enhanced sight, he could barely see it. The only plus to this job was that it gave his mind a break from seeing so many colorful emotions. "That's not what I mean. Like in your head."

"You mean, do I think Jonas is close?"

Yes. That's exactly what Chase meant. He didn't experience such a pull with either of his remaining brothers. Gabe had a theory for this; Gabe had a theory for everything, which was annoying sometimes, but in this case Chase welcomed it. He thought they could feel a pull to Jonas because they were trying to find him—they weren't trying to find each other. Chase knew where to find Gabe and Kaleb, and he didn't worry about them much anyway because they could take care of themselves. He searched for Jonas, though, whether he wanted to or not, just to know if he was okay. Sometimes, Chase saw things he shouldn't see. Trees. Faces. He thought it might be Alex's mind until he began seeing the specks of green ambition and greed. And he knew he was in Jonas's head. What a frightening place to be.

Chase wished he could see Gabe more clearly. "Do you feel him, too?"

"Yeah. He's not far."

"You think he's checking on us?" As angry as Chase felt, a part of him wanted to believe that Jonas cared about his brothers, that what he did last year was unintentional.

The floors creaked above them. Even during the day, the Mansion of Morgues was open for guests. It was a new development this year because of the high demand. This place was still terrifying, even when the sun was out.

"It doesn't matter, Chase. You need to stop letting it in. When all this began, the seeing things that you think he's seeing, I looked into it. It can happen with spirits who have similarly programmed minds, like siblings. There's a reason it's discouraged though."

The door opened and a new group of guests prepared to enter. Chase grasped his pouches of chemicals and prepared to release them, deciding this time to hold his breath since he didn't need to breathe anyway.

"Of all the different workshops and all the different theories, opinions, and teachings, one thing is always the same. Something as complex and personal as the mind isn't meant to be shared."

Chase took one last gulp of air because it was habit. Good thing because he felt the urge to spill his secrets. If Gabe only knew how many people were inside of Chase's mind.

***

Alex tried to ignore the nosy tulips that leaned in closer and closer while Jonas told his story. "You're telling me that my distant relative created a town aboveground for the gifted?"

She latched onto the silver lining. She might be a Havilah, but the gifted didn't need to hate her if she'd been a part of Astor.

Jonas flicked a flower bud. "What better place to imprison spirits? Even if they somehow escaped, the town acts as a natural guard of gifted minds."

Alex's mind flashed to Yazzie dressed as a constellation. "Yes, I heard this story during the festival. Broderick and Brigitta Cinatri wanted their sister to live there. What made the town come above ground?"

Jonas slid a bit further down the bench so he could face her. "That's really why I'm here. These spirits I'm working for—don't give me that look—if you knew who it was, you wouldn't question it."

"Then tell me who it is. I can keep a secret."

"That's a load of crap."

Alex kicked a rock. "You can't tell me. I'm truly shocked. They sent you into a gifted territory? That was really nice of them." She snorted. "Sounds like they care about your wellbeing. How did you get out?"

He scratched his head. "I didn't know it was illegal. The only reason I'm not under the ground right now is because I said I'd relay a message to you."

"Me?"

"Yeah, there's more to your story than you thought."

"I already know I'm a Havilah. I saw the family tree a few weeks ago."

Jonas raised his brows. "Oh yeah? They finally let you see that? Good." He shook his head at Alex's triumphant expression. "They still aren't telling you everything."

His words injected her with indignation, and it spread throughout her being and filled her useless veins with something that made her itch. She ran her hand over the tattoo of blue veins on her chest. "What do you care?"

"Honestly, Alex, I didn't. Until I found out that this was my mission. They want me to do this, so I'm doing it. Shut up and let me talk."

God forbid he do something admirable, something noble. Jack wasn't the only friend she'd misread last year. She might be the world's worst judge of character.

"The first thing I wondered is why these spirits sent me, but I was young enough that I didn't realize the danger of waltzing into a gifted territory. They knew I'd recognize the town."

"Who are *they*?"

"Stop asking."

"Why would you recognize some dumb town in Oregon?"

"You'll love this. It's a duplicate of Parrish. Right down to the light posts in the town square. Astor, Oregon."

Astor. The familiarity of the word caused her mind to shuffle until she held the image of Maori's shop of junk. The coral shield from the Witch Wars.

"This Astor Havilah guy, his daughter was gifted. His family—*your* family—took her away, so he didn't want to live in Parrish anymore. Can you blame him? According to Ms. Portiere, my new best friend, Astor wanted to make amends. He also didn't want his family to be cursed anymore. And he needed a big town with money."

"Why?"

"To buy back his daughter."

Alex took off her hat and fixed her hair that was suddenly very messy. She lived in Parrish her whole life believing the woods were forbidden because of the Jester, when really it was her own family she should have feared. The song about the Havilahs wriggled into her mind.

"How come this isn't common knowledge? Why have I never heard of Astor?"

"I doubt the afterworld knows much about it. They aren't allowed into gifted towns. If they enter, they're imprisoned."

"No one ever mentioned it to me. It makes absolutely no sense to keep me in the dark about everything."

"I thought so, too, at first. But when I was leaving, something about the welcome sign caught my attention. Astor, Oregon. It didn't say founded by Astor Havilah."

"He changed his name?"

Jonas nodded. "Astor, Oregon. Founded in 1842." He glanced around them to see if anyone was around. "By Astor *Raive*."

She didn't move.

"Do you understand?"

She didn't want to. She felt the urge to plug her ears.

Jonas lowered his voice. "Syrus Raive was his son. Syrus Raive was a Havilah, too."

And a murderer. The name was a verbal punch to the gut. She leaped to her feet. She didn't know where she was going, but she knew she couldn't be there anymore. She didn't want to be *her* anymore.

She started running through rows of yellow carnations and continued on through anemones swaying in an invisible wind. Jonas cut in front of her.

"I'm sorry, Alex. You don't deserve all this."

"Every time!" she screamed. "Every time I find out something new, I hate myself even more!"

She felt water streaming down her cheeks. How? How in the world could she possibly produce tears? Nothing about this place made sense.

"That could be why they don't want you to know. This would be a lot for anyone."

"Someone wants me to know! You said that's why they sent you here. You won't even tell me *who* wants me to know this!" Alex fell to the ground and hugged her knees to her chest.

"You aren't related to Sephi Anovark."

Then how on earth would she look identical to her? "You didn't tell them that, did you?"

"No, I didn't tell them."

Of course not. They probably wouldn't have been so nice

to him for knowing her. She bent and scooped up a handful of dirt and threw it at the pretty flowers mocking her. "Why do these people you're with want me to know this? To torture me?"

"They want you to know the truth. And the gifted want you to know the truth. But the gifted, they allowed me to leave freely for another reason."

"Oh, God, Jonas. I can't take much more."

He held up his hands. "This isn't anything about you. This is about the Truce March."

She covered her face with her hands. "What about it?"

"You can't go."

"Why do they care? Isn't it supposed to be about love and harmony?"

"That would sound stupid even if it was true. The gifted would have imprisoned me for crossing territory lines. That doesn't sound peaceful to me."

"What do I do?"

"If it was me, I'd do nothing."

"What?"

"Stop searching. Do nothing. Don't support the Truce March. Don't oppose it. Do absolutely nothing." He sighed. "Let the world sort itself out."

Chapter Nineteen

Alex didn't breathe a word of Jonas's visit to anyone. All Soul's Day approached, and even the most prominent of spirits either worked to finish the final touches in Eidolon or helped in Moribund. Alex hadn't spent the entire month slaving away at the Mansion of Morgues, so the party felt like less of a celebration and more of a reminder that time here aged quickly like dusk.

The longer she was dead, the more fulfilled she felt by information (as long as it had nothing to do with her past). She was an open, empty book, and the more lines she was able to fill, the stronger she felt, so she was relieved when sessions resumed in November and she could have a structured schedule again. And, more than anything, she had Chase back again.

She missed the hum of his presence next to her class. She

missed the notes he'd write on his paper, saying hello or telling her what he was thinking about, even though he could slip into her mind and whisper it to her. There was something childishly fun about looking next to her and seeing him turn his paper toward her to ask if she remembered the time they snuck out at midnight one summer to play pirates on a boat in the Parrish marina. She used a bubble wand as a sword but dropped it in the water, and without thinking, Chase dove in to retrieve it. When he explained his wet, seaweed-stained clothes to his mother in the morning, she hired a locksmith to work magic on his window. Danya never realized that her sons learned to pick locks when they were still in diapers.

Alex grinned reading the story now in Chase's handwriting.

What made you think of that? she wrote on her paper.

Your hair was in one of those braids over your shoulder that night. Like it is now. Well, a little messier.

His brothers used to joke that Alex went around sticking her fingers in electrical sockets. Danya used to buy so many products to try to tame Alex's curly hair. Nothing worked.

She notated Dr. Massin's objectives: *Continue to discuss basic causes for hatred.*

Dr. Massin straightened her cropped blazer and patted the French twist in her hair. "We are an overly intelligent civilization to say the least, but that isn't always in our favor. Our living brains were hardwired a certain way, and it amplifies when the mind is given freedom in the afterworld. We have a basic need to survive, and our survival instincts teach us self-protective actions. Outsiders are threats. That is our natural way of thinking. We aren't comfortable with differences because we don't like uncertainty. We fear it."

Alex followed Dr. Massin's gaze to Pax, who sat straight-backed in the front row, watching their professor through her thick glasses while her pen moved in frenzy. *For what,* Alex thought, *could she possibly use glasses in the afterlife?* Little slouched next to Pax and twirled the pink streak in her brown hair.

"All of that is amplified for us. Do we need to deal with it? Yes." She directed a smile at Jack, Carr, and Reuben.

"The spirited must learn to live together." A light zapped above Dr. Massin's head. "We share the earth with the bodied. A dispute has been going on for centuries, and the outcome is always the same. For our safety and theirs, it's best to keep our worlds separated. They wouldn't understand it. The gifted are hybrids, bodied and spirited, and it's dangerous to allow them to choose which rules to obey. Lost Ones don't follow our society laws. The mentally broken, or banshees, can't understand those laws. That is why we live to exist with the spirited, and the spirited only."

Above her head, one of the objectives highlighted yellow. *Society's system for dealing with deviation and disobedience.*

"Your law training was cut short by extenuating circumstances, so your class of newburies has a limited range of understanding when it comes to our system of justice."

There was a moment of awkward silence for the missing Professor Van Hanlin.

"It's much easier than the system in place for the bodied.

We break a law, and you face several Revealers at different times. Revealers are a foolproof jury; they can tell if a spirit is lying or not. The method is not always consistent, but in various ways, they can see, hear, or feel lies. Some minds analyze tone, some assess body language and impulses or brain waves, and some see effects of truth or fabrication."

See the effects of truth? Like the colors of emotions?

Chase's hand shot into the air. "Is it documented?"

"The findings? Always."

"Publicly?"

"Yes."

He fidgeted in his seat.

Madison flipped over what had to be her ninth page of notes. "Is that how they evaluated the Eskers kids?"

"Way to be tactful, Madi," Linton said, but he grinned to show that he wasn't trying to offend her.

Dr. Massin stopped in front of Joey Rellingsworth's desk. "If those newburies would like to share, they are more than welcome. What you need to understand is that your peers faced the same judicial system as the seasoned spirits around the world, and every one of them was found to be innocent. You can't continue to disgrace them. They were under an influence greater than them. Our minds are vulnerable out here in the open without bodies to protect us."

The ink! Alex wanted to object. *The ink was in all of our books, but only the greedy or the bitter could read it.* This proved something about the differences in the minds of the Eskers kids. Massin was wrong.

"I read something about spirits who are arrested by the Patrol," said Madison. "The news usually says that they're under some influence. Couldn't anyone use that as an excuse?"

"That's where the Revealers come into play because even the most persuasive of personalities can't fool a panel of Revealers."

"Persuasive of personalities?" Madison repeated. "I don't understand."

"The most infamously persuasive spirit was Syrus Raive."

Alex felt a lump in her throat.

"Persuasive doesn't seem like the right description." Linton scoffed.

"Yeah," Tess added. "Serial killer is more appropriate."

Murderer. Alex was related to a murderer.

Dr. Massin tightened her mouth and regarded them momentarily before shuffling across the room to stick her head out into the hallway. She returned to her podium and placed her hands on her hips. "I know we aren't supposed to discuss it, but Syrus Raive was a respected Broderick advisor before the Restructuring. He was *voted* into that position. He was a great man."

Alex felt guilty for being glad of this. The boy in the letters hadn't sounded like a monster.

Linton's voice came out even sharper than usual. "Now I understand why historical figures aren't discussed. Because of bias like yours."

"Watch your tone, Darwin," she sniped. "Even rumors of horrific happenings didn't kill his support. A mind believes what it wants. How does any politician create a following? His words. His ideals. His persuasion." She cupped her cheek and swayed. "I heard Raive speak once. He had a way about him; his words lifted you off your feet and carried you along next to him. It only felt natural to follow the course he proposed."

"And what about when he started killing people?" Linton asked.

"No one believed it." Massin glared. "I didn't even believe it. It seemed like a gimmick created to discourage Raive's following. Finally, he was indicted, and when he faced the Revealers, his actions were exposed."

"What happened then?"

"Detainment. There are detention facilities stationed around the world. Buried alive, spirits cannot move through several feet of earth, and they can't project without seeing where they are going."

Alex's question crawled up her throat. Before she could silence herself, she called out, "And what about the gifted? Is the evaluation process the same with them?"

Every face in the classroom turned to look at her. Pax stretched as high in her seat as she could without standing up.

"Good question. Reuben?" Linton asked. "Do hunters kill the gifted?"

Reuben's eyes bugged at Dr. Massin. He puffed out his fat cheeks, trying to hold in his secrets.

"I'm only trying to speak to Reuben about something I don't understand," Linton said, tilting his head. "Isn't that the whole idea of getting along?"

When Dr. Massin nodded at Reuben, he used both hands to scratch at his head. "Hunters don't kill the gifted. Not anymore."

"Why hunt, then?"

"To herd 'em."

Sparks erupted around Little.

"They don't want the gifted to become spirits."

Chase directed his pencil at Reuben. "*They?*"

Oh, God. Alex covered her mouth with her hands. It was them. It was spirits. "Do *we* hire the hunters?"

Massin yelped and cut off Reuben's response. "No! There are two laws we share. We aren't to enter each other's territories. And we aren't to harm one another. If laws are broken, it's like finding a criminal in the living world."

Reuben's tuft of blond hair stuck straight up. Jack teetered at the very edge of his seat as though he might jump up, but neither of them said a word.

Chase's jaw shifted side to side. *Massin's color is usually turquoise, but now it's getting a little dark. I don't think she's being honest.*

Of course she isn't being honest, Alex thought back to him. *We never hear much about spirits from the past. I'm surprised she's told us this much.*

Alex considered what Linton said about believing a bias. She felt willing to take Massin's word that Raive was a good guy, only because she *wanted* him to be good.

Something Ellington told her churned in her thoughts. Those in power hire others to do their dirty work. The Havilahs did the commanding. The Bonds did the law making, and the Seyferrs did the hunting. Her family would be responsible for hiring the hunters. The Bonds were cursed. The Seyferrs were cursed. What about the Havilahs? What was their punishment?

Was Alex cursed, too?

***

Alex had so much on her mind and found it difficult to concentrate during her monthly brain scan at the medical center. The doctors claimed the visits were for their benefit, but Chase thought they were being used for research. Chase and she always planned ahead and focused on separate things during the hour exam, that way they wouldn't accidentally enter each other's thoughts. Her mind couldn't sit still though. What if the doctors discovered their secret?

"You need a break," Chase said after they returned home.

"Technically, I had one while you and everyone else slaved away at the mansion."

"We were playing a game. Pulling mindless stunts and playing pretend. You were forced to go to workshops and go to the health center." He pulled her off the bed, and a spark shocked them both. "Come on. You too, Rae."

In the hallway, he attempted to position Alex back on her feet, but she imagined herself as boneless and slumped in his arms.

"Cut it out," he scolded as her arms drooped and her head bounced off his chest.

She put her feet down. "You said I needed a break, but you take me away from my comfortable bed."

"Your *mind* needs a break. When you sit and do nothing, you exhaust yourself with all *that* ..." He drew invisible circles around her head. "That curiosity."

Rae perked up and nodded in agreement.

They left Brigitta and crossed the courtyard with Chase leading the way. He said their destination was a surprise, but Alex saw the playing fields flash in his mind. She didn't tell him. In life, she was too frail to play sports, so she hid among the crowd as an outsider looking in. The nostalgia of watching the boys made her happy. Like a Friday-night-high-school-football-game-with-a-thick-blanket-and-hot-chocolate kind of happy. Some of her favorite moments in life involved being an outsider, watching the Lasalles be the stars, while she observed in the dark.

She hadn't thought about that in a long time.

Her shoes made no marks on the grass, a sign that she didn't belong down here. "What am I going to be watching?"

"You're not watching."

"You said I was going to relax."

Rae barreled ahead of them, sprinting across the empty fields.

"You need to have some fun."

"You're kidding, right?" Alex spun in a circle, making sure the stadium was empty.

"Today you get to play."

Chase took off his hat and smoothed back his honey-brown bangs. He turned the hat backward and placed it back on his head. "Catch!"

He tossed her the ball, but it slid through her hands and flipped away from her. She scowled and went to pick it up. "I expected it to be heavier."

"Why?"

"Wouldn't that be harder?"

"Not for the Movers. They could manipulate something made of minerals. If it was a rock, you'd be better at these games than anyone."

But it wasn't. All the more reason for her to go find her seat in the stands. She could count on one hand the number of times she'd thrown a ball, and she didn't want to look like an idiot. "I don't know how to play anything."

"You'll learn. Your first day as a spirit you crushed a bench the size of your bed. I don't think kicking a ball around will be much of a challenge."

"I've seen the way you play. I won't be able to keep up."

"Stop thinking about it so much. You're overanalyzing." He trotted toward her and placed his hands on her shoulders, jostling her lightly. "No one is judging you, and we'll just mess around."

A soccer ball came rolling in her direction, bumping against her shins, and stopping at her feet. Rae stood across the field with another ball in her arms, her brows raised.

Chase nodded at her as if to say, *Good idea.* "Looks like a challenge to me. You want to play, Rae?"

Smiling, Rae set the ball on the ground and stood poised. She took her small hands and smoothed her white hair from her face.

"Hold on!" Chase shouted, racing to the sidelines to grab another ball. His enthusiasm made him seem as young as Rae, who rubbed her hands together before placing them on her thighs.

"Why do I have the feeling she's going to smoke us?"

"Because she's had a century of practice. We should get a head start." A ball flew from Rae's direction and smacked Chase in the side of his head.

"I don't think she agrees."

The three of them lined up as Chase counted down. "Three... two... one..."

It was harder than it looked. Alex moved objects with her mind; she withstood a banshee attack, but trying to run down a field while kicking a ball was difficult. She had a clear view of Rae, dribbling the ball with grace that no toddler should ever display. Alex was left in the dust, but even from the losing end of the race, the breeze that tickled her face and whipped through her hair felt incredible. She understood the appeal of the nightly games.

Rae won easily, raising her short arms above her head in triumph. She ran a lap around the perimeter of the field.

Chase took off his hat and placed it on Alex's head. "Nice work."

"I was terrible."

He angled his head. "Yeah." He spun the hat on her head, turning the brim backward. "Get this out of the way."

He bent to kiss her, and Alex slid her hands under his jersey, running them along the muscles etched there. She loved how the electricity between them tickled her palms. He lifted his head to stare at her, wetting his lips before turning his head in the opposite direction to kiss her again.

Hollowed voices echoed from the nearby tunnel. "You think that's what people come here to see?" Kaleb yelled. "By the way, we saw you two get beaten by a toddler!"

Chase refused to let go of Alex, and she didn't mind.

"Ignore them." He cradled her head with one hand and pressed the other against the small of her back.

"I know who I'm picking for my team!" Gabe bellowed.

Alex pressed her head against Chase's palm and saw Rae continuing her victory lap, whizzing past Kaleb and Gabe, slapping their hands as she went.

Chase sighed, and kissed her one last time. "You're early," he grumbled to his brothers.

Kaleb bunted the ball with this head. "I could do without the PDA, but we didn't want to miss this."

Alex's shoes untied and her clothes wrinkled. She hated that her mind made her discomfort and displacement so obvious. "You came to watch me fall on my face?"

"Exactly. Not to *suck* face. So break it up, you two."

Chase cleared his throat. "No one is asking you to watch."

"We thought we could help. We could teach you a few things."

Chase wiped the side of his mouth with his thumb. "I don't need any advice."

"Not about that, you pervert. I thought I told you to knock it off." He tossed the ball, which bounced off Chase's shoulder. "Keep your lips to yourself here. This is sacred ground."

Alex repositioned Chase's hat on her head. "Is that what you tell Little Gossamer?"

"Yeah right." Kaleb jogged down the field to retrieve a ball but projected himself back. "She's not exactly my flavor."

"She's so nice."

"Therein lies the problem. I have someone else meeting me here tonight."

"Who?"

"Pax Simone."

"Aren't they friends?"

Kaleb shrugged.

"You're such an ass. Did you do that on purpose?"

Kaleb shrugged, passing a football from one hand to the other.

Gabe took a step closer to Alex and leaned over her shoulder. "He doesn't want anyone to assume he wanted a backup for Skye."

Kaleb froze, ball in hand. "Not true at all. Have you ever known me to back down from a challenge?" He chucked the football to Alex. She swatted at it, and it clunked to the ground. "Pax is more ..."

"Authoritative?"

Kaleb considered the word. "Informed is better. Useful is

another good one. I can get some information out of her."

Rae retreated to the hill behind the gap in the stands and began picking daisies. Alex tried to go with her, but the boys wanted to set up a two-on-two. Although she was unskilled, Alex admitted it was fun to run a route to try to get away from a defender to catch a football. It was especially fun when Chase was the defender and she was trying to elude him. After Kaleb threw a ball that stretched at least sixty yards, Alex dove to catch it, expecting to fall flat on her face. Instead, Chase intercepted the ball. He let out a little whoop and winked at her. Alex was so angry at his arrogance that she took off full speed in his direction. She'd watched enough games to know how to wrap her arms around someone and tackle them into the dirt.

Chase flew off his feet and landed heavily on his back with Alex on top of him. A cloud of dust puffed from the turf. Chase lifted only his head. "Not bad, Ash. For a girl."

She didn't like Chase calling her Ash. She wasn't a buddy, and she didn't want to be one. "I took it easy on you," she said, trying to push him back down. He yanked at her arm and used his free hand to pull her closer. "Don't ever take it easy on me."

"Get up, you two," Kaleb groaned. "What did we tell you about that?"

"You know you have an audience, right?" Gabe added.

Spirits trickled out of the tunnel, forming a puddle at the foot of the stands.

"You could stay and play," Chase suggested to Alex.

"You'd like it. Everything you told me about that health center, that's how I feel when I leave the fields at night."

Alex jumped to her feet. "No way."

The veteran newburies, who'd been dead at least two years, played referee and picked the game of the night. Whoever wanted to participate took a place on the field. Depending on the game, some newburies retreated to the skate park or the trampoline park, but most stayed to try their hand at winning. The nightly tournaments served as bragging rights for the following day.

Alex sat alone in the corner of the front row where she could hide and watch the games until Rae finished picking flowers. She didn't get a chance to relax because Jack and Reuben emerged from the tunnel and took a seat on a bench at the edge of the fence. Jack spun around to face the crowd. He studied the spectators, and his haughtiness irritated Alex.

She scooted low in her seat and concentrated all her energy into the bench, lassoing her mind around it and pulling. The stone flew out from under Reuben, and before he could stand up, she slid the bench back to its proper positioning, slamming into Reuben's back and wedging him between the fence and the bench.

He thrashed like an animal stuck in a net. His arms were trapped at his sides, and his big round head was wedged sideways against the fence. All he needed to do was project himself away, but he didn't. Or couldn't.

A few giggles rose above the stands, twisting into the night like twirling kite tails. Alex counted seven. Only seven people entertained by his predicament. Last year, the whole audience would have been howling, and Alex was the one coming to his rescue. What a difference a year made.

Jack spun around to glare at everyone and no one. He squinted at the bench, but he couldn't move it, not anymore. The protégé couldn't do anything telekinetic without his twin around to help him.

Score one for the good guys. Alex thought.

Jack leaned down and said something to Reuben as he tried to move the bench with his hands, but it was no use. Jack straightened, smoothed out his coat, and marched into the stands with purpose. Did he think he was going to find the culprit? He paused at each step, scrutinizing the crowd. No one questioned him. If anything, they cowered away from him.

Alex figured she'd better leave before he noticed her.

"I bet that Reuben kid is the only newbury in Eidolon who cannot wait to be sorted out." Sigorny perched at the lowest bench with her feet up on the railing. "I doubt they'll sort him though."

"Why?"

"If I had to bet, the gifted would find him. Kill him." Sigorny gestured to the lights of the city, hovering to the right of the stadium. "*They* know that." She lifted her pen. "What do you think about Jack's new following?"

"I'm sorry. His what?"

Multiple sets of footsteps clunked down the stairs of the bleachers. Jack had a small army with him, including Joey and Hecker, but there were new faces, too. As badly as Alex wanted to know when newburies began to treat Jack with such prestige, she bit her tongue. Sigorny would twist Alex's questioning and mold it into whatever article she was spinning.

Sigorny leaned forward as far as she could without falling over the railing. When Jack stopped beside Reuben, his army stopped, too. Some were Eskers kids, but some weren't. Carr stood like a bodyguard beside Jack, who said one last thing into Reuben's ear before leaving with his mob in tow. Sigorny tucked her notebook under her arm and chased after them.

Before she could change her mind, Alex projected herself to the space next to Reuben. She directed her energy at the bench and moved it backward. Reuben rolled onto his back to see who had saved him, and his mouth fell open.

"I need to ask you something." Alex checked the tunnel, not knowing how long it would take Jack to return with help. "About your family. Did they know mine?"

Reuben shifted to his side and pushed himself to sit, but he didn't answer.

"I'm just trying to understand."

He studied her. "You never cared to talk to me before. Why now?"

"I tried last year. You didn't want anything to do with me."

"Still don't."

"Fine." She should have left him stuck in the fence. "Nevermind."

Reuben let out a huff. "You don't know it, but you've created two sides. There are spirits who support you and Sephi." He spoke her name with a twang, pronouncing it *Say-*

fee. "Then, there are spirits who don't agree with her preaching, who hated her. Jack is smart. He used that to his advantage. He's now president of your opposing team."

For a moment, Alex couldn't answer. She was too stunned by Reuben's accent. She never heard him speak more than a handful of words at a time, and she hated how a southern twang made him endearing.

"Then he shouldn't be mad that I've given him some friends, should he?"

"He blames you for last year."

"That's stupid. No offense, but *I* didn't try to kill you last year. It was the other way around."

"You were never in any harm."

"Could have fooled me."

"We didn't know it then. Whoever controls Sephi controls the world. Whoever brainwashed us into following along wanted you, not us. We were tricked into thinking we'd be among the likes of the Darwins and other legacies." He pulled himself onto the bench and said with a cluck of his tongue, "A Havilah."

She didn't like the way he spat the name, so she used her mind to nudge at his seat. When it shifted, he grabbed ahold of the sides with his chubby hands.

"Who do you think hired my family back in the day?" Reuben rested his lump of a chin on his hands. "Havilahs. Where do you think the Bonds got the bright idea to hire hunters for the Interactions Department? Havilahs. You're the reason our curses follow us around. You might look like the darling of the nineteenth century, but really you're a chip off the tainted block."

Alex didn't know whether to feel sorry for him or to hate him.

"So you tell me, why am I the one getting the beatings?" Reuben tightened his grip on the fence. "Life might not be fair, but I sure as hell know now that neither is death."

Chapter Twenty

"I can't believe you were talking to him!" Chase said as they climbed the hill away from the fields. "Doesn't it mean anything to you that people are trying to protect you? To help you?"

"You're just mad you got hit in the face with a ball."

He stopped and his face flushed. "Sorry if I'm concerned about your welfare when I see you playing nice with the kid who tried to kill you a few months ago. When are you going to learn, Al?"

She watched her feet as she followed him up the hill. Her prints disturbed the grass here unlike the fields.

Chase reached out for her hand. "You see the light in things and people, and that's something I love about you. I shouldn't be mad, but I don't know what it's going to take for you to be more careful."

"I don't think Reuben is the problem. You want me to hate him? I can't."

"That's not what I'm saying at all. I don't want you to hate. It would change who you are."

"Indifferent then?"

He shrugged. "That's a step."

"I can't pretend like he's not there. He is there. Those Eskers kids will always be there. So why not at least try to coexist? I think that's the purpose of the sociology lessons. It's not about the gifted but about the spirited getting along with each other."

When he didn't respond, Alex peeked at him. His hat was gone, and his hair was smoothed back. Control and order took over again. Part of her wanted to reach out and mess up his hair, and the other part of her wanted to hug him because she loved him so much. Even the neurotic parts.

Once they entered Brigitta, she figured Chase would deposit her at the seventh floor and go to his room, but he followed her down the corridor and stopped outside the frame marked with Eliza Tillerman's name.

She waited for the doorframe to appear. "Don't worry. I don't think I can get into any trouble between the hallway and my room."

"I thought you wanted to give meditation another try."

"Oh!"

Several times over the past few weeks, she attempted to use the sketch to travel to Parrish. The idea that she could investigate her hometown undetected spun excitement within her. It was like being invisible, a fly on the wall. Her concentration lacked though because she'd gotten nowhere. She hadn't even reached that gray area she'd found with Chase.

Chase ran his hand along his square jaw. "I don't mind if you need some space. I can go."

There could never be a time she'd tell him to leave. He should know that by now.

"I want you to stay."

The door swung open for him as easily as it did for Alex. It was a bit more subjective with visitors, even Rae usually kicked it.

Chase threw his bag to the floor. "All right, let's do this before curfew."

"They don't check in on you anymore, do they?"

He rolled his eyes. "Sometimes."

"Really?"

"I'm sure Eidolon wouldn't want to lose someone they could use in the future." His voice carried an undertone of disgust. "Like I said, some things are worth breaking the rules for."

She watched him stretch out on her bed, folding his hands behind his head. The way her stomach flipped embarrassed her. She hoped he couldn't sense it.

"You know," she began. "I was thinking we should lie on the floor. Less distracting."

"I distract you?"

"As if you didn't know."

He rolled off the bed onto the floor. "Hey. When did she do that?"

A new sketch waited on the wall by the floor. Rae was nowhere to be seen, but she'd known where they'd be sitting and what they would need. It was another picture of the Parrish woods, but this time, it was the Frank house. Rae included every detail: the crooked door, the warped paneling, and the thatched roof. Alex could even hear the buzz of the fluorescent sign advertising palm readings.

"Weird," she murmured.

"Hopefully it's a good omen."

Chase lay back, and Alex followed suit, nestling against him. The pings of electricity zapping, whenever they touched, didn't faze them anymore.

"You smell good," Alex said.

"I'm dead."

"You still smell good."

Like cold air and fresh laundry. He lowered one arm to wrap it around her, and he suddenly wore the dress shirt she smelled. The shirt he'd worn on his last night of life. Only half-buttoned and rolled at the sleeves, she wanted even more to bury her head there and sleep, but there was work to do.

"I'm ready," Chase said.

Alex settled into him and focused her attention on the Frank house, well, that and Chase's hand over hers on his chest. Within a few minutes, the outermost edges of the sketch trembled until they eroded, escaping in miniscule pieces like dust. Instead of falling to the floor, they stretched horizontally toward her. She relaxed and allowed herself to be pulled forward. Grayness.

Not again, she was about to groan, but before she could think it to Chase, the Frank house appeared.

The haziness of the world drifted in and out of focus like a watercolor painting behind the breath of life. The colors bled. Chase held her hand, and even that didn't feel real. His touch felt like water.

"This is like a fever," he said. "I don't know if we're imagining this or if it's real."

"I think it's real because it's kind of what I saw when you would visit me before I died."

"Like you're drugged?"

Actually, it felt exactly like that. The distortion and uncertainty increased with each step. Waterlogged voices emerged from the Frank house. The first sounded like Liv speaking from the bottom of a well.

"I grew thick skin at an early age." Her next sentence buzzed, inaudible. A rippling sound followed, perhaps a sigh or a groan. "Could be why I'm an effing size twelve."

Alex's heart constricted upon hearing Liv, and Chase rubbed his chest over his heart and muttered a soft, "Ouch."

"You ... beautiful ... think ... love." Thea Frank's syllables scratched like a skipping needle of a record player.

Liv's curse-word reply came out clear and boisterous. What she said after that hollowed out. Alex strained her ears as much as she could. She felt the ache of the stretch in her mind.

Thea must have scolded her use of language because Liv replied, "Grandma, when you're descended from a line of lunatics, you need some sort of shield to deflect the ridicule ..."

her words cut out and then returned, "... assholes who open their mouths, even the assholes who are faithfully departed."

Chase tugged at Alex's hand and they walked up to the rippling window. But the second Alex focused her attention inside, she traveled like a breeze, bringing Chase along. They landed by the archway between the kitchen and living room, and Alex's head pulsed at the temples.

Thea's arms blurred as she lifted them to fluff her white curls. "You need to spend more time away from here."

Alex couldn't see Thea very well, but she sensed her loveliness. Thea had thrived growing up in an age where curves equaled beauty, and so she always flaunted her magnificently full figure in a way that Liv never had. Thea appeared photo-ready even though Alex knew she rarely left the house. She used to say that when you're never alone, you never want to look like you think you are. In life, Alex hadn't believed Thea's profession as a medium, assuming it was a spinoff of the Parrish legends. She'd been as green as Thea's wallpaper.

Liv's bleary silhouette fell back on the pillows of the window seat. "I used to have friends. Then they all had to go and die. Damn them."

Chase tightened his grip, and Alex saw the colors through him. The glow around Thea tinted indigo, but when she spoke her words escaped in a breath of silver-blue wisdom. All Alex could make out was "lonely."

"Wrong." Liv threw her arm over her head. "I wish I was lonely. I wish I could find some ..." she raised her voice several octaves, "... *peace and quiet* around here!"

A giggle erupted from the far corner, and Alex saw a blurry person with flashes of yellow hair. She elbowed Chase to show him the jester's hat in the boy's lap.

Liv sighed. "How do you put up with it, Grandma?"

"I've heard them since I was old enough to babble." Thea waved off the seriousness of the question, and the gold bracelets on her wrist clinked together.

"I used to be good at blocking out the dead."

Although his features were vague, the Jester's voice was clear, unlike the two living individuals in the room. "You aren't very good at denying your vices." He circled his hand in the air, framing her full figure. Then he mimicked shoving food in his mouth.

Liv's round form jumped from the window seat so quickly a blurred trail of color followed her. "What's that supposed to mean?"

The Jester watched Liv approaching and clutched at the wall. "Earthquake!" He jolted his body back and forth. "Oh sorry, that was you walking."

The first part of Liv's response was muffled. "... hate you."

"Shouldn't have let me into your head, then."

"It wasn't *you* who opened that door. It was Chase."

"You let one in, you let them all in."

Alex felt Chase's guilt as if it were her own.

"No kidding. They come by the truckloads." Liv plopped back to the window seat and toyed with the yellow stones lining the windowsills.

Alex remembered those stones. When she was little,

she assumed they were expensive. Old people always had valuables stashed around their houses. And when they died, their relatives pillaged their belongings and went on antique shows and made a fortune. When Alex was alive, Liv's grandmother told her that voix stones weren't worth anything to anyone who didn't know what they could do. Alex hadn't understood at the time that the dead treasured different things than the living. Looking around the house now, Thea's stock in the afterlife could rival the Queen's diamonds.

Thea's muffled response cushioned the room. Sweet as honey, sticky with concern.

"My friends," Liv replied.

"Your melancholy is misplaced. They're much more alive than you think. Save your pity for greater things."

"Like yourself." The Jester giggled.

Alex felt them falling away from the scene. The colors in the room bled into one another. The objects in the room melted together before they began to blur. Alex held on tighter to Chase.

Don't let go.

She wasn't ready to go yet, so she concentrated on holding minds with Chase.

When Thea spoke to the Jester, bursts of silver-blue and indigo puffed from her mouth like cigarette smoke. "Why don't you go rearrange the pantry like usual?"

"I should padlock it instead," he suggested.

"Or go hide some socks," Liv chimed in. She shifted in her seat to face Thea. "If he wasn't here this place would be perfect."

The boy propped up his feet. "You know nothing."

"You keep quiet," Thea scolded him. "And get your shoes off my table."

"What is he talking about, Grandma?"

Thea kept her thoughts behind her red lips.

Come on, Thea, Alex urged. *Give us something. Why was the Frank name on Sephi's contract?*

"I hope you do like it here," the boy said, and when Thea responded with silence, he grinned. "Since you're never allowed to leave."

Thea breathed sparks of red. "It isn't safe for us Franks out there. Too many spirits who could use us to barter."

Everything in Alex's sight became clearer.

I think we need to go soon, Chase warned.

Jester spun his hat on his finger. "Liv feels a pull toward you, Thea. Or, at least, that's what she thinks. She doesn't realize that she's naturally supposed to be drawn to this area."

Chase tugged at her. Time to go.

The sensation rushing against her back reminded her of the dream where she felt like she was falling and falling.

"Ooooph." She hit the stiff floor, falling back into her rightful mind like the crack of a head against pavement. Her Brigitta room surrounded her.

Chase sat up next to her, rubbing his forehead.

Alex rolled to the side. "I don't feel so great."

Chase reached for her, gathering her in his arms.

"I don't know how you handle those colors all the time.

It's like getting motion sick."

"I'm learning to deal with it."

Rae had returned when they were out. She stood with her back to them, facing the drawing. She lifted a finger and smeared the edges of the woods surrounding the Frank house.

"Or Rae pulled us out." Chase reached for Rae and pressed his thumb against the side of her cheek where a teardrop would be.

"Is she crying?"

"I don't think we're the only ones in the room who called Parrish home."

Rae picked up her charcoal pencil and faced the drawing again. She sighed once before furiously scribbling over the drawing.

She didn't stop until the paper shredded.

Chapter Twenty-One

Sigorny enjoyed lurking around at the Ex House. As the holidays crept nearer, many spirits traded their time at the ball fields for a warm couch at the Ex House. The mild temperatures in this part of the country didn't mean a thing in a mental world. Sigorny's mind made her believe she was cold because her past holidays meant snow, wooly hats, and frostbite. Considering the crowds of people huddled over warm Ex cups, she wasn't alone in her thinking, and this was favorable for Sigorny because eavesdropping on conversations became much easier when she was hidden behind a computer screen or crouched in a corner behind a book.

When she was living, she was desperate and would have forced herself to hang out in the Back Room, the cool game hall, even if she hated it and found it to be primitive. Now that she was *someone*, she didn't need to make such sacrifices, and the Back Room did her no good because it was impossible to hear the gossip over the booming music.

She loved the peaceful bar area of the Ex House with its hazy glow of contentment and dancing music notes. Last week, she'd seen the box seats from floor to ceiling for the first time. Booths protruded from the wall like fields of pods, and spirits projected themselves to the intimate tables. Once the cold weather struck—even if only in their minds—spirits began to absorb the new information in their workshops more effectively because it seemed so appropriate to do schoolwork here ... or read the news. The bright, shiny stream of information stretched horizontally above the bar. Her name was there in lights. A dream come true.

The barista passed her an Ex. "It's on me."

How things change. Sigorny's talent for gossip had paid off. People liked her now. They respected her. She would do whatever she had to do to keep it that way. She couldn't stop trying to outdo herself, make the next story more enticing than the last. And to be honest, she was tired of Alex Ash. How much more dirt could she possibly dig up? She lifted her hands to look at the dirt staining her fingernails.

If she wanted to intern somewhere in the Broderick Square after the Categorization, she needed to keep producing juicier stories than any other journalist, and after her recent success, several other spirits had started sporting notepads and pencils, eager to steal any little piece of Sigorny's success they could get their hands on. People were ruthless. She had always known this, but now she had something to lose. Determination possessed her with an itching anxiety.

Tired or not, she needed to maintain this fabulous new storyline. The other day, she'd been late to leave the ABC classroom because she was arguing with Professor Duvall about a minerals assessment. Skye Gossamer shimmied into the room with her movie-star face twisted in distress. Sigorny waited in the hallway to listen to Skye fret about some incident in the woods, something she couldn't remember. *Couldn't remember?* That didn't happen to a spirited mind, but Sigorny turned to leave because tree-hugger Skye was probably scared of something ridiculous, like uprooted flowers along the side of the road.

She stopped when Skye mentioned eyes internally following her everywhere. Her mind wouldn't let them go. *Luminous eyes*, Skye said before she asked if that meant what she suspected.

Give me more, Sigorny pleaded, but Duvall was no dummy. She must have sprayed some crazy concoction in the air or grinded some of her stones into dust because the conversation silenced. It didn't take long to figure out what they'd been discussing. Research was so much easier with a brilliant mind. Sigorny patted her own head to thank it. When she connected eerie glowing eyes to the traits of the gifted, she ran with the idea, even if she didn't have hard information.

The gifted were here. They'd been spotted by a newbury.

The article went straight to the top of the news ticker. Spirits in the streets began to recognize Sigorny, to *celebrate* her. Some were even beginning to trail her to see where she found her sources. It was surreal! Witch sightings sent the city into a panic resulting in the Chancellor himself addressing the masses, claiming that Ardors were stationed in town, and the Patrol was doing everything they could to keep the city safe.

Sigorny followed up with a quick thought to her fans: why would they need Ardors in town if the Patrol was keeping the peace?

Tonight, she lucked out. She reached the Ex House early enough to disguise herself behind the computer in the corner of the bar. And who came to sit across from her? None other than Alex Ash and Skye Gossamer. The powers that be were shining down on her! She stuffed her mouth with her fist to keep from squealing with glee.

"How are you sleeping?" Skye asked Alex after they each ordered a hot drink.

"It's getting worse," Alex replied.

Sigorny jotted down ideas. *No sleep. Alex is anxious? Addicted to something? Mental disorder?*

"Is it Rae's fault?"

"I don't think so, but I'm worried about her."

"Why? She's older than you are. She should be worried about you."

Alex let out a long exhale. "I worry about anyone who sleeps less than I do."

"What does she do all day?"

"She sketches. Or she visits Duvall, I think."

"I thought she sketched at night."

Sigorny assumed they were discussing the Lost One. No one knew anything about the child, but it wasn't abnormal for a Lost One to set up shop in a city for a few months and then move on. No one paid much attention. Lost Ones were like stray dogs.

"Why aren't you sleeping?" Skye asked.

"Chase's nightmares don't help. He's been having them more and more."

"Car crash?"

"Yeah."

Why would Chase's dreams affect Alex? Were they sneaking around at night? She wondered if that might be newsworthy. Newburies breaking the rules. Nah, that was last year's news. Besides, newburies no longer wanted to hear about each other. They could participate in that sort of gossip in the vestibule. She needed more about Sephi Anovark.

Alex sighed. "There's so much going on around here. When I first died, I wanted to know everything. About me, about Sephi, about my family, and who I was."

Sigorny leaned so close to the computer monitor that the energy from the screen began to tickle her cheek.

"I'm starting to think there's a reason that spirits leave well enough alone."

Skye's arms stretched high enough into the air that Sigorny could see them above her monitor. Skye reached for the classical music notes and caught them in her hands. "What do you mean?"

"Think about it. Information is out there everywhere. Our

world has no limits. There's a reason why certain things aren't shared. And I think there's a reason why spirits don't seek it out, why they don't want to know."

"You're losing me."

"Ignorance is bliss."

Skye released the notes, and they flew to the ceiling. "You're the last person I expected to ever hear say that. You ask more questions than a four-year-old."

"Have you ever been into that health center? You should go. It does make you feel better, but most of the *exercises* aren't about analyzing people or places. They're games, and math, ideas, and progression."

"What are you saying?"

"Whatever happened to history?"

"I hated history."

"Well … me, too. In school. But I'm saying I guess I can see why the professors want to keep the past in the past, you know. I need to take a page out of that book."

"Then you might want to stop reading Sigorny's articles."

Sigorny's mind fluttered. She was a topic of conversation! She saw her reflection in the computer monitor. She was beaming like a goon and didn't care.

"Haven't you wondered why other so-called reporters don't scoop her?" Alex asked. "They report about astronomy and medical advances and the arts."

"I see what you're saying."

"I did all that investigating into my past, and where did it get me? Sleepless because I can't stop having nightmares about home, and the gifted, and the mental hospital where I died."

Mental hospital! Sigorny wrote it down and circled it three times. Once again, she shoved her fist in her mouth to keep from screaming in excitement. Alex died in an insane asylum. This was too good. Right when she thought there was nothing else to write about! Alex was crazy! The masses would eat this up.

"I wake myself to get out of the dream, and I feel like I've run a thousand miles and Rae is holding my hand."

Sigorny didn't need to use her infamous little notebook. The computer sat ready and waiting in front of her. As she began to type her next article, her fingers moved so quickly a haze rose up from the keyboard. She swatted it, hoping Alex and Skye would assume it was steam from an Ex drink.

Chapter Twenty-Two

Sigorny L.
Voice of the Newburies

Ever wonder what happened to the kid last year who couldn't get over his death? You remember him, right? The little boy who would run circles around the courtyard, howling and trying to rip out hair that didn't exist.

Well, I found him.

He's currently a resident of a mental treatment center. Eidolon's medical center refers the mentally cracked of the afterlife to this facility. The most interesting fact about this treatment center? It's for the living and *the dead. You read that right.*

The Eskers Mental Rehabilitation Center opened its doors in the late eighteenth century in Parrish, Maryland. Not only are some of the patients dead, but much of the staff is dead, as well. I suppose when the patients are insane, it doesn't matter if they see ghosts roaming the halls. Half the doctors are Havilahs, and research shows that at one time, half the residents were Havilahs, too.

Their most recent patient was Harrison Blotten, our young courtyard sprinter. Before Room 11 belonged to him, it belonged to a certain Alex Ash.

So my question: will the fate of our world end up in the hands of a lunatic?

***

Rae's sketches wallpapered Alex's room. In fact, in some areas, Rae hadn't even used paper; she'd colored a masterpiece right on the wall. Alex didn't mind. They belonged there, but sometimes in the dark before she fell asleep, the charcoal on her formerly white walls made them seem far too similar to the gray interior of the Eskers Institution with its moving shadows and loud emotions. It didn't help that Alex's dreams kept taking her back there.

On the afternoon of the winter solstice, her mind was at peace, maybe because of the daylight, or because the happiness of the holidays prevented unwanted memories. The pictures in her sleeping mind remained blank. She could feel herself curled in a ball but could see and hear nothing. The only sense was touch. She felt a gentle hand remove her hair tie, and her scalp relaxed as her hair fell free.

Chase's presence arrived like a heat. He raked his fingers through her hair and shifted the pillow under her head. He loved her. The feeling was everywhere, singing to her. She did not budge from that cocoon of melodic warmth.

His hand found hers, but when her fingers opened, she forgot about the note she clutched there, the one she found outside her door that morning with her other solstice gifts. It was a warning. It was a revelation.

And it was from Jonas.

Alex jackknifed awake upon realizing what Chase found in her hand, but the damage was done. He'd only seen the note for a few seconds, but that was long enough.

"He hasn't talked to us in months, and he sends a note to you? How dare he write to you after what he's done!" Chase paced the room in a fury, his hands clasped behind his neck. "And he came to visit you?"

Alex fiddled with her hair.

"That's how you knew about Syrus Raive? I knew it. I didn't think Westfall would tell you something like that."

Alex read the letter. *Spirits already hate you, thinking you are her. The gifted will hate you when they realize you really aren't her.*

"Jonas is right though," Alex whispered. "I don't know what to do."

"We burn that stupid letter. And we keep our mouths shut."

For goodness sake, the Havilah tree outshined the others in the Legacy Room. She found it hard to believe that no one had ever found Raive's name.

"How could you not tell me? You lied to me." His blue eyes cut the space between them, daggering the note in her fist.

She hadn't lied. She just hadn't shared.

"And what the hell is he doing out there? Who is this group sending him on missions? Did he not learn his lesson last time?"

Alex didn't respond to his questions. He looked homicidal, marching around her room.

"Please don't look at me like that."

"Like what?"

"Deer in the headlights. Someone has to worry about you because evidently *you* don't."

She pushed her way into his mind. It was a deep, ugly red of anger and jealousy. The lights on the wall next to her brightened and whined. She stood up and bolted from the room before Chase's fury took shape and burst the bulbs or ignited the carpet. Feelings were contagious; they both knew that.

Alex flew down the ramp and out into the fresh air, hoping the mood of the town would ease Chase's anger. She didn't slow her pace until she reached the sunstones lining the roads through all of Eidolon. They glimmered like diamonds, but their decorations ranged from holiday lights, to flowers, to carvings, to snow. Freestanding sconces hovered above their heads, glowing white and angelic.

"Where is he?" Chase asked. "Did he say?"

"You know as much as I do," Alex replied, skirting around a replica of the earth fading in and out of darkness. "The only information I have is what was written in that note. He didn't tell me anything I hadn't already heard."

Chase caught up to her, huffing and puffing, his breath visible and red in the evening air. Anger never had trouble taking form.

"You don't need to breathe, you know."

"I'm really not focusing on that right now. Jonas is so damn selfish. He knows his brothers are worried about him even after the stunt he pulled last year. I always held my tongue when Kaleb would talk about how Jonas would do anything, step on anyone if it meant he could be boosted a little bit higher. I thought Jonas would come through in the end, but he didn't. He made a fool of me last year not because he attacked me but because he attacked *you*, and I didn't even see it coming. I don't know whether Jonas ever loved me, or Kaleb, or Gabe, or you. He put you on a silver platter so he could step on you on his way up. Kaleb was right from the start."

Alex wrapped her arms around herself, shivering in the night air. She kept moving because that was all she could think to do, turning down a new lane, one she'd never seen before. A glowing semicircle of stairs ascended up into nothingness, so she chose to go straight. She didn't feel like entering the unexpected right now.

"I'm sorry, Chase."

"Don't you be sorry," he barked, pushing ahead of her to open a curtain strung with tiny suns. As he stood under the archway, holding the curtain, he seemed to remember himself, and his fury softened.

"Don't be sorry," he repeated, gently this time. He followed her through the light of the suns. "I'm not angry at you. I'm angry at my ass of a brother. It's not your fault."

It was her fault. She was somehow the product of two extremely dangerous spirits. She wondered where they might try to categorize her now. They could test her, prod her, to see if she related more to Raive or Sephi. She never imagined things could get worse once she found answers. No wonder Rae chose to keep moving, bouncing from place to place. The Broderick officials would never be able to use Rae, or even find her.

What would happen when everyone found out about Syrus Raive? Her adoring fans would turn into a lynch mob. Finally, the people would agree on one thing. Both sides could rally around their hatred for her.

There was her purpose. To be the sacrificial lamb who brought everyone together.

***

Skye leaned out the window of the Broderick Square museum, resting her forearms on the wrought iron railing and frowning at the congestion on the streets below. She'd taken her time wandering through the exhibits, searching for meaning in sculptures and paintings, absorbing the magic of the artists. She didn't feel different here. She didn't feel like she had something to hide. Every object in this building had a purpose, and that was to speak to the people in some way. For once, she wasn't the only one who could understand an inanimate object.

Her gift made her nervous. Her *gifted-loving* relative with the pink streak of hair made her nervous, too. Both things connected her to a group of people this town hated. She would much rather dance around campus and flirt with boys and play dumb. That way, no one would know she was different than the average Gossamer.

She'd spent too much time in the museum. The atmosphere outside had shifted. Spirits in Broderick Square moved too quickly, especially on such a perfect day, one which was supposed to be restful. The piney holiday aroma had been punctured by this frolic and began to burn.

She couldn't exit back through the building because she knew the art would distract her. Time died in this museum; she wouldn't come out until tomorrow. Reluctantly, she blinked and imagined herself on the street below. She fell into the stream of moving spirits.

She caught a glimpse of Alex and Chase but ducked away. She was fond of both of them, but that didn't make it easy to be around them. When they kissed, she found herself staring, enthralled by the raw emotion. Even in a large group, she felt like an interruption. Like a third wheel. Skye wasn't used to this feeling. She was a Gossamer, a bragging right which she flaunted proudly.

Charismatic and amiable, Gossamers got what they wanted. She felt such happiness and acceptance the first time she saw the family tree in the Legacy Room. She was important here, genetically spirited. There was power in numbers. Skye had everything here in death, but Alex and Chase made her feel like she was missing something.

She hadn't decided if her ability was a gift or a curse, but she knew she didn't trust it. Everything she touched was eager to share its experiences with her. Trees. Animals. Books. Even evil, bitter letterboxes. Could they lie as easily as a human?

She should have told Alex—or at least Duvall—what the box showed her. She was still haunted by the maniacal face of the man she witnessed murdering Sephi. The box had to have been there to see the whole thing because it remembered the crime clearly.

She wished she could ask one of her relatives if they ever experienced similar powers, but very few lived within the city. She didn't dare ask that pink-streaked leach. All Skye had to do was touch Little's hand one time to see that she'd lived a picture-perfect life. In flashes, Skye was forced to witness a movie reel of adoring parents, beaches, birthday parties, and cruises. This girl had lived the life Skye wanted, and Skye wanted nothing to do with feelings of inadequacy!

Even the florist was now out in the street. Skye tucked the bouquet under her arm: Forget-Me-Nots for Rae, and shoved her hand into her pocket, extracting the catnip seeds she'd purchased. It could be the protective effects of the catnip kicking in, but something unsettling traveled its way up to her head. Everything became blurry like watching the world through the wings of a hummingbird. It made her dizzy, and she rested her palm on the nearest lamppost to keep herself from falling.

The lamppost shocked her with a memory. "Witch!" it screamed to her.

She gasped.

"Witch!" It repeated.

She snatched her hand away from the lamppost. *Witch.* The lamppost wasn't the only one saying it. The word was everywhere. Skye dropped the catnip and flowers and her vision stopped trembling.

She massaged her temples. The image of an electric-haired girl flashed into her mind. Where did the memory come from? She wasn't touching anything. Except her own head.

Whoever the mystery girl was, she was in the city. Skye placed her hands on the windows of the shops; windows saw much more than doors. No images appeared, just the word over and over. *Witch.* It whistled throughout the air, piercing her ears. A slur. And Skye realized it was an actual whistle and it was coming from the Brigitta campus. It was an alarm, calling all the newburies back home. No wonder there was fear in the air.

She gathered her things and readied herself to run back to campus but spotted Rae. The child stood amid the chaos like a statue, unaffected. She had one arm on her hip while the other arm she twisted around Alex's leg. To an outsider, it would appear as though Rae was holding Alex for protection when Skye knew it was the other way around.

Chase stood opposite Alex, holding her as though she might take flight. As Skye made her way through the crowd to get to them, a large figure swooped in to beat her there. Ardor Westfall was moving with the crowd in the opposite direction, but she heard him bark at Chase.

"Take Alex back to Brigitta *now*. Don't let her out of your sight."

"What is going on?" Chase asked, as Skye stepped in next to Rae and handed over the bouquet. They shared a look of understanding.

"The gifted are in Eidolon."

"The bodied can't get through the gate," Alex argued.

Westfall shook his head and tapped his temple.

Skye handed some of the catnip to Rae. "In their heads?"

The travelers rushed around in different directions, bumping them.

"I'm sure she," he paused, "or *they* love that they've caused panic."

"I won't leave her," Chase obeyed. The determination in his face made Skye red with jealousy.

And as if Rae read her thoughts, she let go of Alex and tucked her small hand within Skye's. Skye didn't realize what would happen, but she was filled with images.

The meadow behind the fields.

Daisies.

Traveling through something bright and scorching.

A girl. With black hair and glowing eyes. And again, the realization struck her that this wasn't the first time she'd seen this face. She saw her own hand brushing against the grandmother Forget-me tree with her crackling, gray bark.

Rae had seen the gifted, too. The day they found her by the gates Skye had forgotten. Rae had given the memory back to her.

Chapter Twenty-Three

Alex never saw so many newburies gathered in the vestibule at one time, and the room didn't like it because the walls turned puke green. She never saw litter either, but she kicked away pencils, papers, and even pieces of rock. Brigitta Hall was losing its cool; the blue flames trapped under the floor whipped and lashed more violently than usual.

Romey sat crisscross on the spout of the fountain, overlooking her children. Her hair stood on end as she searched the crowd for something or someone. When she spotted Alex, the creases in her forehead smoothed. She stretched an arm high above her head and used a finger to pull down a string of data. She typed into the air and then sent the message upward. Alex felt a tightening around her shoulders; she was swaddled in ribbons of warmth.

A group of girls positioned themselves next to Kaleb. Alex could smell their fumes of leather handbags and lust. Skye clucked her tongue as Little Gossamer leaned on her palm, glancing at Kaleb, even during such pandemonium. His attention wasn't on her though.

"Come on, Pax," said Kaleb. "You're the *Interactions* girl. What's going on with the gifted?"

Pax wiggled her bumpy nose. "You act like I'm employed by the government. I'm a newbury, like you."

"No, you're not." Kaleb elbowed her in the side. "You're special! You're Pax Simone!"

Pax curled her lips under her teeth to try to hide how pleased she was.

"It's only us." Kaleb motioned at their small group.

"My family will have my neck if I talk."

"You're dead. You don't have a neck."

"They'll disown me!"

Kaleb draped an arm over her. "They can't do that. Your name is written in diamonds on your family tree, or so I hear."

"You think they can't saw off a limb? If a family wants to, they can chop, burn, or shred whatever family members they cast away."

That answered Alex's question about people seeing Raive's name on the Havilah tree. If Astor was disowned, his son's name wouldn't be on the family tree.

Little caught Alex's attention. "Is this about you?" she mouthed.

Alex shrugged. The invisible hug Romey was giving her

hinted that yes, it was about her, but she mouthed back, "Or is this about you?"

Little winked.

Romey cupped her hand over her ear and faced the entryway, listening although no earpiece was visible. She flicked her chin and the doors responded, closing with a resonant bang, loud enough to frighten the life out of the dozens of excited conversations.

"I'm sure you have plenty of questions, and I will answer them to the best of my ability."

"Is it true?" Madison asked. "We aren't allowed to leave Brigitta?"

"For the night, yes, it's true."

"And the entire city is on curfew?"

"General Brozellos and the rest of the Patrol said it would be easier to do their jobs if the campus, the city, and all surrounding areas are vacant."

"What about the witch?" Carr called out.

The reaction was mixed. The volume of voices swelled, spreading over the vestibule in shadows of panic and fear.

"Way to use an uncivilized term," Linton scolded.

Alex felt the ribbons around her slacken, and she grew cold. Romey was losing focus.

"It was confirmed this afternoon that not only was a member of the gifted sighted, but there was also an unfortunate incident involving a newbury. I don't have much information except that the victim was rushed to Dianab Medical Center."

Kaleb scribbled something on a square of paper and handed

it to Pax. "What kind of incident?"

Little's brown eyes were wide. "A newbury was almost killed. Like afterlife killed. You didn't hear?"

Kaleb shook his head and raised his hand. "Can you tell us who was hurt?"

Gray smoke hovered in the corner of the room where Carr sat with Jack and a few others. Still no Calla. "I'm surprised you don't know," said Jack. He shooed his hand at Little and Skye. "Was the witch one of your cousins or something?"

Skye leaped to her feet, and her red hair snapped like a whip. Her mouth moved rapidly, but her words were muted. Romey had her hand outstretched in Skye's direction, her fingertips pressed against her thumb. Alex hadn't known Romey could do this. Kaleb put an arm around Skye and when she looked at him, he shook his head to imply she should leave it alone.

Tess Darwin coughed loudly. "Who's missing? If he wasn't so large, no one would notice."

A book took flight, arcing over the heads of the crowd, finding its target and slamming into Tess's chest. Following the trajectory of the book was not difficult because there was a rainbow of gray leading to where it originated. Jack Bond didn't seem to mind when everyone stared at him. This time it was Kaleb who jumped from his seat and began to shout a string of profanity so vicious, it slapped against the faces of those nearest to Jack.

Romey allowed this outburst.

Tess gasped and gazed at Kaleb in awe. Little patted his hand. But their knight in shining armor wasn't concerned with chivalry at that moment. Skye yanked at his wrist to remind him that he'd just encouraged her to leave them alone.

Alex was close enough to the fountain to hear Romey murmur under her breath that Jack deserved those words. "Mr. Bond, please see me after our gathering."

Kaleb straightened up and tilted his chin to get a better look at Jack, who was flanked by Carr and a few others, but not Reuben. "I guess we know who the victim was."

"Not a great day in Eidolon to be a hunter," Chase remarked.

Alex grimaced.

"What's wrong?" Chase asked.

"I have a headache."

Romey stood up on the spout of the fountain. "As of now, you are not to leave the building. You are welcome to stay here in the vestibule, and if you feel more comfortable sleeping down here, that is fine. The news tickers will be updated with reports."

"Can you tell us where the attack took place?" Sigorny's nasally voice came from the middle of the crowd. One second she wore a blouse and jeans, but the next moment, her mind projected her into pink, plaid pajamas. She tapped a slippered foot, looking like she had no intention of leaving such a smorgasbord of gossip for the night.

"I am not privy to that information."

"Yeah, right …" Linton muttered.

"Was it an isolated attack?"

"This is not a press conference, Sigorny."

"Of course not, but I'm asking questions everyone else is thinking."

"It was isolated, but there were witnesses. Perhaps you might get some information from them."

Witnesses. There were only two people who paid attention to Reuben.

Sigorny tugged at the collar of her pajama top. "Yeah right. They'll never give me an exclusive."

Jack's head of messy, muddy hair lifted above the crowd. He opened his arms wide, like a scarecrow in a field of contempt.

"I'll tell you whatever you want to know. I'll tell you how Reuben's treatment around here is misplaced. If you've been following the media regarding our very own newbury class, you'll know that there is a member of a much more prominent witch-hating family among us. It's no secret Alex Ash has drawn in quite an eclectic group of tourists, and no doubt the gifted are curious, as well. The irony of your favoritism will condemn you—" His mouth kept moving without sound.

Romey had silenced him, too, but not before Chase snatched the book from Tess's lap and hurled it across the room. The velocity was enough to knock Jack off his feet. Several newburies cheered, but others reached out to help Jack. Alex couldn't believe it.

Romey answered a few more questions before directing them to either behave in the vestibule or retire to their rooms.

Alex wasn't going to stay in the vestibule with the likes of the Bonds and Sigorny. She wasn't in the mood for an interrogation or an exclusive about her defensiveness if she refused to comment. She did, however, have an entire load of books with her, as well as the brilliant mind of Gabe Lasalle sitting across from her. She figured she might as well take advantage of the confinement.

Paleo's latest history assignment was about the early technology leading to afterworld exposure, and there were centuries to cover. It took Alex an hour to finish reading several hundred pages, but by then, the Lasalles needed entertainment, so they helped her construct a miniature replica of Pumapunku, one of the first documented spirited cities. After helping Chase with his debate notes for Law class, which had been taken over by Westfall, Alex attempted to practice her meditating techniques but it was too chaotic in the vestibule.

"We don't have to stay down here," Chase said.

"Are you in my mind or reading my face?"

"A little of both," he said, standing and extending a hand.

"I thought you couldn't let me out of your sight."

"I don't plan to."

Her reaction was a pleasant dread, like holding a promising hand of cards and waiting for her turn, knowing she'd win but unable to control the building anticipation. Chase was a frequent visitor in her room, but if he followed orders, he would be there *all* night. She could only imagine the embarrassing colors exposing her girlish anxieties.

Kaleb said goodnight with a Cheshire Cat grin on his face. Chase smacked the back of his head.

Skye marked her spot in a book about South American plant life. "Is Rae with you?"

"She's probably upstairs. No way would she be down here

in this crowd."

Skye twisted her lips. "Be careful, okay."

"There's no danger in my room."

"I didn't see Rae go upstairs."

Gabe poked his head around his book. "The curfew doesn't apply to her. I guess you guys skipped that section of our Brigitta manual."

"Manual?" Chase mouthed with his back to Gabe.

Alex grinned.

"The wording is specific, and technically, as the laws apply to citizens only, she is supposed to vacate the city in the instance of an emergency."

The word "vacate" echoed in Alex's head. "They'd kick her out?"

"Not likely. They have bigger fish to fry right now, but she shouldn't get in their way."

Chase raised a brow. "I doubt she's going for a stroll in the middle of a manhunt. Or womanhunt."

Alex nodded, hoping he was right.

The seventh-floor corridor was quiet, and the door to her room burst open as though it was in desperate need of company. Alex searched the room for Rae and noticed calm waves of energy rising from her desk chair. They extended like ocean waves might reach for the shore before retracting and returning to their source. Rae was asleep in the chair. Her feet curled underneath her while her head lobbed backward, her mouth ajar.

Alex placed her books on the desk and noticed the box of

Syrus Raive's letters had scuttled further back into the corner under the shadow on the desk. Still resentful. She'd flung it to the ground after it crept into her lap during the meditation. And sometimes now when she dreamed of Sephi, the box would emerge from its cave, wanting to listen.

Chase caught her sizing up the box. "Now we know why you were able to read the letters."

"Why?"

"Duvall said that she thought you were connected to Sephi because they were hers. Only someone connected to her should be able to see them. Wouldn't the same be true of Syrus Raive? He wrote them."

Alex cursed her own stupidity. "I can't believe we told Duvall about the Havilahs. We should have known better."

"You aren't responsible for your family and you didn't know what the Havilahs did in the past."

"I'm not sure how a civilization like this one could have so many technological advances, inventions, and ideas, but they never researched Raive's background. Wouldn't they want to know where he came from?"

"I'm sure certain people do know," said Chase. "You forget that spirits see what they want to see. No one expected him to be a Havilah because he was born in a gifted territory. And on that note, I wonder how my darling brother knew where to go. Who do you think gave him the information?"

"That's the million dollar question." Alex sighed.

"Why do I have the feeling he's doing something he shouldn't be?"

"Because you're worried about him."

Chase's forehead crinkled. "I wish I wasn't. Why can't I hate him?"

"Because you're you."

And that's why she loved him.

Chapter Twenty-Four

Across town, Lucia Duvall crouched down on the endless knot outside the Dual Tower building. She heard movement in the woods beside her and the tree leaves rustled, creating a voice to warn her of the Patrol's presence. She wondered how many officers were stalking her. Most of them were searching the city like she was, but unless the Patrol was losing its touch some of them were assigned to her surveillance. As if she'd been in cahoots with the gifted after so many years.

She folded her legs under her and sat on the knot. She felt the power of three gifted souls, but one was more powerful than the others. She couldn't tell if it was a boy or a girl, but it had left its fingerprints all over the place, which could be due to inexperience or defiance. Duvall would have done the same thing to give the proverbial finger to Eidolon's lawmakers.

The gifted were more trapped than spirits. It was a shame that extraordinary lives could not belong to the soul. A few bruised apples could taint the reputation of the entire orchard.

Judging by the traces, the gifted child was looking for something but didn't know where to look. It had plenty of time. No spirits expected to see it, and therefore, they didn't. That was the tricky thing about a world operated by the mind; the more complicated the ideas, the more nooks in which to hide. Duvall was certain the child had arrived because of Alex Ash. The last Havilah was dead; the gifted were celebrating. At the same time, they wanted a peek at the new Sephi.

"But you needn't fear them," Duvall whispered to the shadows in case the Patrol—or even the gifted—could hear. "Their intention was not to harm. They must have been taken by surprise."

She dug into her pocket and felt the tickle of lycopodium. She curled her hand into a fist and grinded the small plants against her palm. She extracted her hand and opened it at her mouth like blowing a kiss into the wind. The particles escaped and stuck to the air like static, revealing what she already knew. They uncovered the fingerprints stuck like graffiti.

Handprints appeared one at a time, pressed against the bricks of the buildings and glowing like fire. They blended together to form letters, and those letters formed words. Finally, when the prints ceased, Duvall took several steps back to look at the message that spanned three buildings.

Acta, Non Verba.

Duvall cocked her head. *Actions, not words.* They had

used quite a bit of effort to write such a vague message. And for what reason would they use Latin?

Duvall inspected the ground and the words etched into the stone at her feet: *Si Monumentum Requiris, Circumspice*. The message was inscribed during the construction of the city to remind spirits of the legacy of the town. *If you seek monument, look around.*

The small handprints covered the word monumentum and instead spelled out malum. Crime. Evil. Damage.

If you seek evil, look around.

***

Jonas flicked the drooping branches of the large tree as he passed it, hating it. Bad memories came by the truckloads in Parrish. He and his brothers used to hide their loot under the roots. His initials loomed larger than the others because he thought the size of them would make him bigger, more significant, but that had never been the case in the Lasalle family.

He never wanted to come back to this godforsaken town, and he never thought he'd have to. And now, less than two years after his death, he trekked through these same damn woods again.

He was bitter that they threw him to the wolves in Astor, Oregon, but they were pleased he made contact with the gifted.

We needed to send you. You were the only one innocent enough not to offend them.

There were different spirits each time he went back to Home Base, as they called it. All of them were pleased he made contact with Alex. Some gathered together looking over documents. Others pinned up maps with shaded regions or blueprints with notes all over them. He didn't know what they were doing, but he'd seen the spirits in charge, and that was enough for him. For now, at least. He would do whatever they wanted. Even if it meant going home.

He argued that there wouldn't be witches living in a witch-hating town, but thinking twice, he had a hunch. He stood at the threshold of Thea Frank's old shack and attempted to ignore the jingling of bells. Damn Jester. He forgot who he was dealing with because he walked right through the door and appeared on the other side, thinking he couldn't be seen.

Liv squatted on the floor by the fireplace, trying to get the logs to ignite. He blinked and sent a jolt of energy her way. The flames erupted with a whoosh, like the sound of shaking a bed sheet.

Liv turned and her mouth fell open. "Jonas."

Shit.

Chapter Twenty-Five

The thrill of the lockdown had worn off. Now that Alex was safe in her room and Rae was accounted for, she felt nervous about the sleeping arrangements. Chase draped himself over Alex's loveseat as though this was no big deal.

"It's *not* a big deal, Alex."

"Stay out of my head." She took her books from her bag and placed them on the shelf above her desk.

"Calm down." Chase massaged his temples. "You're going to give me a headache." He stood up and walked toward the door.

"Where are you going?"

"Back to my room."

"You said you wouldn't let me out of your sight!"

The desk chair slid in front of him, but he walked through

it. "What sort of trouble could you get into hanging out in your room? I'll come back after you're asleep when you're not so..." he waved his hand around, "... analytical."

The door didn't open for him at first, and Alex saw Chase's shoulders rise and fall as he sighed. The hinges creaked as the door popped out to give him a crack through which to escape.

Alex flopped down on her bed, fiddling with the edge of the comforter and trying to fight the disappointment rising inside of her. This was their chance. Westfall had given them an order so they couldn't get into trouble if one of them didn't stay in their own room that night. She'd blown it. Regret surrounded her in a cloud, and when she swatted at it, it thickened.

She slid off her bed to get away, but the cloud followed her until she reached the door, which still hadn't shut after Chase's exit. Actually, it was open even wider. She took it as a suggestion and headed out. The cloud dissipated.

She'd never ventured above the seventh floor. She assumed all the hallways were the same, resembling a hotel or dorm, but not the eighth floor. It looked like a door showroom. Some propped against the wall. Other doors were freestanding or flat on the ground. They were painted all different colors and shaped like keyholes or diamonds or crescents. Some had knockers or locks, wrought iron designs or windows with nothing on the other side. She stopped in front of her favorite one, a distressed orange door with ivy around the frame. It swung open to reveal Chase waiting with his arms crossed.

"I wondered how long it would take you."

She knew him better than that. "You were worried."

"Your door didn't close when I left. Dead giveaway."

"Can I come in?"

He stepped back with an outstretched hand.

Alex felt her pulse quicken, though without a body she felt detached from it. The stronger feeling within her was Chase's anticipation as she took in the scene. She spun around to face him.

"Really?"

He shrugged and ran his hand over the top of his hair. It was his room in Parrish. Every single detail was the same even the family and sports photos pinned to the wall next to his ball caps and concert tickets. On his desk sat the picture of him with his arm slung around Alex, and they smiled so wide their toothless grins took up their whole faces. A note in Danya's handwriting stuck to the desk, telling him to please finish his laundry. Next to that was a sticky note that said she loved him. Atop the laundry pile was his white dress shirt from the night of the dance. Also from that night, Alex's blue dress lay in a heap on the floor by his desk.

He stared down at it, too. "I didn't want to move it. I didn't ever want to forget that night because what if you never showed up here? What if this was all I had to remember?"

Alex ran her fingers along the note that Danya had written. Those simple words stretched from the page and reached out to her. They wrapped themselves around her heart.

"I'm sorry." Her voice cracked.

"I know." He lifted himself to sit on the desk.

Over his shoulder, a photo of Chase and Jonas caught

Alex's attention. They held up fishing rods on their family boat. It must have been late summer considering their deep brown tans and sun-scorched hair.

"His pictures are bigger than they used to be. I guess that means I'm thinking about him."

"You don't sound happy about it."

Chase placed his hands on Alex's waist and pulled her to him. "When we were at the haunted house, I asked Gabe about this feeling I had. I knew Jonas was nearby. I get it with all my brothers. It's nowhere near as strong as what we do." He drew an invisible line between her head and his with his free hand. "But it's there. I wish it wasn't because I'm guessing that was the day he came to find you and didn't bother visiting us."

Alex thought of a way to ease his worry. "Do you want to try to find Jonas right now? We don't have to stay long. You can … we can … you know."

"You mean meditate again?"

She nodded.

"I don't know. Last time my head hurt for like a week."

"We make sure that we only stay for a minute."

A dimple struck his cheek as one corner of his pink mouth lifted. "Are you suggesting we do this because you're nervous to be in here with me?"

It shouldn't be a big deal. They slept side by side so many times but as children with Popsicles staining their faces or marshmallows from the fire pit stuck in their hair. And sure, lately he wandered in to her room at some time during in the night, but there was something so intimate to Alex about tucking herself under his arm for the entire night. In his bed. Lying against him while she was still conscious and aware of the setting. His brothers would look at them differently, knowing the arrangements, whether they were sleeping or not. In life, Alex always thought those couples stuck out when they had that closeness. You could see the secret hiding in the space between them, or lack thereof, an affection that bound them, separating them from everybody else.

Chase kept his head low. "We already have that, Alex."

She should have known that he'd hear her thoughts. "I know."

"Let's try to see if we can find Jonas. It won't take us more than a few minutes. Then we'll come back."

"Anything weird, we get out."

"Agreed."

This time, it wasn't as alarming to fall away from reality. They walked the same path as before.

"Why are we in Parrish?"

"I'm beginning to think that we're obsessed with it."

"Or it's obsessed with us." Alex felt something odd stirring within her. In life, anticipation felt like trying to breathe with a barbell on her chest. This sensation struck her when they reached Thea Frank's house. Chase suddenly ran forward, yanking her along.

She blinked, and they stood in Thea Frank's blurry living room yet again.

Jonas was the only clear figure in the room. He looked worse for wear. Strands of long hair fell over his face as he leaned over the table separating him from Thea, who puckered her bright red lips.

Her image, though more visible than the last time, still seemed like a colored pencil sketch. "Your past begins much earlier than your date of birth."

Jonas groaned. "No more riddles. Spirits really love to beat around the bush, and I'm sick of it."

Footsteps erupted from down the hall, and the form of Liv appeared. "You're still here?"

"Shut up, Liv." Jonas took a seat on Thea's desk. "What were you doing back there?"

"Practicing some of the things my grandmother's been trying to teach me."

Their voices are too clear, Chase said. *Is your head hurting?*

It was pounding, but Alex wanted to hear more.

Jonas crossed his arms. "What sort of things?"

"Why do you care?" Liv asked.

"The gifted are breaking into spirited cities." He glanced from Liv to Thea. "Judging by the looks on your faces right now, you hadn't heard."

Liv sat down next to Jonas. "How do you know?"

"My people know everything."

Thea's image faded in and out of clarity. Alex tightened her mind and held on to her silhouette.

"Please tell me you haven't left Parrish, Liv. I told you—"

Liv jumped up. "I didn't! Not really. I went somewhere in my head. With Rae."

Rae?

"It's illegal," Thea warned.

"I don't think she meant to. I was thinking about something, and she was there with me, and it just kind of happened."

We have to go right now. Chase squeezed Alex's hand. *Don't you feel like you're going to pass out?*

Alex blinked and saw gray. Only gray.

Chase?

Nothing.

Panic set in. Barbell on the chest times ten. She shoved against her mind with her thoughts but it didn't budge. She clawed at the gray around her and it scraped away like mud under her fingernails. Where was she? Where was he?

She felt a pressure against the front of her and prayed it was Chase. She began to dig at the foggy coffin with more ferocity.

She was stuck.

"Alex!"

Her eyes popped open to find Chase lying on top of her. "What happened?"

He lifted himself up and grabbed her hand to pull her upright. "We stayed too long, that's what. Where did you go?"

"It was like the first time we meditated. Gray. But you weren't there."

"No kidding. I was here and I could feel you, but I couldn't see you."

A wave of dizziness struck her. "I don't think we should meditate like that anymore. Did you hear Liv mention Rae?"

"Yeah." He smoothed the hair from her head. "We might never find out why though because we can't meditate again. You want to go back to your room?"

"No!" She didn't want to be alone. The familiarity of his room comforted her: the chipped edge of the dresser where Jonas had chopped it with a light saber, the overflowing laundry basket, and Kaleb's college banner.

She opened her mouth to ask a question, but Chase held up a hand. "I don't want to talk about Jonas. My head hurts enough already."

"I wasn't going to ask about him." She pointed at the dresser. "What do you keep in the drawers now that your mind dresses you?"

"It's the same stuff I had there in life."

She opened the top drawer. "I thought you said you lost that sweatshirt," she said, looking down at the logo for the University of Maryland.

"I lied. I kept it in there after you wore it on the boat that one night."

"Why?"

"Because it smelled like you." He combed his fingers through his hair. "How's your head?"

"Ouch. Yours?"

He nodded. "I need to lie down."

She slid from his lap and they both stood, staring at one another. Alex fiddled with the ends of her hair and followed him to his bed. She couldn't figure out which throbbed more, her head or her heart. He leaned back on his pillows with an arm open and waiting for her. They both left their shoes on.

She gazed up at a ceiling of stars. In Parrish, they spent a week positioning glow-in-the-dark constellation stickers all over his bedroom. Now they shone and twirled.

"Are those real?"

"They seem like it. I had to have some fun with the place, didn't I?"

She watched clouds pass over the stars. "What was your favorite memory in this room?"

His chest moved up and down and she wondered if they would always continue to breathe out of habit. "Isn't that obvious by the setting?"

"The last night?"

"The last night. And my teenage mind of possibilities."

She lifted her head and placed her chin on his chest. "What's your second favorite?"

"This could take all night. A lot happened in this room."

She got comfortable, placing her cheek right over his heart. "I've got nothing but time."

And as surely as she could feel his chest rising and falling, she could feel his smile.

Chapter Twenty-Six

"That was anticlimactic," Kaleb groaned the next morning. "We don't even get to miss any workshops."

Gabe whistled beside him, clutching the straps of his backpack. He seemed overjoyed to be returning to the learning center.

Alex rubbed her hands together. "At least my architecture project is finished. Thanks, guys."

Kaleb stopped next to the fountain to inhale some of the mist. "I'll invoice you the bill for my help."

"Gabe did most of the work."

"A deal is a deal. You know I hate schoolwork."

"Fine, I'll pay up in promises. I'll show you the memory mine."

"That's my girl." Kaleb pumped his fist. "And, by the way,

I'm sure homework isn't *all* you accomplished last night."

Chase coughed.

"So, you two, what is your idea of fun?"

Chase's lips were right next to Alex's ear. "Don't worry, Al. He's about to get his payback."

Right as he said it, Kaleb nearly collided with Little.

"Hi, Kaleb," she chirped. "Are you heading to the history workshop this morning?"

He sidled sideways, scooting away, muttering about jailbait. "No. Sociology."

"Great! I need to fit in one of those sessions, too. Walk with me?"

"I don't know. You're going to get me into trouble with all your admirers," Kaleb teased, but lifted his gaze over her head and pleaded silently for his brothers to help him.

"Oh, please." Little giggled, touching Kaleb's arm.

"I'm not sure I can fend them off."

"I heard you took on a group of twenty-five last spring. I think you'll be fine." She sidled even closer to him.

"Anyone else want to join us?" Kaleb asked through gritted teeth.

"Sorry," Alex said. "I already went to Soc."

"Me, too," Chase added, slinging an arm around her.

"I don't even know why I bother with you two. You're so far stuck up each other's—"

Gabe jumped in between them. "I'll go with you, K."

Little beamed. "Great! I get two cute escorts."

Ever the gentleman, Kaleb gestured for Little to exit first, but he twisted back toward them. "After class, we're meeting to go up to that—" he hesitated next to Little, "—*place*, right?

Alex nodded. "A deal is a deal."

In the entryway of the learning center, they broke away from Chase's brothers and entered the tunnel leading to history. Chase ran his fingers along the whispering stone walls. "You know, Kaleb might have finally found his match."

"She's persistent. I'll give her that. I'm still rooting for Skye though."

Chase reached the doorway. "Speaking of."

Skye was already in the classroom, leaning against the wall and talking to a group of boys. She spoke with her hands and they followed every movement. Her hair rippled and seemed to let off some sort of intoxicant. Each of the boys leaned closer to her, inhaling.

Alex slid into the closest row, peering over the railing of the tier to survey the rows below them. No Bonds. No Eskers kids. She relaxed and took out her notes. Skye excused herself and breezed across the room, the boys' attention following, caught in her tide of captivation.

"Where is everyone else?" Skye asked.

"Off to Sociology with your mini-me," Chase replied.

Skye let out a humph, turning to the front where Paleo began the lesson. She might be the only spirit in Eidolon who was not excited about relatives becoming newburies.

Architecture was not Alex's forte, but she drew the diagrams while Paleo lectured. After an hour, she had the schematic of the lower half of the city, the government square named for Broderick Cinatri, and the learning center campus named for Brigitta Cinatri. Before hearing Yazzie's story about the Cinatri siblings, Alex assumed that they were married. She had a romantic image in her mind of them running away and building a city together, a city of dancing towers and parties. Instead, they were bickering siblings.

Paleo fiddled with the large glasses that sat on her big nose. "Siblings have similar brain structures, and that's why they are more connected than average spirits. The Dual Tower means 'two,' but it is also a pun to indicate dueling. The Cinatris argued over many aspects of the city, which is why one decided to focus on governing and the other on education."

"If they fought so much," Madison said, "why would they build a city together?"

"They were strong because of their sibling bond, and other spirits knew it. Their abilities were respected. Mass fear for the gifted began in the late 1600s in Salem, and man began to hunt both the gifted and spirited. We needed somewhere to turn for safety."

Skye twirled a strand of her hair. "Didn't the Cinatris have a gifted sister, though?"

Paleo's wide nostrils flared. "Off topic. Back to landscape architecture. Now the rosebushes by the stone rings—"

"How come spirits never want to discuss anything controversial?" Linton asked.

Alex cringed. She didn't want to know. Not anymore. History was better left buried.

"Interrupt again, Mr. Darwin, and you'll be asked to leave."

Linton threw his hands in the air. "I'm not trying to disrupt; I'm trying to understand. The spirits who built this city had a gifted sister, and now we're wondering how the gifted are getting into the city? Doesn't seem like rocket science to me. There's a chink in the chain somewhere."

Madison twisted in her seat to look at the rest of them. "They're probably celebrating at our expense right now."

Paleo lifted her chin. "You have so little faith in your elders. You forget that for years the gifted attempted to gain access to Eidolon in order to speak to the first member of the gifted to enter our gates: Lucia Duvall. They never got in. Now back to the rosebushes."

Skye muttered something under her breath.

"What?" Alex asked.

"Nothing."

"Did you say something about Rae?"

Skye furrowed her brow. "Yeah."

"What about her?"

"Lost Ones are friendly with the gifted, and it can't be coincidence that the gifted showed up the same day that Rae did."

"Whatever."

"That tree messed with our heads, Alex. One second, we're running for our lives, and the next we're dashing home and wondering where Rae came from."

"Wait. Is that why you freaked out?" She had trouble keeping her voice low, and Chase began to elbow her.

"Yeah, I think so."

Alex flung her pencil onto the desk. "I'm so confused."

"Do you not remember what we were doing that day? The bark from those border trees makes you forget things. I didn't remember it until Rae showed it to me."

Chase propped his elbow on his knee. "Right next to a thought-stealing tree is a mine that keeps those thoughts and memories?"

His hand shot into the air.

"Yes, Mr. Lasalle?"

"You said the rosebushes are there for protection. If the gifted can't get into the city, why do we need protection on our side of the gates?"

"In case they decide to project themselves. You have to be able to see where you're going. The walls prevent it."

"How could living people project themselves? You mean meditate?"

Madison straightened in her chair. Her voice quivered with excitement. "That's why the gifted were only seen in flashes, right? They were meditating?"

"What do flashes have to do with meditating?" Chase asked.

Paleo wiggled her big nose. "Because that's how meditation works, of course. Hasn't Banyan Philo talked to you about this? I'm sure you've witnessed it. One can only exist in the field of meditation for a few seconds."

Alex didn't need to look at Chase to see the dread on his face. They meditated much longer than a few seconds.

"What's wrong?" Skye asked.

"Nothing," Alex replied, but she threw her hand into the air. "Why is that, by the way?"

Paleo sighed so heavily that the collar of her blouse fluttered. "Because the mind won't come back. This is extremely off topic! Meditation is something to bring up in your Meditari session. Moving on!"

Alex felt a breeze whip past her. It was followed by the sound of a door slamming, causing each of them to jump. Everyone shifted in their seats to see who had entered, but no one was there. Alex couldn't remember her questions. Her mind felt like it was being held in a straitjacket. Paleo meant what she said. Conversation over.

Chapter Twenty-Seven

The memory mine had grown since the last time Alex had been there. She watched Chase as he sighted the field for the first time, watched his expression contort to surprise as the emotions went straight to the vein.

Kaleb's voice was hushed as he said, "What is this place?" She felt triumphant. Kaleb didn't impress easily.

"I can't believe that vagabond guy is the memory miner." Skye moved her head every which way to see if he was around. "I used to see him wandering around the city."

"He's the storyteller too, right?" Gabe extended his fingers toward the field of the floral crosses even though they were several feet away. He wiggled his fingers through the air. "I wonder if that's where he gets all his stories."

For a knowledge scout like Gabe, a field full of stories was better than a library. Many of these would be stories never shared. Secrets. Sigorny would love to get her hands on some of these.

Alex scoured the area. She hoped during the midday chaos, Yazzie would be parked outside the health center. She'd been surprised that the boys hounded her more about seeing the mine over a gym for the dead, but Kaleb claimed they had the playing fields for mental stimulation, and he curled his nose when Alex mentioned calculus, even after she tried to convince him how great she'd felt after leaving the center.

"Can we get closer?" Kaleb asked.

This was what Alex was worried about. That Kaleb would want to do more than see the sights. She assumed Skye would refuse, she *hoped* she'd refuse. Because it was Skye's discovery, it was her decision. Growing up, if one of the boys uncovered a fun, new hideout, an abandoned boat, or climbing tree, 'founder's rule' applied. Whoever made the discovery made the decisions there.

Skye studied the open mouth of the mine. "I *have* been wondering what it looks like in there."

Kaleb laid a hand on her back. "Let's go, then."

Skye leaned into him as she took a step.

Alex tugged on Gabe's arm. He wouldn't condone this. But then he, too, took a step forward as though the scent of emotion had latched a hook around him.

"Chase?"

"I know," he replied. "But I don't think it'll hurt. We won't let them go past the entryway."

A pathway appeared right under her feet where it hadn't been a moment before. It urged her to journey forward, and this was the only reason she took that first step. The closer she inched toward the mine, the more the emotions jumped on her, ghosts in a graveyard, sirens tempting her to listen. They begged to be pulled from the ground and heard.

Her emotions pinballed from elation to remorse, from heartbreak to regret.

"I can't imagine burying pieces of people's minds day in and day out," Kaleb said, shooing at the voices around him.

Chase touched his ear. "You know what? I kind of can."

Alex could too. She wondered if that was the reason Yazzie had lived so long, not because of the health center but because everything he learned about people from the thousands of narrative whispers. What could make the mind stronger—learning or *understanding*?

"What colors do you see?" she asked him.

"All of them. Smudges everywhere."

Kaleb and Skye stood shoulder to shoulder at the mouth of the mine.

"What do you feel?" Gabe called to them.

"Nothing."

Skye, who rested her hand against the lip of the opening, didn't look like she agreed. She whispered something to Kaleb, who whipped around.

"What?"

Alex caught a strong scent of cigars in the moment before Yazzie's face appeared in the mine. Skye stumbled backward.

Yazzie came into the light, clutching a bag in one black-stained fist and a pickaxe in the other. "Well," he remarked. "This is more visitors than I've had in a decade."

Alex couldn't catch her words. They left her without making a sound. Yazzie's gaze flickered around as if he could see her unspoken thoughts.

"I'm sorry," Skye stammered.

Yazzie shook his head. "You've been peeking through the border for a year now. It was only a matter of time." He clutched his hip and gesturing to Alex. "You brought the sunlight with you. So you're forgiven."

All of them turned toward Alex like flowers leaning toward the sun.

"I wondered when you'd come to speak to me, little bird. You like answers, and memories are the only real truths."

Kaleb ran his fingers along the edges of the mine. "That's an interesting way to look at it."

"The mind is programmed to think a certain way. Your news will make sure of that. They give your newbury reporter a voice now, just to get you to follow. Soon, they will be feeding her the information though she won't realize it. Memories, however, they cannot be manipulated. They tell you the story. That's all." Yazzie opened the small bag in his hand. When he lifted his arm to wipe his brow, the scent of birthday cake floated from the bag.

"Is that a memory?" Skye asked, gravitating toward it.

Yazzie nodded. "Would you like to help me bury it?"

Skye nearly fell over. Kaleb held out his arms to support her, leaving his hands on her hips because she was too preoccupied to notice. "Can I help, too?"

"Sure." Yazzie chuckled. "Even though I suspect your interest is not so much in this task but for the girl beside you."

Yazzie hobbled along the pathway until he reached the edge. A few more bricks added themselves to the road. The path grew with the memories. Alex stood with Chase and Gabe as Skye and Kaleb squatted by Yazzie.

"The hole doesn't need to be wide," he instructed, handing them a shovel the width of a child's plastic beach toy but the length of a pole vaulting stick. "But it needs to be six feet deep."

Kaleb got to work digging the hole while Skye nestled the memory in her hands. "Why six feet?"

"Always seemed like the right amount."

Gabe watched in wonder. "Do you know who it belongs to?"

Yazzie nodded. "I've been getting many from this particular source."

"Today?"

"In the past few months. Memories are like the fish in the Klamath River down there past those trees. The salmon cruise the river, laying eggs before they die, leaving them behind. When the fish are born, they swim free, kind of like our memories after we die. Not all the memories are strong enough to find something to latch onto. But many make it here."

"Was it the bodied or the spirited?" Gabe asked.

"Spirited."

Kaleb gritted his teeth as he dug, more justified in his task now. Skye looked up at Yazzie, the memory still in her hands.

"I know him, don't I? I can feel it."

Yazzie's mouth became a thin line.

"Who is it?"

"That memory belonged to your own Professor Van Hanlin."

Alex gasped. "You told me when you found my mother's memories, you knew she had died. Van Hanlin is gone?"

Yazzie shrugged. "I report every memory to the Office of Mental Health. They haven't declared him dead yet. Guess we have to wait to find some more."

Alex bowed her head in respect. Chase knelt on a knee, and Skye curled the memory into her chest.

Gabe refused to look at anyone, pinching the bridge of his nose and turning away. It could have been him. Van Hanlin had been attacked at the same time he was.

Kaleb stopped digging. "How could there still be an investigation against him?"

"Because many of his memories haven't reached me. There are less of them than there should be. Could be a cover-up."

"You said there were a lot."

"An entire life and death of memories should be more than a dozen. They might not have traveled here yet. Time will tell. Sometimes, memories take their time and latch on to other things first."

Skye mumbled a prayer under her breath before she tossed the memory down into the earth.

Yazzie scooped up a handful of dirt and let it trickle through his fingers into the grave. He muttered, "For dust thou art, and unto dust shalt thou return."

They each took their turns sprinkling dirt down into the darkness, paying their respects. Kaleb took the shovel and began the process of replacing the ground. "They haven't reported much about Van Hanlin."

"It would scare people," Gabe said. "They've kept the focus on Alex."

Skye sat down in the middle of the road and hugged her knees. "Out of sight, out of mind."

Kaleb kept shoveling. The group was quiet for so long that when he said, "Finished." Alex jumped.

When they left, she considered reaching out to touch one of the flowers, but it scared her. This place was a cemetery, and although she knew what was buried under the ground couldn't reach her, that didn't mean it couldn't affect her. Harm her.

It's the things you can't touch that hurt the most. She'd learned that a long time ago.

Chapter Twenty-Eight

Sigorny L.
The Voice of the Newburies

Happy midweek. I would like to express my sincere gratitude to Broderick Square for attempting to avoid an overexaggerated game of telephone, and prevent you from receiving false information. I'm pleased to announce that I've been given an opportunity to work closely with such wonderful minds and provide you with more information than ever. As always, I'm honored to be your voice of reason.

I do hope everyone enjoyed the eventful sleepover otherwise known as a lockdown. I know I did. There are several pieces of knowledge I gained from the experience, and it's my pleasure to share them with you.

Only one gifted soul made it into the city. *Rumors are circulating about a group. Representatives from Broderick Square want you to know that this is false. I repeat, false.*

There was only one, and the Patrol is on top of finding out who it was.

Our gates do not allow entry for the bodied. *So how did he/she get in? I went to our very own Ardor Westfall about this one. He informed me that the gates surrounding Eidolon are indeed secured. The only possible entry would be through meditation tactics, and the perpetrator must be pretty skilled to succeed in this feat.*

He/She was only seen for seconds at a time. *If you've been paying attention in Dr. Philo's class, you should know the reason for this. But for those of you who are ignoring your accelerated brainpower and writing love notes in class, here's your answer. Haven't you noticed that we can only flicker in and out of our meditative states for several seconds? This is why the bodied believe that spirits are invisible. Even the most practiced meditation specialists can only leave their projective bodies and travel elsewhere for a matter of seconds. I spoke with Dr. Philo specifically:*

"Meditation is only momentary. Anything else would be unnatural. We shouldn't be in two places at a time."

My next question: what would happen if we could, to which he replied:

"I suppose the mind would get used to it. Why would it return to its projection when it likes being free?"

The witnesses who spotted the gifted last week saw only flashes, but it was enough.

The saga of our tattered relationship with the gifted seems to be the theme of this very peculiar year.

***

Alex decided to focus on Sigorny's latest article during her monthly brain scan. Chase memorized the Invisiball Field Rule Book and said he'd recite it over and over. They hoped if they kept their thoughts separated, whatever the doctors inspected wouldn't show a link between their mental activities.

Each time they reported, the white-coated doctors attached sticky suction cups all over their heads. Multicolored wires and visible current connected Alex and Chase to clunky devices and high-tech monitors. The lines, dots, and shapes on the screens looked more like video games than a scientific study.

In December, the doctors evaluated them in the same room, but Alex couldn't concentrate. In January, they were separated. Chase's doctor took him to a different floor, making Chase more suspicious than ever. In February, their devices waited for them side by side. Alex was pleased, but Chase grinded his teeth as the doctors arranged the gadgets. He leaned into Alex's ear and urged her to only think about Sigorny.

When they were finished, Chase grabbed her hand, and they left. He looked back only once as they exited.

"Good," he muttered. "They seem upset."

"What if they really are just making sure we're okay?"

Chase snickered. "You don't see them bringing back every patient who ever had a head injury, do you?"

She poked her head through the doorways of every room they passed, hoping to see another spirit hooked up to a mind machine. She found something better. She pulled away from Chase and marched into a room without hesitation.

"What are you doing?" Chase called from the hallway. "I don't think you're supposed to—"

He must have seen Reuben, too, because the second after Alex reached the bedside, Chase appeared next to her.

"He's not sleeping."

"I'm sure he's not," she said. "What color is around him right now?"

"Dishwater gray, like usual."

"Wake up, Reuben. You owe me."

Reuben opened one slit of an eye.

"Can you see me?" She asked.

"I don't need to open my eyes to see. You're bright enough as it is."

Chase leaned forward. "Meanwhile, you have *no* light around you. Let down your guard, Reuben. Show us your true colors."

"Ain't you guys done enough to me? Leave me alone."

Alex could have smacked him. "Stop feeling sorry for yourself. Because of you, we have to come back here every month like a bunch of lab rats. So no, we won't leave you alone."

Chase's mouth fell open.

"What?" she asked.

Never heard you make demands like that.

Reuben sniffed. "*You* feel like a lab rat? What do you think they're doing to me?"

Alex glanced around the stark-white room. Besides his bed, it was empty, lifeless. No energy lived here. She couldn't imagine what he did all day without any entertainment.

"Did the gifted kid knock you out?"

"*They*," he corrected. "I didn't get taken out by one witch. They ganged up on me."

Alex nudged Chase's foot. Sigorny had lied. Or been misinformed. "Did *they* say anything to you?"

"Yeah," he snorted, "we sat down for a nice cup of tea before they beat the crap out of me."

Two chairs appeared behind Chase and Alex. Plain and plastic, they unfolded themselves and scooted forward.

"Did you do that?" Chase asked Alex.

She shook her head; she wouldn't conjure something so uncreative.

Chase sat and folded his arms. "Lonely, Reuben? I'm willing to bet that none of your little Eviar buddies have come to see you."

Alex sat, worrying that the chair might bite.

"Did Jack come?"

Reuben didn't answer.

He's letting down his guard, Chase thought to her. *The ideas swirling around him are turning black.*

What does that mean?

I see a lot of black when we're in group therapy.

Nothing good?

Hurt or loss. But it's something. Nice to know he has emotions.

"I'm sorry they attacked you, Reuben," Alex said.

"You should be. Wanna know why Jack hasn't been by? Because I don't agree with him anymore. He thinks we should be trying to get you into trouble. He wants them to take you away somewhere. Like Calla. Me, I'm only trying to stay away from you."

Alex tucked her hands into her lap. She didn't know what to say.

A monitor attached to Reuben began to beep until he shook his head around. "I'm damned if I do, and I'm damned if I don't."

Chase propped one leg over the other. "Reuben, you're a witch hunter. They are witches, excuse my choice of words. You can't blame them."

"You don't know me."

"Am I wrong?"

"My *family* hunts witches. I never fitted in with them. Look at me." He spread his arms wide and tried to sit up, and Alex noticed a thin thread trailing along his forehead, which explained why he hadn't lifted his head higher than a few centimeters.

"I never killed one of them."

"How did they know who you were?"

"Can sense me as much as I sense them. I don't remember all of it; I don't wanna. It comes back when they talk to me here though. Don't know how they do it, but I end up swiping the air and fighting nothing."

"Sounds like PTSD," Chase said.

Alex frowned. "Not the same at all."

"Isn't it? It's all in our heads. It happens to me, too. Things we fight to forget but can't because the memories remind us."

After months of Chase being angry at her for refusing to hate Reuben, now he was the one defending him?

Reuben twisted and untwisted the sides of the sheet beneath him.

"Why are they restraining you?" Alex asked.

"You noticed that, eh?"

Chase's eyes searched the bed. Alex drew an invisible line across her forehead to indicate where it was.

Reuben touched his fingers to the string. "Like I'm dangerous or somethin'."

"You're a Seyferr," Chase argued.

"I've never belonged, like I said already. Do you see danger when looking at me? Yeah, me neither. Seyferrs are natural born hunters. But not me. I had asthma. I'm fat. I'm weak. Other hunting families, they used to call me 'Bakery' because of my dough rolls." He rubbed a hand along his belly. "My mom gave me different food, and she got up early with me to run around the property while no one else was watching because I was slower than a slug, and when I'd breathe my chest would burn.

"When I found a witch at the glen by my home, I thought it was a stroke of luck. The girl couldn't reach her bike pedals, and she was old blood, like a trophy. But she already found her gifts because she snapped my neck like a chicken before I even pulled my weapon."

Reuben still didn't look at them. He scratched at his arms and kept his gaze on the ceiling, telling the story to himself. "I was nothing in life. That's why I aimed to be better as a spirit. Thought being in the afterlife meant I was special after all. Couldn't wait to tell my dad. After I got here, I broke the rules and went home with the proof I'd been searching for all my life, that I was a Seyferr through and through.

"But my grandpa told me, he said, 'Sure other Seyferrs could have lived on too, but they made the right choice. You shamed your family.' Hunters are supposed to keep the unnatural out of the world. They said I was no better than the witches."

"They didn't let you stay?" Alex asked. "Your family?"

Chase interrupted with a huff. "What makes us unnatural? The fact that we are different from them? Just because you don't understand something, doesn't make it unnatural."

Reuben regarded him for a moment, stone-faced. Then he continued without addressing Chase's comments. "I came back to Eidolon to face my punishment. Would rather be dead than here. That's why I wanted Eviar to be real. I would have done anything to stay in that group. They gave us tasks, and I knew I could lead them. I knew better than anyone how to hunt a person. I knew your face the second I saw you," he said to Alex. "To kill you would be a reward. I could have gone home with that star on my record and been forgiven by my family."

As Reuben went on about his desire to kill Alex, Chase's

hands clenched the sides of the chair.

Reuben stared hard at Alex. "I should've known better. A face like yours is impossible. Unless you been cursed."

"What?"

Reuben wore smugness like a prize. Alex was sure he enjoyed this moment of being needed.

He pointed at Alex but spoke to Chase. "I haven't felt a heartbeat in a long time, but even now looking at her face ..." He stopped to pat his pudgy hand over his chest. "My heart, it goes so fast. Instincts."

"Why?"

"She has some sort of magic in her, even if she is a Havilah."

"We know that at least one of the Havilahs was gifted," Alex said.

No, Chase warned her in their minds. Reuben's face glowed. "Yeah? That's something new." He drummed his fingers together. "My family has known the Havilahs a long time, but that's a piece of their history I never heard."

There was plotting in his voice, and Alex regretted giving him any verbal ammunition.

"We're getting off topic," Chase intervened. "What did you mean by cursed?"

Reuben scratched his forehead under the thread. "You're the last Havilah."

"And?"

"Havilahs die young. I know that clear as the sky is blue. The gifted made it their business to turn them into what they hate."

Alex suddenly understood. "The gifted wanted the Havilahs to become like them."

Reuben scrunched his red nose. "My dad always said that the worst thing you could ever do was become something you hate. If only I'd understood that on the day I died, I might not be suffering now."

"The Havilahs are cursed because of Parrish?"

"Parrish is a devil town. They do the buying and the selling. Esker Havilah was a boss for the hunters. His town made him a killin' by selling witches to the highest bidders and blamed the profit on something called an Anil plant or indigo, whatever it's called."

Reuben kept twisting his head—as much as he could under the wire—to scrutinize Alex from different angles.

Chase cleared his throat. "What were you saying about her appearance being a curse?"

Reuben grimaced and rolled his eyes to the ceiling.

Chase sighed. "What will it take for you to tell us?"

"I'm needin' to get out of here."

"Out of the medical center?"

"No." Reuben glared at them. "Out of Eidolon."

"No offense, buddy. But I think you'll be sorted in a few months anyway."

"They won't let me go. Even to a colony. Those places are all the same. Jack says it's Eidolon's offspring."

Alex's emotions seesawed in regards to this boy, and it was exhausting. She didn't have the energy to play games.

"What specifically are you asking?"

Reuben looked at her, and for a moment he flinched like he used to. "Figure out something, some place for me to go."

Alex cocked her head, trying to make sure she understood. "And if we promise, will you tell us what you know about curses?"

"Yessss."

Alex looked to Chase for reassurance. He had his hand covering his mouth in thought, but he shrugged one shoulder. *Why not.*

"Fine."

"Great." Reuben made small circles in the air around her face. "Chances are if you look like her," he crinkled his nose in distaste, "then the curse was made by her."

"That's it?" Chase asked in a mundane voice.

"No," Reuben answered. "When I was little, I used to get spooked during the hunting trips. I still had to tag along. Family tradition," he added, ignoring Alex's humph of disgust. "My big brother used to tell hunting legends to distract me. I can remember one he told me 'bout a curse. Those bedtime stories, they always had lessons, and this one warned us to always, always know the heritage of who we're hunting."

"Why?"

"The longer their family line, the harder the fight. It's scary what they can do: make you see things that ain't there, believe things you wouldn't usually believe. With this legend I'm thinking, the hunting family chased down a Kindall girl. Now the Kindalls," he said with a tremor in his voice. "The Kindalls are as old as the Havilahs. This girl warned them that she'd haunt them in a way that would tear them apart, snap their family line. She even winked at them before they killed her. The youngest hunter in the family married that next year. He had a baby girl, and he lost his damn mind, saying the devil was alive in his child. He drowned his own baby in the same place where that witch girl died. They say the baby was winking at her daddy, that she had the same eyes as the witch girl."

"I don't get it," Chase said.

"Says the story, each time a baby was born in that hunting family, some part of the child looked like the witch. The hunters kept killing their own children or killing themselves. That witch cursed them something awful. It broke their minds."

Chase clasped his hands on top of his head. "How is it possible for a person to alter the appearance of someone who isn't born?"

The story cooked in Alex's mind, turning over and over again until it blackened in her thoughts. Magic was all tricks of the mind. What if Sephi was powerful enough to imprint the image of her face in the minds of the hunters? What if it was powerful enough that they married someone with at least one of her features?

You're beginning to think like a dead girl, Chase remarked in her thoughts. She hadn't realized he was there.

Reuben looked past them as though he expected someone was listening. "It ain't all so bad. Alex is part Havilah and part witch. She's a piece of two families who hated one another."

"You're saying you think people will look on the bright

side, and see the glass as half full?"

At that, they each lowered their eyes to the floor, realizing how ridiculous this sounded.

Chase rested his hand on Alex's knee. "You think that's why Alex looks like Sephi? It might be something like that family in the story?"

"Sephi was a Kindall girl." The smugness in Reuben's tone blotched the space around him. "I think the family in that story *is* Alex's family."

Chapter Twenty-Nine

The remnants of Alex's body still influenced her mind. Her nonexistent heart still pounded, and the memory of her mortal throat worried itself dry each time she had to walk the green mile to ABC. She believed Duvall would be pleased to know that the line of her history began so far back, to swaddle herself with that line like the threads of the thin shawls she loved. Instead, Duvall seemed more likely to tighten that line around Alex's throat. If looks could kill. Even months later, she refused to speak to Alex.

Little waved Alex to a table. Pax Simone hurried across the room to take a seat next to them.

"Hey, girls. Don't forget the Legacy meeting this afternoon. We need to make final plans for the Truce March. My family is excited to meet you, Alex."

"It's still happening?" Alex asked. "The March?"

Pax lifted a palm. "Why wouldn't it?"

"The gifted broke into the city and attacked a spirit."

"That was an isolated incident." Pax waved her hand. "Definitely not from a civilized group."

Duvall exited her office with a projection hovering above her head like a thought bubble. *Balance*, it read and teetered left to right, up and down. She clapped two stones together in her hands. The first row sat up straighter, then the second and the third, and so on until an invisible jolt forced Alex to fix her posture.

"We have much to accomplish this morning, newburies. And I even prepared a lab, so let us begin."

Goggles appeared over Alex's face. She must have projected them there without realizing it because no one else had them. She ripped them off.

"Balance," Duvall began. "Such a light word with such heavy meaning." Her gaze skimmed her audience. "Stability is what makes the world able to stand on its own two feet without toppling over. Often when it reaches its tipping point in either direction, something occurs to pull it back. People react. Nature reacts. Or history reacts."

Balance. Alex wrote the term in her notebook and watched as her pen began to transcribe everything her brain conjured upon considering the word. A gymnastics beam, a cat, the term: equilibrium, a scale, exercise.

"The bodied have their version of such beliefs. The most prominent example derives from nature: the predator versus the prey. The lion never runs out of antelope to chase, to eat. Yes, Tess?"

"What about extinction?"

"There are exceptions to almost every rule. So how does the idea of balance apply to your friendly neighborhood alchemist? Balance provides insight."

"I don't understand." Madison voiced Alex's very thoughts. Alex wouldn't dare to raise her hand in class anymore. As things stood, Duvall wasn't treating her as low as the Bonds, but Calla used to sit with her hand in the air the entire class without so much as an acknowledgment from Duvall. Embarrassing. Alex's proverbial skin was not thick enough for that.

Above them, the word balance turned green and melded together into a single stone.

"Jade." Professor Duvall began to march backward, slowly down the center aisle, facing the projection. "Don't be fooled. It isn't always green." She snapped her fingers, changing the tone from green to orange to white and back to green.

"You are aware of the healing effects of jade, but then there's its counterpart." The image shifted from brilliant green to a muddy lime. "Edaj, like its foil, is prominent in Egypt, in the old tombs since much of it was mined long ago, and the substance is rare. Probably why you've never heard of it even though both were discovered at the same time as one cannot form without the other."

"Do you have an actual edaj stone to show us?" Linton asked.

Duvall let out a small yelp and slapped her hand over her

chest. "The substance is illegal, and even if it wasn't, it's far too dangerous to be handled so flippantly. Did you ever pass around nuclear explosives in school when you were alive because they were the topic of a lesson? No." She shook her head, muttering about stupid questions.

Alex couldn't help but smile. She missed spending time with Duvall.

"Professor?" Madison's desk sprouted five new pencils. "What does that have to do with insight?"

"Patience, my dear. Two sibling stones. One used for healing, and one used for harm. When combined, they bestow euphoria."

As Alex wrote, her mind supplied her not only the facts Duvall presented, but her immediate inferences, connections, questions, and hypotheses. Add water to fire and you have smoke, and even that dissipates. Add good to bad, and you get indifference, which is again, nothing. Why would the sum of these two parts equal *anything*?

She longed to ask.

"Now, for your lab."

A mortar and pestle appeared on Alex's desk, surrounded by various ingredients and directions.

Duvall stood near the glass wall of the aquarium, and a family of sea horses swam toward her to watch over her shoulder as the newburies fretted over the lab.

"As you learned before, the voix stone means what?"

"Insight," several newburies replied.

"And truth. Take the voix stone and turn it in your hand four times," Duvall instructed.

Alex picked up the yellow stone and did as she was told.

"Place it in the mortar. Pick up the ignarus stone and spin it four times in the opposite direction."

Alex selected the gray rock and obeyed. Duvall instructed them to follow the rest of the directions. Alex worried she would screw up somehow. There were at least two dozen lines of intricate commands. It wasn't just adding honey to the mixture but grinding the stones together for twelve minutes and one second before adding the honey, dripping the stream as thin as thread for seventeen seconds. Water had to bubble for twenty-two minutes while flower petals were broken into seven increments.

During the process, Duvall continued to lecture about the ignarus stone and the use of its services to provide silence. She told stories of its appearance throughout history from monasteries to libraries to secret operations. Alex almost dropped the petals she was supposed to dispense at a rate of one petal per six and a half seconds when Duvall explained that the ignarus stone was used to silence their signals out in space.

"We travel much further than the bodied, but we must be discrete so as not to frighten them. There have been glitches, however. A large one occurred in 1977."

"Are you talking about the Wow! signal?" Linton asked, pausing with a handful of petals.

Duvall cackled as she continued to stroll aisle to aisle, fixing a mixture here and a wrist flick there. "We need to keep ourselves silenced out in the field, and sometimes we need to silence people who see more than they should and attempt to share it with the world."

"What do you mean, Professor?" Madison yelped as her water boiled over.

"Sometimes, the bodied see pieces of our world. Plants, for instance. Many species are only seen by a dead eye. Anyone ever heard of the Voynich manuscript? Oh, we might need to discuss that. Even after we silenced the guy because he could see with amplified eyes, he went ahead and wrote out his findings in one of our earliest languages. He must have been able to hear us, too. The bodied don't know the language so it wouldn't matter except that he drew illustrations." She shook her head. "What a waste."

It took nearly a full hour, but Alex finally finished the lab. She plopped back in her chair, staring at her creation based on voix and ignarus. It contradicted. It was bright but brown. It smelled bitter but sweet. She felt a sad happiness when a realization washed over her.

Was that the combination of truth and silence? Realization. Duvall didn't hate her. That was Alex's instant realization.

Duvall resented the Havilahs, but she couldn't feel the same about Alex, which was probably infuriating.

Duvall's hands were balled into fists, but her glare softened. "There isn't only black and white, my loves. There are areas of shaded gray. The combination of jade and edaj, healing and pain, provides variations of contentment. The combination of voix and ignarus will give you clarity from what is hounding you."

A lumped formed in Alex's throat. She was painful to Duvall; she was a reminder of hatred and loss.

No one wants to stare that in the face every day.

Chapter Thirty

On the day Rae disappeared, there was a silence Alex hadn't heard in months. She didn't realize how much space Rae took up until that space was empty. It took her an hour to track down Skye. Alex begged her to work her magic, to do whatever she did to know when things happened.

Alex thrust Rae's blanket into her arms, and Skye's expression twisted with sadness. Rae was gone.

"You didn't do anything wrong," Skye whispered. "Lost Ones never stay still. And sometimes they don't choose if and when they travel; it just happens."

"Where will she go?"

"I doubt she knows. Spirits like Rae don't travel conventionally." Skye petted the blanket. "Meaning Rae could be standing right here in the same spot, but we aren't here anymore. She didn't travel over a length of space; she traveled over a length of time."

"I don't understand."

"For Rae, time may not be linear. It folds, and she might pulse in and out of then, and now, and later."

Alex laid her head on the arm of the couch. "How do you know? Did someone tell you that?"

"I saw a few things when Rae would hold my hand."

Alex looked down at her hands, remembering the energy of Rae's warmth in her fingers. "You think she could talk to us that way?"

Skye stepped back to examine the sketches covering the walls. "There's more than one way to communicate. She seemed to like this method a bit better. By the way ..." Skye gestured to the door. "Did you know Chase was outside?"

She did know, but if he wanted to come in, he would. She could see inside his head, and he was afraid that his sadness would be magnified if he entered the room. He was smart. Rae's absence was heavy. It felt like trying to remember something you were supposed to do, and knowing you're in the right place, but you can't remember what it is.

Alex sat in silence, absorbing the emotions of the sketches. Most were abstract without defining pictures or figures. In some of them, she could hear music. Senses were eager to overlap now. Kind of like in life when Alex could walk into a kitchen and tell how something might taste because of the smell. Here, she could see music. Hear art. Taste the feel of something.

The sketches above the mantel fluttered. "Will she come back?"

Skye had her chin on her hands. "I guarantee it."

"You said she can't choose."

"Alex, this world is mental. I'm sure if Rae thinks about it enough her mind will take her back here eventually."

Alex mulled over the word: eventually. She hated waiting for things.

Chase still hadn't entered the room, and Alex figured she'd better check on him. Without moving from her sullen spot, she opened the door between their minds. There, she could see his memories; he was walking up the hill by the fields, Rae at his side. He bent down to wipe stray pieces of grass from her ankles, and she placed hands on his shoulders before throwing her arms around his neck. Chase's surprise and fondness filled Alex with warmth, even now, and even though it wasn't her memory. Rae was special to Chase, too.

A *whishing* sound brought her back to herself. She glared up at the sketches. "Shut up," she murmured.

"What?" Skye asked.

"Not you. Rae's art is noisy sometimes." An idea occurred to Alex, and she jumped to her feet. "Skye, if you were to touch a sketch with those magic hands of yours, would you be able to see what Rae saw?"

Skye looked horrified. "I don't touch art. Or music." She scooted further away from the black box in the corner. "Or writing. It's too much."

Alex pressed her lips together.

"Don't pout. Try to do it yourself."

"I can't touch something and know what it is thinking. That's your job."

"I'm not asking you to." Skye shoved her hands in her pockets. "What is the noise you hear?"

"Huh?"

"You said the sketches are noisy. What do you hear?"

"Whishing."

Skye stepped closer to the pictures. "Like rain falling?"

Alex shook her head. It was too gentle to have the force of rain.

"Wind?"

That was closer.

"More like …" Alex crinkled her forehead, "… sand."

The way the pictures fit together, the images pressed together in the center formed what Alex tried so hard not to see.

Another hourglass.

At the pinch of the hourglass, Rae had drawn a mess of lights and objects on shelves.

"What is that?" Skye asked.

"It's a shop in Moribund. The one Little showed us."

"And who is that?"

Alex snatched a sketch from the wall. Next to the Moribund sketch was a drawing of Thea's house. Rae *had* been there. In the archway between Thea's kitchen and living room, Liv was being held by three men. One man held a rifle butt high above Liv's head, which slumped at a ninety-degree angle. Thea was on her knees with her hands clasped together, her mouth open and screaming.

"Oh my God."

The higher sketches of the hourglass looked hollow, empty. The lower sketches were dark, nearly reaching the pinch of the middle. All the "sand" was at the bottom.

Time was up.

Chapter Thirty-One

Alex didn't dare meditate to get to Liv and Thea. Duvall was out of the question; even if they were on good terms, there was no way she'd be willing to help the family that signed away the lives of the gifted. They couldn't use the emergency exit outside of Van Hanlin's classroom because it was sealed after last year's events.

Moribund was their only option. The town was holding its annual art fair and Chase suggested they try to escape through Maori's. Rae might have placed the sketches together for a reason.

Alex assumed Westfall and his security team would prohibit her from leaving Eidolon. She lied through her shaky voice, saying she'd be more than happy to spend extra time at the health center while the others enjoyed a break at the beach.

She couldn't very well enter Gramble Station without the travel agents sounding the alarm, but Skye had showed her not only how to pass through the gate, but how to project. It took them half the day, but Chase and Alex finished walking and projecting their way through Redwood National Forest and into Moribund.

The beach was vacant because every person, dead or alive, crowded the main streets to watch artists with their water colors, spray paints, pencils, and sculpting clays. Spirits and bodies twirled together down the road to the music coming from a bandstand at the end of the street. The fair gave Alex a chance to hide. She and Chase hurried past the end of the paved road and stepped through the glass of Maori's store.

They stopped beneath a group of swaying amulets, and Chase dropped her hand. "Calm down, okay?"

She tried to stop her tapping foot and settle her racing heart, but she couldn't control it. She wanted to get to Liv *now*.

"Where do you want to start?"

"I guess we should look for Maori." Alex's voice echoed all the way down the center aisle of shelves. The reverberation mocked her: *Maori, Maori, Maori?*

Chase tugged her forward. She didn't want to look at Sephi's framed trade document, but she did anyway. There were similar pages on the shelf beside it. Sephi's age was listed as fourteen in 1862, but on some of the other documents, the ages of the gifted were as young as three or four years. Alex shuddered.

She heard a flapping behind them, and she and Chase both

spun around, but there was nothing but air to greet them.

Alex turned back to find a black-cloaked figure hovering inches from her nose. "Whoa!" she cried out and would have stumbled backward if it hadn't been for Chase holding on to her. Alex composed herself, her eyes drifting upward ... and upward. Towering above them was a giant man with a height to rival the redwoods. He held up his arms that were lanky and bony like tree branches. His large palms faced them in defense.

"I am sorry," he croaked. "I did not mean to frighten you." His sharp syllables stuck to his tongue.

Chase found his voice before Alex could. "Are you Maori?"

The man raised a bushy brow and bobbed his head of wiry curls.

"Yes." In a snakelike way, he drew out the *s*.

Alex gulped. "We came to see you a few months ago. You weren't here."

She stopped speaking as the man's expression of confusion grew deeper. "And you were able to enter?" He released a thunder boom of a laugh. "I'm sorry. It's interesting that the store would allow customers without my permission."

Why is that funny? Chase thought to Alex before taking a small step forward. "We aren't sure whether we're customers or not, to be honest. We have questions."

"You don't think questions come at a price?" He brushed past them and began to walk down the dark aisle. "Come."

We don't have time for this! Alex wanted to scream. The hunters could be coming for Liv right now!

She stepped on Chase's heels through the abyss of lost

treasures, shields, masks, papers, vases, and scrolls until Maori stopped outside of a tall, thin door. He fumbled with a key and whispered, "I cannot concentrate with all that noise. It is distracting."

Alex glanced back over her shoulder at the quiet store, but no one was there. Chase's lips were set in a tight line, but Alex locked her mind and blocked out his entry. She didn't want to know what he thought about all this; she didn't want the colors to spoil their chances to figure out why Rae wanted them to go here.

They stepped inside a simple room with only a desk, a chair, and a light. "Since we are away from all that racket," Maori said, "I can hear properly now. You are customers because you have questions. Your payment shall be in the form of answers. Do we have a deal?"

"Yes," Alex replied. "So—"

"I go first. Tell me a secret."

Really?

"Um," Alex lifted her palms, "I'm not Sephi Anovark. I'm the last of the Havilah family."

Maori pursed his large lips. "This I had heard, but coming from you, it is better. So what is your first question?"

"It's kind of strange."

"Good questions usually are."

"Okay." Alex's knees trembled. "Do you have an exit here? A way to get to the outside world?"

He tilted his head. "I mean, you are free to leave whenever you would like."

Chase took Alex's hand and rubbed her fingers with his thumb, trying to calm her. "She means a travel system."

"No." He clutched his chest. "I only carry items of extreme value."

Damn it! They were wasting time! Alex wondered how quickly they could escape. She heard a click, and her gaze darted across the room to the knob. Did he lock them in?

"My question! What are they filling into your head at that dead city of yours?"

"Knowledge? I guess?" She didn't want to play this game anymore. "We have to go to classes every day."

"And they tell you stories there too?"

Not if they can help it.

"Your hesitancy is my answer. Pity. That city doesn't change. You may take a turn now."

We're stuck, Chase thought to her. *You may as well ask some good ones.*

"Okay," Alex said. "What is the significance of hourglasses? Do they mean something special to the afterworld?"

"Right." His *r* rumbled. "You are a Havilah. The word Havilah, itself, means *a stretch of sand*. Havilahs considered themselves to be one with the earth and the dirt and the land. Now the hourglass, I cannot offer a definitive answer, but you are the last Havilah, yes? So there's your significance. If the sand has run out, your time is up. You're dead." He exaggerated wiping his hands against one another. "Done."

Alex sighed. "But I've been dead. Why would the hourglasses be appearing everywhere? Like in my pocket?"

Maori shook his finger at her. "You might see hourglasses if your mind is attempting to decipher your past. It is telling you to look back home with your family."

Alex glared at Chase. That was precisely what she'd been telling him.

Maori drummed his long fingernails on the desk. "My turn! What is going on in there?" He made a circular motion around Alex's head.

"I don't understand," she replied.

"Do not lie. There is enough energy up there to power a small city."

"I'm anxious. We have somewhere we need to go."

He stood and reached high to lower a device from the ceiling that hadn't been there moments before. With a long pipe attached to two handles, it looked like a periscope. "May I, *bitte*?"

Alex shrugged.

He grabbed the handles, pressed his forehead against the pipe, and slowly rotated around Alex. "Do you have a memory stone on your person?"

"No."

"Have you ever? You are a Havilah, after all. That family simply adores rocks."

She clasped her hands, tapping one finger against the rest. "I never met anyone from my family."

He muttered under his breath in a language Alex didn't know. "My machine tells a different story, but the energy doesn't come from jewelry or from somewhere on your body.

It is coming from your head. This interests me."

Alex, Chase pulled on her hand. *I don't like where this is going. He's looking for something he can use.*

Maori retracted from the periscope and glared at Chase. "My boy, you do not have to stay. You aren't contributing to the purchase anyway."

Chase's mouth tightened.

"Actually, I have one more question," Alex said. "It's about the gifted transactions. Can I show you?"

"Oh. All right." Maori released the device and watched as it flew to the rafters. He opened the door. "But out here I cannot hear those marvelous voices coming from your head."

Creepy.

Alex exited the office, and in thinking about Sephi's document, she projected herself down the aisle. She blinked and found that she was brushing shoulders with the glass protecting the weathered contract.

"The Frank family," Alex said. "What do they have to do with the exchanges?"

"You know them, eh? My question first." Maori rolled up his sleeves. "Is that clown still hanging out in those woods or has he finally checked himself into the mental ward?"

"He's still in the woods."

"I have lost a bet then." Maori clucked his tongue. "Okay, the Franks. They are the bridge between the gifted and the spirited. No exchange was complete without their judgment. Selfish fools. They cannot leave their town or the gifted would surely find them and kill them."

He was right. Liv never left town. She never went on vacation or visited relatives or traveled.

"Why would they do that?"

"It was an agreement to keep them out of the holding centers and to keep the family together." He knocked on the glass. "See."

Currency offered for Lorraine Havilah from the council of Parrish, Maryland to Astor, Oregon. Sale completed.

It was signed by Abigail Frank.

The lettering burned Alex's eyes. "That's a Havilah being sold. This was ... was this Astor Havilah's daughter?"

It said she was sold to Astor, Oregon. Her father must have gotten her back after creating the town Jonas visited. Alex's heart lifted finding a positive piece to the story.

"Do you know Rae?"

An invisible wind whipped through the aisle, rustling Alex's hair, cradling her in her own shock.

"What did you say?" Chase asked.

"Rae. She wanders into town sometimes."

"She was with us the last time we were here," said Alex.

"Ahhhhh. That's how you gained entry."

Alex couldn't get the words out fast enough. "She knows you?"

He cocked his head, casting a shadow over them. "That's her contract." He snapped his fingers and the light brightened below the document next to Alex.

"*She's* Lorraine Havilah?"

"Why, yes."

No wonder Rae attached herself to Alex. She was a Havilah, like her. The document said that Rae was three when she was sold. Her spirit projection couldn't be older than three, so how did she die without her father getting her back? It was written there in black and white that she was sold to Astor, Oregon. If the sale was completed, she should have been alive.

When Alex asked Maori, he shrugged a high, bony shoulder. "We should probably be thankful she didn't live much longer than three, knowing who her *brother* turned out to be." He shook his head. "The last thing we need in this afterworld would be another Syrus Raive."

Alex looked down at her feet. Indeed.

Chapter Thirty-Two

Alex and Chase doubled back through the aisles of illuminated treasures. Alex might as well be an item for sale. She should snatch a firefly light and dangle it above her head with a price tag.

"I guess we were wrong about the exit," Chase said. "Rae might have meant something else by sketching this store. I'm sure there's a telephone in this town somewhere. We could travel that way."

On the other side of the glass, not one piece of the sidewalk was visible under the feet of the crowd gathered outside.

Why is the Patrol here? Chase thought to her.

Where?

He flicked his chin in the direction of the sidewalk. *Follow me.*

They fell into the masses and zigzagged around singers, artists, dancers, and observers. Alex kept her head down and a hood covered her head to conceal her. Halfway down the road, the crowd parted.

Chase scooted sideways, pulling Alex along, to avoid whatever was coming. They stumbled into an easel, and Chase muttered an apology to the girl sitting on a stool. The girl set down her paintbrush, adjusted her earbuds, and slid her easel closer to the building.

Alex and Chase were trapped between the shops behind them and the crowd moving as one, shuffling further away from the street, which was now filled with the sound of stomping feet.

Dozens of voices harmonized in a chant: "Equality now. Equality now."

"Those aren't spirits," Chase warned.

Alex stood on tiptoe and saw white squares rising and falling in the air. On one of them, thick red letters spelled out *Soul = Soul*. Her hands began to shake. "Are they from Moribund?"

"Moribunders wouldn't be picketing in their own town. This is as close as the gifted can legally get to Eidolon."

"It's the gifted?"

The white signs reached them, and Alex swayed side to side to find a hole in the crowd. She wanted to see them. Would they look like Duvall? Eccentric and whimsical. Would like act like Liv? Angry and confused.

"Protesting," Chase replied. "Yes."

She crouched down to see through the legs of the people in front of her. The marchers ranged from tiny toddler feet to giant combat boots.

"Oh no," Chase muttered.

Alex stood up. "What?"

Chase zipped his lips. Above the heads of the crowd, the white signs continued to bob up and down but these signs had photos on them ... of Alex's face. The caption: *CHANGE IS NOW.*

Alex spun around to face the store, cupping her hands around her eyes and looking into the window. The door displayed a sign saying, *At the Festival. Visit us by the bandstand.* There could be a phone inside though.

"Alex, we need to try to project."

"But we can't see where we're going."

"We need to try. We have to get out of here now." Chase grabbed her hand. "Focus on that lamppost down the road. We can do this gradually."

Alex wasn't sure this was the best idea. What if they separated? She wiped her forehead with the back of her hand and hoped for a better solution. She stepped closer to the painting girl, who wasn't bothered by the chaos surrounding her. Alex tapped the girl on the shoulder.

She removed an earbud.

Alex inched toward the easel, which held art supplies and a cell phone. "Can we borrow your phone?"

"Oh my God!" a voice shouted beside them. "It's her!"

Alex wished she knew how to alter her appearance. She

retreated into Chase's mind to see muddy colors. These people weren't going to ask for her autograph. They were afraid of her.

"Why is she here?" A woman wrapped her arms around the shoulders of her children and began to back away from Alex.

The rest of the crowd did the same. They gave Alex a clear view of the street and the protesters ... and Jack's gang across the way.

Jack stepped into the road, bringing the march to a halt. Carr followed him, linking his arm through Jack's. Hecker did the same. And several others. They stood as a fence, dividing the march, blocking the gifted from their mission.

The crowd on the sidewalk didn't make a sound, waiting to see what would happen next.

The gifted stopped. They looked like normal people: kids wearing sports shirts, fathers with children sitting on their shoulders, teenagers with perfect hair and makeup. Someone whistled, and Alex flinched, expecting the worst.

Instead, the gifted continued forward. They resumed their chants and marched, walking right through Jack's barricade. They stepped through Jack like he was invisible, and Alex felt the urge to run out into the street and march with them.

She took a step closer to the street. Bad idea. Jack met her gaze before shouting. "It's Alex Ash. Look! Over there! Sephi Anovark!"

A violent wave of wind barreled through the street, jostling everyone gifted, spirited, or neither. For a second, no one moved. There was no telling where it came from, but then a sharp jolt shook the ground under her feet; someone had struck. Both sides retaliated. Bolts of energy rocketed from everywhere. People screamed and ran. Chase grabbed Alex and pulled her back, but not before she saw the Patrol flood the street. They seized the gifted and pinned their arms behind their backs.

"No!" They didn't do anything!

Chase cursed and reached for the phone on the easel, but the girl snatched it up. Both sides of the street converged like oil and water, mixing together in a tide of scalding madness.

Alex reacted. She screamed. She let it out louder than she ever had at the medical center. From her nonexistent gut to the depths of her soul, she opened her mouth and allowed it all to be free. It launched out of her like a separate entity, causing the town to tremble. The spirited fell to the ground while the unaffected living gawked at her in confusion.

Chase snatched the phone from the girl's grip and punched in a number. "Get in."

Alex didn't stop screaming until she felt the shock of the radiofrequency waves.

Chapter Thirty-Three

Liv's grandmother said this was a calling, that it was in her bones. Liv wasn't so sure, but she belonged here more than she belonged with the giggling, flirty lemmings at her school. She didn't like people, especially the ones her age who called her a freak and made fun of her weight. She couldn't fit into trendy clothes, and her hair didn't flip in a peppy way. If it did, she'd cut it off.

She emerged from the back room, tapping on her phone. "Damn prank call."

"For such an outspoken child, you've been rather lost in your thoughts recently."

Liv plopped down on the window seat and rested her chin on her hand. She couldn't tell her grandmother that she hated life. She was surrounded by dead people, so a comment like that would sound ungrateful. "I like the woods," she said, looking out the window. "No matter the scary stories."

"Don't be thinking that since you can't see all the things that go bump in the night that they aren't there. Those woods aren't safe for you. There are more horrors out there than you can imagine."

Liv wanted to die. Was that crazy? Yes. She couldn't say it out loud or she might end up in that asylum like Alex did. She didn't belong in this world; she belonged with Alex and the Lasalles. They'd always been larger than life like they were too crazy, too free, for this world. When she tagged along, it felt like watching a television show or reading a story. And when they were gone, all she wanted was more. To see them. To watch them. She never stopped thinking about them.

She couldn't measure up to their personalities, but they were the only people on this earth who made her feel like she mattered. How many times had they braved the edges of the Parrish woods to find a better hiding place for buried treasure? Even when Kaleb and Gabe were older, they would play along with the younger ones because there were ways to make the games thrilling. Upping the stakes. Teasing the spirits in the Parrish woods. She shuddered to think what might have happened to them if the Jester didn't patrol the trees.

"Why are bad things allowed to exist?" Liv wondered aloud.

"Because nature is a siren. We are all built differently. You ask why horrible things exist, but terror wonders why people like you exist. Gatekeepers and caretakers are necessary."

Liv reached for a yellow voix stone and spun it in her fingers.

"We are appraisers, and that is what we are meant to do. Sometimes people have to be brave enough to accept a life that isn't ordinary. Your friends understood that. It's all a part of fate."

A gnarled voice interrupted them. "Fate schmate."

Liv hated that stupid clown slouched in the doorway. He sat sideways with his longs legs propped on the doorframe.

"Get your feet off my walls," Thea commanded.

"Technically, I'm not really touching it."

"Of course you are. Don't you ever wonder how things get so dirty? It isn't only the bodied who make the messes."

"A doorway isn't furniture," the boy argued, but he lowered his feet nonetheless.

Thea looked at him in dismay. "And what's your issue with fate? You don't think Sephi knew what she was doing?"

"Oh, she knew."

"But you scoff at it?"

"The things that Sephi predicted she helped to create. How is that foreseeing the future?" The Jester began tossing Thea's shoes down the hallway. "She predicted that the way this town operated would drive the residents insane. There's a mental institution here now."

Liv stood up the retrieve the shoes. "Sounds like she was right."

"The institution was created because the Havilahs went insane after Sephi cursed their daughters to look like her!

When they weren't hurling themselves off cliffs, they were drowning their own babies."

Liv stopped in her tracks, looking around the corner of the hall and then under the couch. She felt the haunt of hidden eyes. She owned a cat when she was little, and sometimes it would hide in the strangest of places like under pillows or in between shoeboxes in the closet. Liv would know the cat was there watching, but she couldn't find her. She had the same feeling now.

Thea took out a tube of lipstick and reapplied. Then she opened her compact mirror and puffed up her short curls.

"What are you doing, Grandma?"

"Tell your friends to sit down."

"What?" Liv glanced at the door where the Jester still slouched.

He snapped his fingers at her. "Why are you looking outside? You don't have friends who need to use doors." His shoulders slumped. "Aw, man. They didn't bring their pretty friend this time. Where's the Gossamer girl from last year?"

Liv never understood what it meant to feel a heart skip a beat until now. She spun around and looked in the foyer to find Alex and Chase standing hand in hand. Liv clutched her chest as her heart felt a happy devastation. They were dead but together.

Alex's innocent eyes grew wider than usual. "Thank goodness you're still here. Can you see me?"

Through her tears, no, she couldn't. "I can hear you."

"Hey, Liv," she heard Chase say.

"Oh, my God, Chase, I'm so sorry." Her voice cracked. "I'm so, so sorry. I couldn't save her."

It should have been her. She would have traded places with Alex in a heartbeat. Then she'd be free of this body and this cage her grandmother calls "a calling."

Something covered Liv's hand. It was like dipping her fingers into a current of energy. Tears spilled out of her. Chase was squeezing her fingers.

"I didn't expect you to," he assured her. "I'm the one who's sorry. I'm sorry I put you through all this."

Liv swallowed a sob. "I've missed you guys." She felt energy surround her when Alex touched her shoulder.

"We miss you. You were so important to me. You still are."

To hear beautiful, tragic Alex Ash say this to her felt overwhelming. Alex didn't need more than Chase. She chose to like Liv. Here was proof that Liv was likable.

She couldn't stop staring at them even when they sat down in the living room. The Jester crept closer to listen even though he pretended not to care. Chase sat next to Alex, leaving no space between them, just like he had in life. It made Liv happy.

"Thea," Alex began, "the hunters can't take you, right?"

Her grandmother was happy, too. Liv could tell. She also seemed proud. Her shoulders were back, and she beamed at their company. "No. We're protected by history and this town."

"Because we saw something. About Liv."

"They can't take her either."

Alex's face creased with worry. "Did Rae show you the way to Eidolon?"

Liv couldn't believe her ears. They knew Rae?

"She's the one that told us—well drew us a sketch—of Liv being taken."

Liv's heart raced. "I never left town, not really. Rae took my hand when I was meditating, and I was thinking of you, Alex. It was only a flash and then I was back in my room. Grandma, you said everything would be fine."

"It will be," said Thea.

"I wanted to find you," Liv said.

"I wish we could take her to Eidolon with us," Alex said to Chase.

Liv's heart lifted. She could have her friends back. She could live somewhere she belonged.

Thea took off her glasses and wiped them with her shirt. "The Cinatris divided the world into three: living, dead, and gifted. Eidolon, Parrish, and Paradise were constructed together. Separate but equal. They'd never allow intermixing."

"So stupid," said Alex.

"Sephi thought so too."

"Are you sure they can't take Liv?"

"Where would they take her? She's already a prisoner here."

Liv knocked on the window separating them from the woods. "But they could put me down there!"

Alex yanked her head in the direction of the window. "Down where?"

Thea sighed. "Underneath us. They needed a place to send the lawbreakers. Balin Cinatri was the first resident of Parrish's underground paradise."

Liv saw Alex's hand fly to her mouth.

"She kept trying to get into Eidolon. The first rule established by the three cities was that no one was to cross into another's territory. I let them be traded. I let them be tortured. Bought. Sold. To keep us safe. They can't take Liv."

The Jester jumped to his feet. "No time for talk. They're coming!"

"Who is coming? What's going on?" Liv put a hand on her grandmother's shoulder.

"The hunters," the Jester said. "They're right outside the door."

Chapter Thirty-Four

Alex tapped her foot against the floor of the hallway, disturbing the dust. "Liv needs to run."

The Jester sat opposite them with his back against the wall of the gray hallway. His long legs stretched toward them, forever molded with that thin knobbiness of a boy who still had some growing to do. "You can't run from these people. They aren't normal. Those are witch hunters."

Alex shifted in the tight space. "She should hide."

The Jester shook his head of white-blond hair. "Weren't you listening? They aren't allowed to take her. That's a written law. They're probably here because there was a sale."

Chase put a hand on Alex's arm. "Can they hear us? See us?" He asked the Jester.

"If they really wanted to, but they aren't looking for you,

so chances are they won't notice."

With that small bit of reassurance, Alex poked her head around the edge of the hallway wall. She could see Liv still poised on the window seat, but Thea was at the door. Her wrinkled knuckles turned white as she clutched the doorknob.

Moments later, Thea entered the living room with a middle-aged couple. She introduced her granddaughter and Liv's shoulders relaxed as she offered to go make some tea for their customers.

"Customers," the Jester sneered. "My ass."

The man on the couch hunched his shoulders and shoved his hands in his pockets. His physique was impressive for a man of his age, but despite his size it wasn't his presence that filled the room. It was the woman at his side who twisted a handkerchief in her trembling hands as she sat on the couch. It was she who wanted to be here, not him.

"We appreciate you seeing us in light of our history. I just, *we* just didn't know what else to do." The woman continued to twist the handkerchief, wringing out the scent of grief.

The woman couldn't be a hunter. Her voice was as sweet as southern tea.

Alex felt Chase tug at her arm. She pressed her back against the wall again, but she didn't like the disadvantage. She watched the Jester, whose expression hardened.

Chase jutted his thumb behind them. "You know them?"

Jester nodded.

"Is everything okay?"

He shrugged one shoulder.

Alex couldn't help herself. She twisted her torso to get another look.

"It's my boy." The woman's voice cracked. "I was wondering if we might be able to speak to him through you."

Thea was solemn. "Hunters do not linger in between worlds. I know that much about your beliefs."

"He's not gone," the woman assured her.

"How do you know?"

The woman rested a hand on the man's knee, which was jerking up and down. "He tried to come to us, but he was turned away. We didn't know."

"How long ago did he die?"

"Almost two years have passed."

Alex elbowed Chase. The Jester jumped to his feet and hurried away, bells jingling.

"Where is he off to?"

Alex was already looking around the wall again. All four people in the sitting room had turned in the direction of the Jester's departure, as though they could hear him.

"He's still around," the man remarked. "With his blasted bells."

"Of course," Thea said. "He never leaves." She leaned forward. "There are ways to summon your son, but I'll warn you that a spirit so newly buried might have difficulty arriving."

"Why?" the man barked, causing his tear-streaked wife to jump in her seat.

"There are rules."

The way the man curled his nose gave Alex the creeps.

"Please," the woman begged.

"Mrs. Seyferr, I'll do what I can."

The Jester flew back into the hallway, his hair whiter than ever. "The others are coming, Thea. I don't know why. They'll arrive momentarily."

Liv stood and crossed the room, blubbering about the tea.

Thea shifted in her seat and clutched at her hip. She reached for a cane Alex had never seen her use. "Why are you really here?"

Mrs. Seyferr sobbed into her handkerchief. Mr. Seyferr reached into his pocket and handed a document to Thea. "We got orders to deliver a boy from underneath."

Thea tut-tutted. "He arrived not too long ago."

Alex looked at Chase. What were they talking about?

"There's an offer. If accepted, we got the delivery schedule with us. But we are also s'pposed to investigate a bounty issued for this area. Have any of your kind traveled within restricted boundaries?"

Alex's being grew icy cold. She scrambled to her feet and ran to the kitchen to Liv.

"You know I'm not allowed to leave."

The man waved his hate-stained hand. "I don't think we are here for you, Thea. But rules, they've been broken. You aren't hiding any refugees in the house again, are you?"

"You'd sense it if I was."

He wiggled his fingers before using them to shove his own chin sideways, cracking his neck with a teeth-grinding pop. "You know my senses holler at me within ten miles of this place."

"If you wish to speak to those you sense, knocking on their doors might be difficult." She held out an open palm to the window overlooking the woods. "If you want to risk your neck down in Parrish's underground, be my guest."

"I reckon no witch buried in your tomb city could have *thought* her way into a spirited city."

"You've lost me."

"Don't play me for a fool."

Thea seemed to find this amusing. "I play you for a lot of things though a fool isn't one of them."

They regarded one another with revulsion for several unbearable moments. Liv started to leave the kitchen doorway, but Alex stepped in front of her.

Mrs. Seyferr gasped and jumped to her feet, crouched in a squat on the couch. She clung to her husband's arm and shrieked at the empty floor.

Mr. Seyferr swiped his hand in front of them. "Whatever you see, it ain't real. She's trying to get rid of us." He regarded Liv as he passed her. "They say the villain is a young witch. Tell me, how old is your granddaughter now, Thea?"

"You can't—"

Seyferr interrupted. "My hunting corps is waiting outside. Gather the boy."

He stomped out, leaving the door ajar for Thea to follow. Alex flew across the room and wedged herself behind the open door, moving the window curtain aside. Over a dozen hunters circled the property, armed with long-barreled guns. The man in the middle resembled Reuben, if Reuben had been cut from an ideal mold. Unlike Reuben's toupee tuft of blond, this man's marine-short hair appeared as no-nonsense as he did. His broad shoulders bulged under his shirt as he held his aim steady.

A wrinkled hand slapped the curtain back into place. "Don't. If they knew you were here ..." Thea took a deep breath and walked out the door.

"Where is she going?" Alex asked Liv, who stared at her toes.

"If one of them has been sold, she has to release him."

"Wait," Chase said, his face twisting in disgust. "I thought Thea had to approve some sort of paperwork."

"Maybe in the old days that's how it was done, but there aren't any Havilahs left to look out for us. They stay in the treatment center. We have to do what they say."

Alex watched through a small slit in the curtain. Thea crossed the yard to a large monument Alex had never seen. Moss covered most of the aged granite in the shape of a preaching Esker Havilah. Thea disappeared through a door in his stone podium. There was nowhere for her to go but down into Parrish's version of Paradise. That was the entrance.

"My grandmother says they're sent here if they've been caught doing something wrong, but their sentence can turn into servitude if someone pays the price for them. I'm not so sure I believe that anymore. I think if they're out in the open, the hunters snatch them and make up a lie."

"Where will they go?"

"They're bought by research facilities, or corporations with money, or by governments."

The pounding in Alex's mind felt like a wooden beam had landed on the crown of her head. Thea emerged from the tomb followed by a barefoot boy with bony knees and ankles shackled together. A bag covered his head, and his hands were bound.

This isn't right! Alex's conscious screamed so loudly she barely felt herself step through the open doorway. "I'm not letting you take him."

The bag on the boy's head turned in her direction. He could hear her!

Thea shook her head at Alex. "Go inside."

"No," Alex replied.

"You don't even know where he's going! For all we know, his own family could have bought him back."

Liv stepped out next to Alex. "The last time that happened you ended up with a gravestone in your front lawn."

Alex searched the yard but found no such gravestone. Chase appeared beside her, squinting at the hunters. She could feel him analyzing their colors.

Seyferr faced his troops. "Take the granddaughter too."

"Absolutely not." Thea stamped her foot. "It's illegal."

"The Havilahs won't stop me. Their legalities mean nothing now."

One by one, the hunters raised their guns. They aimed at the house. Liv looked around fearfully.

"We won't let that happen, Liv," Chase said.

Thea's voice shook. "There was nothing on that paper of yours that specified my family."

Seyferr didn't waver. "She won't be imprisoned. She needs to be questioned."

"Over my dead body."

"This ain't really the place to joke about that."

Thea hobbled back toward the porch in a steady rhythm of 1-2-3, cane, foot, foot. She stopped at the bottom of the steps with her back to the kids. She spoke over her shoulder. "You need to stay inside."

Mr. Seyferr joined his ranks and slung a rifle over his shoulder. "Is her granddaughter the only one she's speaking to?"

The hunter standing closest to Alex lowered his aim, revealing a baby face with fresh stubble. "There are a few, sir. One is the Anovark girl."

"You mean the Havilah." Seyferr chuckled. His eyes searched the property, not knowing where to find Alex. "Thank you for ending the lineage, girl. You've passed the prestige to a more suitable family. The Seyferrs are now the oldest living line of hunters."

"Congratulations. Shall we inscribe a trophy for you?" Liv gestured to the tomb. "Or how about one of those trophies? I'm sure we could pick out a nice headstone."

Alex had been in awe of Liv's fearlessness since the day they met, but school bullies and cranky, premenstrual teachers were much different than an army of hunters. They stood still as statues without blinking or flinching like the little green army soldiers the Lasalles treasured as children.

Seyferr regarded Liv with surprise. "I should think you'd

be glad to be free of your bondage."

"The Havilahs aren't really dead," Thea said calmly, even while addressing a fortress of loaded guns. "Alex is still technically alive. As are other Havilahs."

"They are without bodies," Seyferr growled.

"Get ready to run," Liv commanded.

Alex's voice crawled up her throat like a cough. "What's going on?"

"I can feel what they're feeling. Something in my bones tells me that they're getting ready to come for me. It's the ultimate high for them. The Most Dangerous Game. I'm sure they'd rather us run so they get to hunt us down."

"Liv?" Thea whispered.

"I didn't do anything wrong, Grandma. I was trying to find Alex and Chase."

"By meditating."

"Leaving my body. I told you how much I enjoyed it. It was a dream come true to escape this tub of lard."

Alex understood what it was like to feel trapped within her body. She didn't blame Liv.

Seyferr stepped forward. "You crossed territory lines."

Liv frowned. "No, I didn't."

"They issued a bounty. She attacked a spirit!" Seyferr barked.

Liv's hands went straight to her hips. "I didn't do that. I didn't even make it past that gate. I never went in."

Alex counted the hunters hiding behind hedges and trees. Twenty.

"Where's the Jester?" Chase asked. "We could use all the help we can get."

"He never intermingles," said Liv. "He stays out of everything."

The baby-faced hunter who could see the dead had relocated himself without Alex noticing. He was now whispering into Mr. Seyferr's ear.

Thea repeated herself. "Alex, you really need to go inside. Get to my phone."

"Why?"

She whispered even lower now. "You're worth a fortune. I'm not sure yet if they know quite how much."

"They can't catch a spirit, can they?"

Thea's voice dropped several octaves. "Believe me, I—"

She never finished her thought because something clicked from the forest behind her. Whether the cue was intentional or not, the hunters opened fire. Chase leaped sideways to force Thea to the deck while Alex shoved Liv backward through the open doorway. Torpedo-like darts pelted the siding while small copper rocks bounced to the deck. Glass snapped and shattered, falling down on them like rain.

Alex and Liv rolled to their stomachs. Liv's face paled to a bleached white, and her green eyes glowed like a burst of sunlight behind a stained-glass window. Her black hair stood on end. Energy shot from her like fireworks, merging forward into the ground where a tornado of dirt rose, twisting and spitting rounds of gravel at the hunters. Some of them dodged while some tried to withstand the shots, aiming their weapons at the house. Alex picked up one of the copper rocks to use it for ammo, but it stung her with its heat. She yelped and dropped it.

The hunters moved as one, inching closer. Seyferr Junior fell to a knee and took aim, but a burst of fire erupted in front of him, setting the ground aflame. He rose and stepped through it without flinching. More flashes of fire burst from areas around the attackers, but it didn't affect them whatsoever.

"We know your tricks," Seyferr called. "We know what's real and what's not."

Lightning struck from sky to ground in a crooked cobweb of a threat, but Seyferr shook his head. "You're actin' like we never hunted a witch before." He lifted the barrel of a misshapen rifle and aimed it right at Liv.

Alex ran forward, but Chase pulled her back right before a hunter took aim and shot a copper-colored rock in her direction. "Don't let those hit you!" Chase bellowed.

Liv flicked her chin and the rifle directed at her flew from the hunter's grip. He chased it, and five more hunters appeared behind him. There were too many of them. Alex couldn't turn her back to one side because another would move in. Chase cursed as a copper bullet grazed his shoulder. They weren't going to win this. The hunters walked slowly forward without fear, only a few feet away now.

Through the dust, Alex saw a hunter fly off his feet, shoved by an invisible force, and in the same blow, Seyferr Junior's body lurched sideways. Alex and Chase both looked left to right in search of who had come to their aid. In the hunter's place, stood Jonas, his arms extended. In her moment of shock, Alex stood long enough for another hunter to fire at her. The copper stone hit her arm, burning like fire. She howled and bent forward, clutching her head where it hurt the most because her arm no longer existed.

Chase lunged for her, but a steady flow of copper rain formed a barrier between them. Alex felt a hand snatch her by the collar and drag her into the flames. She flailed in panic as the yellow and orange fire immersed her, but she stopped when she felt nothing but a breeze. The flames weren't real. She looked through the blaze to find Professor Van Hanlin. Van Hanlin! Alive! He ran off, projecting himself in different areas of the grounds closest to Thea. He joined Jonas, knocking guns into the air and kicking hunters from their feet.

Why? How? Alex scooted back to the nearest tree and scrambled to her feet where the Jester stood, observing the fight.

"You won't help?" she cried.

"I can't," The Jester replied. "I can't risk my freedom. It's my job to protect the woods and that's all."

The ground exploded in front of them, dust and dirt flying. Alex took the opportunity to move. She tried to mimic Jonas, flickering to various spots around the hunters, appearing only to disappear again. They couldn't take aim long enough to get a good shot. She hoped it would at least distract them.

From behind the barrier of the porch, Thea rose. She lifted her cane high and made her way down the steps without so much as a wobble. She twirled the cane around her head, creating a halo of sparks and anger. She fell to her knees and slammed the cane in the ground, causing the air to quake. Giant globs of rain fell from the sky, accelerating into sheets. To Thea's right, several hunters pinned Liv facedown in the dirt, but large, jagged rocks barreled in from the nearby cove and came zipping in the direction of Liv's assailants. With resonating cracks, they made contact with the heads of the hunters, and Liv scooted away.

Thea's eyes became an orange-brown fire. Chase ran forward to help her, but Thea cried for him to get back with Alex. She threw her cane to the side and lifted her hands in the air. Several of the hunters screamed as blackness leaked from their eyes. It trickled to the ground at their feet and spread like death through the dirt. It rose like night and stunk like winter.

The last thing Alex saw was Jonas with Van Hanlin, who grabbed the boy with the shackles, ripped the bag from his head, and took off into the trees. Then, darkness shrouded everything.

Alex blinked, and it made no difference. She was blinded. Brutal silence accompanied it.

"How did it come to this?" Thea asked. "Sephi said these times would lead to peace."

The Jester's voice interrupted the darkness. "Sephi also said things would get worse before they got better. That boy must be important for rebels to come rescue him. The hunters could have taken Alex, so this was necessary."

"They weren't here for her." Liv couldn't have been standing more than a foot from Alex. "They wanted their son or did everyone already forget that crying mother?"

She was right, Alex realized. They had a bargaining chip no one had considered. "Can any of you hear me?" The sound of shuffling feet and muffled conspiring ceased. "I have something you want."

Mr. Seyferr's voice moved through the darkness. "Who's speaking?" He was closer than Alex thought.

She didn't hide her surprise. "He can hear me now?"

"Take away one sense." Thea's voice cut through the blackness with sparks of yellow. "Heighten another. This will open his mind. This will make them *see*."

"Is it you, little Havilah?" In the blackness, Seyferr was moving closer.

Alex felt the urge to move backward, but she couldn't see where the doorway began, where the porch ended, or where she was at all.

"I have a trade."

"Not much need for trades."

"I've heard information is more important than anything else."

His voice traveled closer. "Not sure who's been fillin' your head, but it ain't hunters."

"I want you to go. Say the boy ran away and leave here."

She felt the presence of someone in front of her. She panicked until she felt Chase press against her front and then reach back a hand and wrap it around her waist. He was a barricade between Alex and the hunter.

Chase finished Alex's thought. "And we can return your son to you."

Somewhere, in the depths of the woods, a woman muffled a sob.

"What do you know of my boy?" Seyferr hissed.

"He's tortured for being what you forced him to be," Chase said.

"We know him," Alex said. She paused and allowed the words to travel, to reach the ears of the woman sobbing. "We've known him for a whole year."

"You threatening me?"

Alex didn't understand. Chase's thoughts rushed into her head.

He thinks we're threatening to harm Reuben. He thinks everyone is as vicious as he is.

"We can bring him to you," Alex said. "Send him home. We know he wants to come home."

The sobs grew louder.

"I give you my word."

Like a light switch, it was day again. Reuben's brother rested his hand on Seyferr's forearm, and in a flash of color, Chase's mind showed Alex what she couldn't see. A haze of colorful hope puffed around the father and son.

"They'll accept the trade," said Chase. "He isn't lying."

"How did you do that?" Alex leaned toward Thea. "The darkness?"

"Oh, child." Thea shook her wrinkled head. "All I did was expose their minds. Their blindness. Funny, right?" She picked up her cane and clutched her hip. "Perspective is so much more powerful than force."

Chapter Thirty-Five

Like a summer storm, as quickly as the hunters arrived, they were gone, leaving an overcast sky and small rumbles of thunder in their wake. Alex sat cross-legged on the ground outside the Frank house, waiting. Rae would come here. She knew it. Rae had sketched the pictures. She'd led Alex to Parrish to find her.

"Alex, we need to go soon," Chase urged.

"I know," she whispered. The humid air stuck to her, trying to trap her there.

"I don't know why you think she's here."

"I feel her," Alex said. "It's weird, Chase. It's like those letters. There's a string attached, and I know if you wander into my head, you'll feel it."

Chase mumbled something she couldn't hear, but he

plopped back in the grass, yielding. "We're going to be in so much trouble."

"What else is new?"

The door of the house squeaked, and Liv emerged.

"How often does this happen, Liv? The selling?"

Liv sat on the grass a few feet away. "I only found out about this a few months ago. This is the first time I've seen it."

"How are they getting away with it?"

"They say a crime was committed. The gifted child was sent here for punishment."

"You agree with this?"

"No one said that. If I don't follow these rules, though, I'll be down in the Parrish Paradise and sold within a day."

Alex glanced at the woods, and her mind livened with memories, stories about the things that went bump in the night. She remembered the lights that sometimes erupted from the trees, or the way the ground shook. How many times had they sat out here as kids? They played on the steps and climbed the trees and picked the flowers. They never knew what hid under their feet.

"Liv, you said you knew Rae?"

"She's always here."

She knew it. Alex jumped up. "Where?"

"Next to you."

Alex spun around but found no one.

"You have to look for it. There's a tombstone right over there."

Buzzing filled Alex's head like a flatlined heart. She thrust her arms over her face, refusing to believe it.

"Alex," Chase whispered.

She removed one arm. Then the other. And she saw a kneeling angel carved from gray stone.

Liv scooted closer. "The bodied imprison them. The spirited sell them. The gifted attack both of them. There are riots. And there's a Truce March next week. I hear Sephi Anovark is going to be there," she snickered.

"She won't," Alex said. "I won't."

Thea's footsteps came from the porch. She scuttled out and landed on the porch swing. The siding next to it was punctured with holes. "I wonder if this is what Sephi had in mind. She said everything comes full circle."

The Jester appeared next to her on the swing.

"It's beginning again," she said. "Time is up."

"Things change," Chase said. He met Alex's gaze. *If things come full circle, we'll end up exactly where Sephi and Raive did. I can't accept that.*

"It will repeat."

"Things change," Chase repeated with too much force.

The swing creaked under Thea's weight. "You played sports in life?"

Chase sighed and nodded.

"What is it called each time you try something new with your teammates? With different formations or what not."

"Like a play?"

She snapped her fingers. "If a play doesn't work the first time, what do you do?"

"Try it again, I guess."

"Exactly. Like anything else, history has a mind of its own. History will keep trying until it gets it right."

Alex tugged at Chase's shirt, trying to get him to calm down. "Why does it feel like everything leads back here to Parrish?"

"Because it always leads back here."

"That can't be coincidence."

"The Havilahs had a hand in each world. So many parts of them are sprinkled throughout this life and the next. You're the last one. And Sephi always said the last one would be the most important one. Sometimes we don't see right until we try all the wrongs."

"No offense," Chase said, "but if Sephi knew what was so wrong with the world, and everyone loved her so much, why didn't she fix everything herself?"

Thea dabbed at her smeared lipstick, using her cane to push the swing back and forth. "Because Sephi allowed someone else into her mind, and it ruined her. Evil infected her in the form of love and lured her to her death. It imbalanced her. You are Sephi's creation of balance. You are Havilah and Anovark."

But Alex's thoughts were not her own either. Not only did she share them with Chase, but Chase had a link to his brothers.

"I can't imagine what your Havilah family thought when your father carried you through the doors of the Eskers, half dead. I knew though, when Liv told me you were taken there, I knew with that face of yours that you weren't coming out alive."

The Jester kicked his feet to make the swing go higher. "She didn't listen. I tried to warn her to stay away that night they drove into my woods. I even left my post and gave her a house call."

Alex glared at him. "You weren't very specific."

He ignored her and hummed the Havilah rhyme.

On the nights when the breeze stinks of indigo
Shut your window tight on the sill.
The Havilahs dance in the shadows
Leaving fingerprints shaped like Anil.

Alex's hands fell into her lap. "I don't know what I'm supposed to do."

"Oh, child. I think that's the entire purpose."

***

Alex didn't have much time, but she needed to walk at least a block in order for the street to feel "real" again. She watched her feet as she stepped over the lines of the sidewalk. She saw no cars in the street, no kids at the park, no birds in the trees because she didn't want to. She didn't need to. She was only here for one thing.

As she stepped onto Lullaby Lane, the only movement came from the memories. She saw four towheaded boys trampling through the flowerbeds and a small girl trailing behind. The smallest boy fell back to help her. They vanished like ghosts to be replaced with Danya Lasalle scooping a small Alex off the pavement with a rip over the knee of her ballet tights.

An image of David Lasalle appeared, throwing a pitch to Kaleb, who smacked the baseball with enough force to shake the memory away. And she saw Chase ... as a three-year-old holding her in a wagon being pulled by Gabe. She saw him as a five-year-old holding her hand as they stumbled up the giant steps of a yellow school bus for the first time. She watched Chase hand her a snow cone while red, white, and blue fireworks exploded overhead.

None of the memories included the man on whose doorstep she now stood. So many times, she witnessed her father searching for her mother. He'd mutter her name in his intoxicated sleep. He'd rush around corners in the house and ask where she'd gone. Alex wondered if Logan Ash had actually seen his wife from time to time. Now that she knew it was possible.

She lifted her fist and knocked four times on the chipped door. She looked nowhere else for fear that things would change. She'd see who had moved into the Lasalles' old house. She'd see a new driveway or a different paint color, new pavement or fresh mailboxes. And she didn't want to see that.

The door flew open like an opportunity. Loss, bitterness, and alcohol had aged her father well beyond his years. He poked out his graying head and turned it left to right. Alex did not move. Even after he slammed the door, muttering about stupid kids.

He didn't see her. He still didn't care to look for her.

***

Chase considered Thea's words again and again. She said the line between life and death was like the line of the horizon over the bay. They were equally vast, equally gorgeous, and separate.

How, Thea asked Chase after Alex left, *would he feel if the waves bled into the pink and purple sky, making a pinnacle to the other world?*

Scared, he replied. He thought about that question now as he glanced at the redwoods towering above Lazuli Street. The trees breathed life into Thea's words, reaching their fingertips to the heavens above. Alex sat in front of him on the rickety staircase, one that led to nothing. She leaned back and rested her elbows on his knees.

She sighed, and he didn't want to do anything to ruin her air of happiness. He kissed her head, keeping his lips shut.

Right, Thea had said, *because the ability doesn't exist. But we're all looking at it the wrong way. Which world do you live in, Chase? The one that belongs to the earth or to the sky?*

The earth, I guess.

And what of the bodied?

The same.

That was Sephi's mission. To make the spirited see that we were all one and the same. Our worlds don't have to be separated. We could help one another. And the world keeps trying to make it so. Sephi was not the first. She was an ending in the same old cycle, as is Alex. They all end the same.

Recalling these words, Chase grew cold.

Alex turned to look at him behind her. "What's wrong?"

"Nothing, why?"

"Your hands are like icicles."

He rubbed them together as if that might do something. He looked to the sky, but the sun could find no way to break through the clouds today. He could do with a little light.

You say it will repeat, he'd said to Thea. *Is that why you told me this after Alex left? You're saying she'll die.*

The prophet always does.

He refused to accept it. And he'd do whatever he needed to do to change it. Whether Alex agreed to it or not.

"I have a theory," Alex announced. Her caramel hair fell over the side of his thigh.

"Oh?" He worried she would bring up something he didn't want to discuss.

"If we climb these steps to nothing, we will exist on nothing."

"I'm confused."

"We'll walk on air. That's why the stairway is here."

He wasn't convinced. "We'd have to really believe it was possible for it to happen."

"No kidding. We only exist as projections, right?"

He stood up and held out a hand, helping her to her feet. "All right, Houdini. Let's give it a try."

She clasped her hand in his. "Together."

"Of course."

With each step they took, he realized how ridiculous they looked, one foot at a time, one step at a time, like a wedding march.

"Don't let Pax see you up here," he joked. "She might try to shove you off the steps."

"Yeah, I ruined her perfect little Truce March, didn't I?"

"I think the riot did that, but the Legacy group needs someone to blame."

They didn't stop when they reached the last step. On either side of them, he could see the ground so far away. At the peak of the staircase, their only company was skepticism.

"Westfall took it better than I thought he would," Alex said.

"He was a little distracted with the new information we were able to give him."

"That Jonas is fighting some war we didn't know existed?"

Chase looked at her. "That Van Hanlin is still alive and fighting it with him. What did Westfall tell you?"

Alex deepened her voice to mimic him. "You keep living. You keep fighting. You keep purpose." She looked over the edge. "On that note ..."

After the last step, they both tumbled forward. They didn't walk on air; they fell. Chase pulled Alex close and wrapped his body underneath hers as they flew down. Nothing would hurt her. And because he believed it in his mind, when they hit the ground with a thump, his head pained, and she giggled.

"Well, that didn't work, did it?"

On the contrary, his experiment tested out perfectly. He proved Thea wrong. Nearly everything he'd learned since death emphasized the power of belief. If he believed he could protect Alex, no harm could come to her. As he lifted his aching head to press his lips against hers, it didn't seem like anything could ever change that.

Because he loved her. And that was never something he had to force himself to believe.

Epilogue

In her dream, Alex was back in the desert, the one with the footprints, except this time the sky was purple. Chase appeared and intertwined his fingers with hers.

"Hi, Chase." His name still tasted like sunlight, and the sky brightened, once again.

He squeezed her hand. "There are a lot of footprints in the sand now."

Parrish's legends were hard at work. "We aren't alone. I don't think we ever were."

"Think some people will see the footprints in the morning?"

They would if they were looking for the right ones.

Alex was more concerned with the sand dunes, and her hopes rose as they traveled closer to the bonfire. Finally, beside the dune with the tousled beach grass, Rae huddled and hugged her knees, just like the sketch. When she spotted Alex and Chase, she leaped to her feet and ran forward, opening her arms and barreling into them.

The kids playing volleyball near a bonfire—four brothers and a sickly undersized girl on the sidelines—didn't notice. But someone else did. Near them, an open-mouthed Liv Frank froze in place, staring at them.

Alex waved her hand, gesturing Liv to come out to the water.

"What are you going to tell her?"

There was so much she could say. That they were going to die. That she doesn't need to look for them, and she shouldn't try. That they loved her.

"I'm just going to hold her hand," Alex replied. "And have her walk with us."

A. LYNDEN ROLLAND

A. Lynden Rolland was born and raised in a picturesque town obsessed with boats and blue crabs. She has always been intrigued by the dramatic and the broken, compiling her eccentric tales of tragic characters in a weathered notebook she began to carry in grade school. She is a sports fanatic, a coffee addict, and a lover of Sauvignon Blanc and thunderstorms. When she isn't hunched behind a laptop at her local bookstore, she can be found chasing her two vivacious children. She resides in Maryland with her husband and young sons.

OTHER MONTH9BOOKS TITLES YOU MIGHT LIKE

OF BREAKABLE THINGS
THE LOOKING GLASS
ENDLESS
LIFE, A.D.
MY TETHERED SOUL

Find more awesome Teen books at Month9Books.com

Connect with Month9Books online:

Facebook: www.Facebook.com/Month9Books
Twitter: https://twitter.com/Month9Books
You Tube: www.youtube.com/user/Month9Books
Blog: www.month9booksblog.com
Instagram: https://instagram.com/month9books
Request review copies via publicity@month9books.com

Of Breakable Things

A. LYNDEN ROLLAND

Find the diary, break the curse,
step through the looking glass!

THE
LOOKING
GLASS

JESSICA ARNOLD

"A TRULY MODERN GHOST STORY THAT TAKES THE READER DOWN
A RABBIT HOLE OF SUSPENSE."
- LAURA BICKLE, AUTHOR OF THE HALLOWED ONES

ENDLESS

AMANDA GRAY

LIFE, A.D.
Life, After. Dez.

MICHELLE E. REED

DOROTHY DREYER

MY
TETHERED
SOUL

REAPER'S RITE - BOOK TWO